Been There, Done That

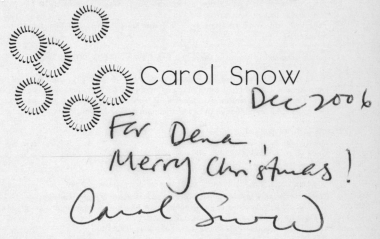

Carol Snow

Dec 2006
For Dena,
Merry Christmas!
Carol Snow

BERKLEY BOOKS, NEW YORK

THE BERKLEY PUBLISHING GROUP
Published by the Penguin Group
Penguin Group (USA) Inc.
375 Hudson Street, New York, New York 10014, USA
Penguin Group (Canada), 90 Eglinton Avenue East, Suite 700, Toronto, Ontario M4P 2Y3, Canada
(a division of Pearson Penguin Canada Inc.)
Penguin Books Ltd., 80 Strand, London WC2R 0RL, England
Penguin Group Ireland, 25 St. Stephen's Green, Dublin 2, Ireland (a division of Penguin Books Ltd.)
Penguin Group (Australia), 250 Camberwell Road, Camberwell, Victoria 3124, Australia
(a division of Pearson Australia Group Pty. Ltd.)
Penguin Books India Pvt. Ltd.; 11 Community Centre, Panchsheel Park, New Delhi—110 017, India
Penguin Group (NZ), Cnr. Airborne and Rosedale Roads, Albany, Auckland 1310, New Zealand
(a division of Pearson New Zealand Ltd.)
Penguin Books (South Africa) (Pty.) Ltd., 24 Sturdee Avenue, Rosebank, Johannesburg 2196,
South Africa

Penguin Books Ltd., Registered Offices: 80 Strand, London WC2R 0RL, England

This is a work of fiction. Names, characters, places, and incidents either are the product of the author's imagination or are used fictitiously, and any resemblance to actual persons, living or dead, business establishments, events, or locales is entirely coincidental. The publisher does not have any control over and does not assume any responsibility for author or third-party websites or their content.

Copyright © 2006 by Carol Snow
Cover design by Annette Fiore
Cover photo by Cosmo Condino/Getty Images
Book design by Kristin del Rosario

PRINTING HISTORY
Berkley trade paperback edition / August 2006

Library of Congress Cataloging-in-Publication Data

Snow, Carol, 1965–
    Been there, done that / Carol Snow.—Berkley trade pbk. ed.
        p. cm.
    ISBN 0-425-21006-5 (trade pbk.)
    1. Women journalists—Fiction. 2. Investigative reporting—Fiction. 3. Prostitution—Fiction. 4.
College students—Fiction. I. Title.

PS3619.N66B44 2006
813'.6—dc22

2006042799

PRINTED IN THE UNITED STATES OF AMERICA

10 9 8 7 6 5 4 3 2 1

To Andrew, of course

acknowledgments

My agent, Stephanie Kip Rostan, signed me shortly after the birth of her first child; how anyone can be so smart and capable on so little sleep astounds me. She has been a tremendous advocate and sounding board.

Cindy Hwang, my editor at Berkley, did more than simply improve my finished manuscript; her insightful comments and direction have made me a better writer.

My parents instilled in me a love of language and laughter. As for my siblings, Tom Snow and Susy Snow Sullivan are two of the funniest people I know, while Kim Snow, my second set of eyes, started things rolling when she taught me my ABCs a long, long time ago.

Dan Goodman, Kim Rueben and Melissa Karl Lam read my manuscript in its infancy and provided valuable feedback and encouragement.

Finally, Andrew Todhunter inspired, cajoled and ultimately shamed me into finishing this book. He is my rock and my inspiration. Plus, he keeps the computer running.

To all of you: many, many thanks.

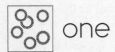 one

Getting carded would have been okay if I'd been out for a glass of wine with my friends. Funny, even. They'd throw around the Oil of Olay jokes. I'd give thanks for good genes and poor lighting. I'd hand over my license, wait for the waitress to marvel at my birthday, toast the fountain of youth.

But I wasn't out with my friends. As *Salad* magazine's new education editor, I was interviewing Donald Archer, Mercer College's dean of admissions, for an upcoming profile, "Keeping Pace with Changing Times: One School's Journey." I was supposed to be a serious reporter. Serious reporters do not look nineteen, even if they are nineteen, which I am not. Serious reporters have frown lines and prematurely gray hair from time spent in war zones and inner-city emergency rooms. Dean Archer had just ordered a Manhattan. And as all good reporters know, when they drink, you drink, even if it's barely past noon. Or you order a drink, at any rate—just to show camaraderie—then you let it sit there and wait for them to loosen up.

The waitress had a nose ring, which made things worse. I passed the legal drinking age long before facial hardware came into vogue. When I passed the legal drinking age, this chick was still playing with Barbies.

I pulled my leather bag off the shiny fake-wood floor, plopped it onto my lap and dug around for my wallet. If that bimbo knew anything, she'd know that no one under twenty-one can afford a Coach bag. I rooted around the extra tapes, pens, rumpled Kleenex: no wallet. I peered under my chair to see if it had fallen out. I stuck my hand in my blazer pocket (as if anyone under twenty-one wears a blazer), knowing full well it wasn't there but feeling I had to do something, anything, because times were becoming desperate. I was about to dash to the phone to report my stolen credit cards when I remembered where my wallet was. It was in my pocketbook. In my apartment. Really, really far from here.

"I had a date last night," I blurted to the dean. "And I put my wallet in my pocketbook and forgot to switch it back." I looked at the waitress, lowered my voice. "I'm thirty-two."

The nose ring quivered. "I'll have to see some ID."

"I am so much older than you."

"ID."

I smiled at the dean, tried to laugh. "I'll have a seltzer water. With lime."

I took a deep breath, looked around as if fascinated by my surroundings. We were in one of those nouveau pub chain places decorated with antique kitchen implements and rusted farm tools. On one wall, an enormous, homey sign proclaimed, without a hint of irony, LIKE NO PLACE ELSE. It had taken two weeks for my boss, Richard, to approve this expense account lunch, but he only allotted twenty-five dollars (which I suddenly, horribly, realized was at home in my wallet). It was this or Wendy's.

The dean settled back into his heavy wood chair, laced his hands over his generous stomach, and smiled benevolently, as if to a freshman in for counseling. Somewhere on the far side of middle age, the dean had the look of a former football player: bulky shoulders straining against his suit, a neck as wide as his oddly square head. What had once been muscle had softened but not shrunk. Some women might find him attractive. I didn't, but his face was kind, with crinkly light eyes and ruddy cheeks. A thatch of thinning strawberry blond hair topped it all off. From what I'd seen, Dean Archer was indeed warm and kindly. He was also boring as hell.

The article had seemed like such a good idea when I'd discussed it with Dr. Archer's dog trainer wife, whom I'd interviewed for an earlier feature, "The Four-Legged Tutor: A Guide Dog Opens Educational Doors for a Boston-Area Teen." Evelyn Archer had practically begged me to write about Mercer, whose applications dwindled each time their tuition went up, which is to say continuously. Evelyn gave such good quotes ("With a Seeing Eye dog, it's not just about having an extra set of eyes. It's about freedom. About acceptance. About love.") that I'd foolishly assumed her husband would be likewise brimming with pithy comments. I had 180 minutes worth of tape with me, but I wasn't sure that was enough to catch one quote-worthy statement from Dr. Archer.

"I had you pegged at twenty-two, twenty-three," he said to me.

"Good genes," I said reflexively. "Bad lighting." It *was* rather murky in here. And loud from all those voices bouncing off the tin ceiling. "So you were saying about colleges today, student apathy, the root problem . . ."

"Thirty-two. Wow. And not married? How was your date last night? A nice boy?"

"Nice. Nothing special. So the real problem with kids? You said . . . let me check . . . more far-reaching than absent parents and drug experimentation . . ."

"I think I was going to say TV. Too much TV. But that doesn't sound quite right. Maybe it will come to me later. Wow. You could pass for one of my students."

Women sometimes ask what kind of skin care products I use, assuming my youthful appearance must be something I either work at or purchase. Really, though, my skin is nothing special, unless you consider the light spray of freckles across the bridge of my nose. My eyes are big and blue. I'm on the short side, which may explain why I got into movies on a child's ticket until I was sixteen. I have tiny breasts and almost no hips. I keep my brown hair longish for fear of being mistaken for a thirteen-year-old boy.

For years, I wished I looked my age, if not older. A fifteen-year-old doesn't want to look eleven. A twenty-one-year-old doesn't want to look fifteen. Now that I'm getting older, I'm suddenly glad to look young. Except for today. Today I want to look forty.

The waitress brought our drinks. My seltzer had a lemon instead of a lime. Dr. Archer's Manhattan came in a frosted beer mug. I hoped he wasn't planning to drive back to western Massachusetts too soon after lunch.

Dr. Archer held up his mug. "To youth."

"To youth," I replied.

Two chicken Caesar salads and another super-sized Manhattan later, I'd learned that Mercer had a top-notch archery team and a junior year abroad program in an Eastern bloc country I couldn't pronounce. I'd digested the rationales behind ever-increasing tuition costs—something about a commitment to low student-teacher ratios and a state-of-the-art computer center. My tape recorder had run out of tape. I had found nothing worthwhile to say about Mercer College and how it was adapting to changing times. Even worse, I had no idea how I was going to pay for lunch.

The waitress dropped the check on the table—in front of Dr. Archer, no less. It almost made me like her, even though it did no good. He let it sit there. I let it sit there. He smiled kindly and started talking about affirmative action and what a stupid idea it was. I couldn't take it any more. "Dr. Archer?"

"Yes?"

"I appreciate your taking the time to talk to me."

He beamed. "The pleasure was all mine." (No argument on this end.)

"I'll send you a draft of the article before we print it so you can be sure I've portrayed your views adequately."

"I'd appreciate that," he said. He smiled. I smiled.

Finally: "Dr. Archer."

"Yes, dear?" (I'd turned into "dear" about a third of the way through the second Manhattan.)

"I don't have any money with me."

He roared, his face getting even redder, and pulled a money clip from his suit pocket. "Don't you worry about a thing, dear. A pretty little girl like you shouldn't have to pay for lunch, anyway."

It was enough to turn a person back to Lifestyles. I was good at Lifestyles. Home décor, food, entertaining—it was shallow, it was fluff, but it was fun. Besides, it was comp heaven: samples of this, free admission to that. But how could I turn down a promotion? Sheila Twisselman, the editor-in-chief, guarded the Lifestyles section closely, and she would never leave. In the midst of building a ten-thousand-square-foot "cottage" on Boston's North Shore, she needed all the Mexican tile samples she could get. She couldn't string two sentences together, but since she was married to Richard Twisselman, the publisher of *Salad* magazine ("A mix of fresh ideas"), chances of a layoff seemed slim. So when the previous education editor, an abrasive middle-aged woman who had long maintained she was underappreciated, quit the magazine to teach high school, declaring the pay better than *Salad*'s and the students more polite than Richard, I dug out my college notebooks, convinced I could do a better job. I had taken a handful of education courses during my brief save-the-world phase, and they supplied me with enough jargon to sound like I knew what I was talking about, at least when talking to Richard, who knew even less than I did. The job was mine.

To be honest, I never truly understood why *Salad* had an education section in the first place. Richard claimed it was indispensable because, "Boston is the education capital of the world." Most likely, Richard kept it because it allowed him to pretend that he ran a serious magazine. Or maybe it was a shield for even deeper insecurities. Far too many of his sentences began with the words, "When I was at Harvard . . ." For a long time, I took that to mean that he had, well, gone to Harvard. And he did: he took an extension class there. In creative writing. Anyone can take an extension class at Harvard. I once took an art history class there. It was an excellent class. But I would never say I went to Harvard.

My new job wasn't the self-actualizing, world-changing power trip I'd hoped for. I liked the title, of course, but my raise barely covered the cost of an extra frapuccino per week. I missed having interior designers (never call them decorators) back to my place for a little input on paint color. My bedroom's red accent wall is nothing short of inspired. And what I'd counted on as the biggest perk—an assistant—meant being subjected to a twenty-two-year-old named Jennifer saying things like, "You know NutraSweet? Like they put in diet soda? It causes cancer in rats? And I drink, like, ten Diet Cokes a day?"

When I got back to the office, Jennifer was hunched over my computer. Her own outdated model had crashed last week, and none of the former English majors who populated the office had the slightest idea how to fix it. Today Jennifer wore a cropped navy-and-lime striped shirt. Bent over the computer as she was, her shirt rode up in the back, revealing half a foot of freckled white skin, a long, bony spine, and a blue butterfly tattoo. One could only assume it had flown out of her ass.

"What you working on?" I dropped my bag in the middle of the desk as a way of reclaiming my territory. Then I nudged it to the side when I remembered the work I'd left her. "Those the interview notes?"

"My novel."

"How's that coming?" I tried to sound like I cared, but not too much.

"Really, really great." She leaned back and stretched. Today's navel ring was a lime rhinestone. Her powers of accessorizing never ceased to amaze me.

"And the, uh, interview notes? How are they coming?"

"I didn't get to them yet. But your article? About magnet schools?" She jabbed at they keyboard until she pulled up the file. "Okay . . . you've got: 'Ask whether magnet schools are a good thing or a bad thing, and you'll get a different answer depending on who you're talking to.' It would be cleaner if you just said, 'Ask whether magnet schools are good or bad . . .' Then, technically, it should be, 'to whom you're talking.' But that sounds kind of stuffy. So maybe we could reword."

I understood why my predecessor had hired Jennifer, who never listened to writing teachers who advised their students to write they way they spoke. Jennifer spoke like a moron. But she wrote like—well, like a writer. The problem was, I didn't need her to write. I already knew how to write. I wanted someone to free up my time so I could write more. I wanted a good typist with excellent phone manner. I wanted a woman who found inner peace through the creation of color-coded file systems. When I'd been sick the week before, Jennifer cancelled an interview by saying, "I'm calling for Kathy Hopkins. She was going to meet with you today. She's got to reschedule because she's got, like, a major case of the runs."

I moved my briefcase back to the center of the desk. "That's just the first draft. I hadn't gotten to the editing stage yet. Did anyone call?"

She stuck one electric blue plastic platform shoe on the edge of my desk. Jennifer has a preference for colors not found in nature. She smiled. "Not officially. But some guy named Dennis? First he said to tell you he called to say he had a great time last night. Then he said, no—just tell her I called. Then he said, no, never mind, I'll just call her later."

She grinned up at me and tapped her orange gel pen on my desk.

"Anyone else call?" I asked.

"Is that Dennis Stowe? From the ad agency?"

"Yes. Anyone else?"

She uncovered another scrap of paper. "Some guy named Tim McAllister. He left his number."

My face must have frozen—or shined or grimaced, or something—because she said, "Is this bad news? Or good news?" She dropped her foot off my desk and leaned forward.

"Neither," I said. "Just an old friend from college."

A few minutes later, when Jennifer had finished backing up her novel onto a disk, I returned my calls. I dialed Dennis first. I took that as a sign of growth and healing; I didn't particularly want to talk to Dennis, so I must really, really not want to talk to Tim.

I got Dennis's voice mail. I love voice mail. It means you get credit for calling without actually having to talk to anyone. "Hi, Dennis. It's Kathy, just returning your call. Thanks again for last night. I'll be in and out of the office this afternoon, but maybe we can catch up later in the week." In truth, I didn't plan to leave my desk all afternoon, except maybe to visit the candy machine, which had just been restocked with Three Musketeers bars.

I'd been supremely annoyed when Richard first instructed me to work with Dennis, who had several clients willing to place ads only if they were assured of getting positive mention in the editorial content. "People don't trust ads," Richard explained, as if this were a big revelation. "They are more likely to believe something if they read it in an article. They figure it's un-, un- . . . that the person writing it is giving their own opinion."

"But an article is hardly"—I looked him in the eye—"*unbiased* if we are, in effect, being paid to write it."

He shrugged and put up his hands, as if in defeat. "It's the way the game is played."

Still, I'd liked Dennis immediately. (Just not, you know, *in that way*.) Until he asked me out to dinner, I'd smiled every time I heard his voice on the phone. The date had ruined everything. It's not that he was ugly; I just didn't find him attractive. At all. And now that I knew he wanted more than friendship from me, I felt profoundly uncomfortable around him.

I took the message from Tim and centered it on my desk. I stared at it for a minute and then picked up the phone. As I dialed, I was dismayed to discover that my heart was throbbing all the way up to my esophagus, and my armpits were growing damp. The receptionist answered, "*New Nation?*" I hung up and trudged down the hall in search of a Three Musketeers bar.

 two

Sometimes I wish our society encouraged arranged marriages. This free will stuff is a pain in the ass. Tim could have been forced to marry me, or I could have been forced to marry Dennis. It wouldn't matter. It would be a done deal, with no guilt involved, no hours spent wondering about missed opportunities, no relatives patting my tummy and saying, "Any men in your life? Tick, tick, tick!"

I said as much to Sheila Twisselman in the health club locker room as we were swapping silk for lycra. Half naked women were everywhere. It was five-thirty, and we were all determined to work off the bulging sandwiches and dressing-sodden salads we had eaten for lunch.

I pulled on a faded Cornell T-shirt, trying to remember when it had last seen the wash. Sheila yanked on flesh-sucking, lemon yellow shorts and a sports bra to match. Yellow, she swore, was the next Big Color, and she wanted to be ahead of the trend. Since she'd spent an hour a week in a tanning salon ever since she was about three, the color didn't look bad on her. "Oh, noooo," she said in response to my arranged marriage diatribe. "Then I might not have married Richard." She pulled her hair (also yellow, and in need of a touch-up) back into a ponytail and smiled. Rumor has it that last year, when Sheila said she was going to tour the American West for decorating ideas involving shed antlers and distressed beams, she was actually recovering from her first face-lift—a present to herself for her forty-fifth birthday. I believe it. Every time she smiles, I think, "Oh! I thought she was already smiling!" Her grin reveals crooked eyeteeth. She hates the imperfection, but I like it; it makes her seem less manufactured.

"Why did you and Tim break up, anyway?" she asked. She knew all about Tim, since we were still living together when I'd started at the magazine.

"We had a difference of opinion," I said. "I thought we should be together forever, and he thought eleven years was long enough." I've used that line before. One of these days, it's going to get a laugh.

"You and Richard seem like a good couple," I said, not so subtly changing the subject. Was Sheila really in love with Richard? Or with his trust fund? The buzz in the office was that Richard's father had made his fortune manufacturing the Porta Potti. Whenever Richard sent down some especially loathsome ruling, we called him "The Prince of Poopness" behind his back.

Sheila pulled a compact out of her bag and began applying pink-tinted powder to a face that would be dripping with sweat in about five minutes. "We're more than just spouses. We're partners."

She snapped the compact shut, popped up and did a little jog in place. "You ready to work off that candy bar?" Women were irritating enough when they talked relentlessly about the food they shouldn't have eaten. But a woman who polices another's fat intake is nothing short of evil.

I once believed that if I attended step-aerobics classes regularly, I would grow to enjoy them, or at least to stop confusing my left foot with my right. I believed that when our instructor, Stacey, shouted, "FEEL—THAT—BURN! DOESN'T—THAT—FEEL—GOOD? OH—YEAH!" I would work that much harder instead of just entertaining fantasies of whacking her over the head with one of those hateful plastic steps. Now, after coming three times a week for six months, I no longer dreamed of hurting Stacey. I merely pondered how much nicer it would be if I were shopping.

After a half-hour of stepping up, down, forward, backward and sideways in time to some horrid techno music, Stacey had us take our pulse and drink water. At the water fountain, Sheila, her hair plastered to her skull, said, "Here's an idea for an article: home gyms. Like it?"

I did, and I told her so.

She drained her paper cup and threw it in the wastebasket. "Maybe Richard and I should put a gym in the cottage."

"That would really help you on the article," I said, trying not to smirk. I would love to see Richard and Sheila's tax return. Against her inflated income, she deducts the typical journalist write-offs: the computer paper, the stamps, the steam room, the koi pond . . .

Stacey gave us oversized rubber bands and instructed us

to lie on our sides. Then she told us to stretch our foot out against the band. This hurt so much that my Stacey-bashing fantasies returned. She turned on ocean sounds intended to focus us but that instead made me realize I needed to pee.

"So," Sheila grunted. "How's. Education. Working out."

"It's really. Challenging." I replied to the back of her head. The industrial carpet reeked of disinfectant that didn't quite cover up the sweat of so many yuppies.

Stacey told us to release our legs and turn to the other side. Now Sheila was looking at the back of my sweaty head. "You have any. New. Story ideas?"

"Yeah. Not exactly. Fleshed out. Yet. But. Soon."

Stacey told us to relax, lie on our backs, spread our legs out straight and jiggle them. They felt wobbly, but it was near enough to the end of the class for me to feel virtuous.

"These story ideas," Sheila continued. "Are they like the ones you've done so far? Or are you going to do anything, you know . . . racier?"

That's when I knew. Richard had set her up. Sheila and I pretended to be friends, but she was, first and foremost, my boss's wife, mouthpiece and spy. And my secret was out. Most of the time, Richard didn't know squat, but even he had recognized what I'd already suspected: that my articles about education were deadly dull.

No, they were worse than dull. They were uplifting. The first article I wrote profiled Cassandra, a blind sixteen-year-old who attended a regular high school with the assistance of Fritz, a German shepherd trained by Evelyn Archer. I quoted her parents ("She is our inspiration.") and her math teacher ("It's incredible how much she has taught me."). I neglected to mention the kid who sneezed her way through French class because she was allergic to Fritz. Exploring that angle might have made a better article: more provocative, more honest. But it just seemed mean.

After that, I wrote about a local high school that required students to perform community service as a requirement for graduation. I spent a lot of hours at nursing homes on that one. I wrote about a fifth grade teacher who spent Saturdays teaching illiterate prisoners to write their names. (I took the teacher's word for it; a trip to the prison just didn't fit into my schedule.)

Stacey dimmed the lights and turned up the ocean. "IT'S TIME TO COOL DOWN AND CALM DOWN!" she shouted, as she did every class, lest someone get carried away and doze off on the stinky carpet. I tried to visualize the ocean, but the waves kept knocking me over. I allowed myself to be swept ashore, only to be attacked by biting flies. This was hopeless. All I could think about was how badly I needed to pee.

"Maybe Richard could help you brainstorm," Sheila murmured. I squeezed my eyes shut and pictured diving back into the sea, swimming as far down as I could and holding my breath till I burst.

One good thing came from obsessing about my inadequate job performance: I stopped obsessing about Tim and the reason he'd called. As my evening at home wore on, though, the doubts about my career and my future began to overwhelm me. So I called Tim.

I had his home number; he'd been in the same apartment

since moving from Boston to D.C. three years ago. I'd called him a couple of times to update him on mutual friends—an engagement here, a baby there. Those were excuses, of course. When you've been close to someone for so long, it's hard to just break things off forever. It's not that I expected to rekindle anything with those phone calls. But he'd been there for so long: the first person to hear about all of my failures and triumphs, the friend with whom I shared all the best gossip and speculation. I thought that talking to him would make me feel less alone. After every conversation, though, I felt even more disconnected. He'd tell me about his job—he was the star writer for *New Nation*, an on-line publication that focused on politics and other "serious" issues. He'd go on for a bit about, oh God, social injustices in Zimbabwe, say, then I'd take my turn with, "The current trend in master baths is to do away with a door from the bedroom. It's supposed to make things look more open and airy, but I think it's dopey."

Finally, I stopped calling. Since he never started calling—at least until now—we hadn't spoken for over a year. As I dialed the phone, my heart boomed and my throat constricted. The phone rang once, and I hung up. I went into the kitchen and put water on for a cup of Sleepytime tea. The phone rang.

"It's Tim," he said, as if I wouldn't recognize his voice.

"Hi!" I tried to sound surprised. "Sorry I didn't call you today—just got too caught up in things."

"But you just did."

"Excuse me?"

"I have Caller ID."

I hate Caller ID even more than I love answering machines. "Right." I tried to laugh. "I decided to make a cup of tea. Then I was going to call you back." I had a sudden vision of myself as he must imagine me: hunched over, wearing a moth-eaten cardigan, surrounded by fourteen cats.

"You're probably wondering why I called you," he said. And then I knew: he was getting married. I clutched the counter.

"I hadn't really thought about it." I was trying to maintain a last shred of self-respect.

"Oh." He sounded miffed? Even as he was about to get married? Bastard. "It's a professional call, actually."

"Oh?" He was still a bastard—I mean, that I knew—but perhaps not on quite the scale I'd been imagining.

"I heard you were the new education editor at *Salad*."

"I am." I enjoyed a self-esteem rush. Free tile samples be damned—I had arrived. I've never been one of those people whose lives center around living up to their parents' expectations, but I'd never gotten over trying to impress Tim. I accepted his congratulations as nonchalantly as I could muster. Eventually, he got to the business at hand. "Do you have any contacts at Mercer College?"

I made a face at the phone. How had he found out about my humiliation at the restaurant? Was he stalking me? The thought of Tim stalking me was more appealing that I liked to admit. "I had lunch with the dean of admissions this afternoon," I said as casually as I could manage, as if I was keyed in to every institution of higher learning in New England.

"You always had a knack for networking," Tim said, absurdly. When we were together, this translated into: "How can you stand to spend that much time talking to gay men about upholstery?"

"I've got a lead on something going on at Mercer," he announced. "Could be big. Interested?"

For one surreal moment, I thought an alarm had gone off in my head. Then I realized it was simply the tea kettle whistling. "One second. I've got to get the tea." I put the phone down on the counter even though it was portable— and even though I could have easily reached the kettle, mug and sugar even if I were restrained by a cord. (My apartment is drop-dead charming, but it isn't exactly what you would call large. Even with an old-fashioned corded phone, I could have stayed on the line while I brushed my teeth and climbed into bed.) I poured water over the bag, dunked it a couple of times and let it sit. I took a deep breath and picked up the phone. "Sorry," I said. "This big story—what is it about?"

"I don't feel comfortable discussing it on the phone."

"Oh, come on."

"Not while I'm on my mobile. I was going to come up later this week. Maybe we could talk it over. Thursday afternoon work for you?"

My heart surged with even more adrenaline. I almost said yes immediately, but then I remembered how busy I was covering our nation's collapsing educational system. "I could move some things around." Very, very cool.

"I gotta run now, can't really talk. But you know, Kath, I'm really . . . it'll be nice to see you."

"Same here. And, Tim? Just out of curiosity, why do you think I might be good for this story?" I braced myself for the bullshit about how much he respects my mind and my writing, how pleased he is that I've finally focused my career on something worthwhile. I steeled myself against the warm fuzzies and a nasty flutter in my heart.

"Why? Well . . ." He sounded momentarily baffled. Then, the truth: "It's hard to do this story from D.C. and you're, you know—there."

three

The first time I saw Tim he was wearing aviator eyeglasses and a paper hat. We were in a Cornell dining hall; I was eating, he was working. I wanted ice cream—vanilla soft serve, to be exact—but the machine was empty. Tim, wearing a red Cornell T-shirt under a white apron, stood next to me, replenishing paper napkins. He tilted his chin toward the hulking stainless steel soft-serve machine. "I'll refill that."

"You don't have to," I said. "I'll just have the chocolate."

"The lady wants vanilla, the lady will have vanilla." He gave me a huge smile. There was a slight gap between his two front teeth. I smiled back because he was cute in a goofy sort of way and because no one had ever called me a lady before.

And then he was gone. I stood there uncomfortably, feeling like everyone was looking at me, although, of course, no one was. I gave him at least ninety seconds before I snagged a brownie and scurried out the door, feeling oddly rejected.

The next morning, I was sitting alone in a crowded auditorium, waiting for my Intro to Shakespeare class to begin. I'd chosen an aisle seat about a third of the way back: close enough to hear, but not so close that I'd risk eye contact with the professor. My notebook sat poised on the swing-arm desk.

"Anyone sitting there?"

I said no and moved my knees to the side without looking to see who'd be sitting next to me.

"You stood me up yesterday," he said, and I looked up, shocked. He was wearing a dark sweater, and he looked much more serious without the paper hat. I felt my face flush. He grinned, and the gap between his teeth made me think of Howdy Doody.

I settled back in my chair and raised my eyebrows. "Did you expect me to wait for you forever?"

The day after Tim's phone call, I did what any woman in the midst of an emotional crisis would do: I went shopping. The minute the clock struck five o'clock (okay, it was four fifty-eight), I made my way to Washington Street. My goal was to find an outfit for Thursday, something chic and sophisticated—or, barring that, at least something that fit right. I was getting a mushy tummy, compliments of my candy bar and cookies diet.

"You are not fat," assured my friend Marcy. "*I* am fat." Five months pregnant with her third child, she was still carting around excess thigh and butt baggage from kids one and two, who were home with a fifteen-year-old girl who lived down the street. An associate lawyer toiling on the partner track, Marcy's husband, Dan, risked jeopardizing his career if he left before nine.

"Dan's worked weekends for the past month," Marcy said. "The boys and I were in the Walgreen's parking lot a couple of weeks ago—I was buying Tucks pads; don't ask—and Joshy spots this tall guy and starts yelling, 'Daddy! Daddy!' The guy didn't even look like Dan! He was blond, for God's sake! So I tell Dan, 'Your own son can't even remember what you look like.' "

"Guilt is good," I said.

In the dressing room, I peeled off a ribbed T-shirt dress that revealed me to be curvaceous in all the wrong places. I tossed it to Marcy, who shifted uncomfortably on the hard bench. She stuck the dress back on the hanger.

"You are not fat," I assured her, staring at my white body in the full-length mirror. "You are filled with life. I, on the other hand, am filled with Doritos and TV dinners." Normally, I am not comfortable traipsing around in my undies and inspecting my body in front of other people, but Marcy was my college roommate for three years. She has seen me vomit, and she has seen me through my big hair phase. Nothing can shock her.

"You look great," she assured me.

"I was so much skinnier in college," I sighed. I saw her narrow her eyes. "Okay, except for that fat phase freshman year."

"And junior year," she snorted. "You look a hell of a lot better now than you did junior year."

Dan, who I've known almost as long as I've known Marcy, once declared that he'd give anything to hear what

Marcy and I said to each other when we thought no one else was listening. I occasionally worried that he would—and that our mystique, such as it was, would be gone forever.

In truth, I'd been feeling neglected by Marcy of late. For years we spoke at least once a day. Now she forgot to return my phone calls and apologized for not having more time to spend with me, even as she amassed a small army of minivan-driving mommy friends. She had missed my birthday two years running.

In the end, I picked out a brightly colored scarf to go with a black shirt and stretchy black skirt I already owned. This would draw the eye up to my youthful face. If I chose a dark restaurant for lunch, Tim might not see my body at all.

I got in line while Marcy went off to the baby section to look for some stretchies. I felt a tap on my shoulder and turned. There was Dennis, smiling and holding the shirt of my dreams: pale blue linen, sleeveless with a Chinese collar. "That for you?" I asked after a moment of awkwardness. His face, already ruddy, turned apple red, starting at the neck and working its way up. From his reaction, I wondered for a moment if he actually did enjoy a little cross-dressing.

"It's for my sister's birthday." He smiled, revealing straight, tiny teeth. I feel bad for red-haired guys. You take one look and think, "Here's a guy I could never take to the beach."

"It's pretty," I said, eyeing the blouse and wondering if it would fit me. "Were there, um, any more? Maybe in a smaller size?"

"No, this was the only one," he said. Damn. "The scarf you're buying is nice, too. Is it for you?"

"Yes, it is."

"It's pretty."

"Thanks."

We smiled at each other. When we'd gone out to dinner the other night, our conversation had run pretty much along the same lines: What looks good to you? I was thinking about the salmon. I love salmon. And you? The pasta special or maybe the steak. Everything looks so delicious. Sure does. Pretty place. Sure is.

The evening was so pleasant, it made me want to spew profanities and run naked through the street.

The crazy thing was, we had never run out of things to say to each other before he'd asked me out. He'd call to give me a phone number for an interview, and we'd end up yakking for half an hour about how to remove red wine stains from upholstery or what movies we wanted to see or which celebrities we found most annoying. The minute he'd tried to move our relationship out of the platonic zone, I found myself clamming up in his presence, wishing desperately we could go back to the way things were.

I checked the girl at the cash register. She appeared to be on sedatives. And there were two people ahead of me in line. "I talked to John about you," Dennis said. "My boss."

"Oh?" My stomach churned. His boss? Was that a trial run for telling his mother that he had a new squeeze? In my head, I began to construct my "Dennis, you're a really nice guy, but—" speech.

"He'd like to have you in for an interview."

I squinted at him, confused for a moment, then: "Oh! About being a copywriter." Before our dinner—back when we used to have normal conversations—I'd vented to Dennis about Richard's cheapness, stupidity and nepotism.

"I appreciate that, but with my promotion, well, I'm happy at *Salad*, at least for now. Besides, I'm a writer. I don't want to do anything else."

"You'd still be a writer."

"Yes, but it would be—different." I'd learned long ago that advertising is populated by would-be novelists, and it's best to avoid touching delicate nerves by stating the obvious: that crafting words to sell, say, foot powder isn't exactly reaching your literary potential.

"Not necessarily," he said. "We've got a fabric and wall-cover client—you'd be perfect. He wants us to give him some advertorials, you know, ads that look and read just like articles." His voice grew suddenly lower, more confident, like he was telling me that he could sell the movie rights to my as-yet-unwritten novel for five bazillion dollars.

"That's nice, Dennis. But the things I'm writing now really *are* articles."

That stopped him cold. There's something about a lousy salary. It makes you passionate to defend your career choice (since you're obviously not in it for the money). It also makes you snotty and mean.

"Forget it, then," he said, hunching over and pulling at the blouse. "I didn't mean to push."

"No, I'm sorry. I didn't mean to sound so . . ."

"Superior?" He was holding his lips tight, standing his ground. It was my turn to blush.

"I was going to say defensive, but maybe that's how it sounded." I scanned the room for Marcy. Where the hell was she? "I'm stressed by my new position, is all. It seems important—it is important—but it's taking a lot out of me to get up to speed, and I guess it's making me testy." I didn't say that the best part about my job was that

Richard had not yet thought to sell ads to Seeing Eye dog trainers.

Dennis laughed and then—God help me—beamed. "I'm glad you feel comfortable telling me the truth. So tell me this. Will you go shopping with me this weekend?"

He caught me before I'd had a chance to come up with an excuse. "I'd love to."

He smiled, showing me his little teeth once again. "Guess we've had our first fight."

 four

My new scarf really did look good with my black shirt and skirt. It looked so good, in fact, that when the weatherman declared Thursday "a scorcher," I wore it anyway, telling myself that I'd be traveling from air-conditioned place to air-conditioned place. For lunch, I'd chosen a bright, airy restaurant that featured potted palms, crisp white tablecloths and California cuisine. By the time I got there, I had completely sweated off my makeup, and my hair, which I'd actually taken time to style, was limp. The scarf stuck to my neck. Had I been meeting anyone else, I would have peeled it off. At least it would help catch the perspiration droplets from behind my ears.

As I'd hoped, Tim had gotten there first (I was intentionally five minutes late). Either because he forgot how much I detest the heat (he never really cared for me, never paid attention) or because he wanted me to be miserable (heartless bastard), he had chosen a table outside. "The ones with the umbrellas were all taken," he said, standing up as I approached.

"Not a problem," I said, diffusing any memories he may have had of me as a whiner. My heart was pounding. We hugged and kissed in a superficial, "Darling, it's fabulous to see you" kind of way. For the quickest moment, I thought I could pull it off—I could convince myself (and him) that bygones were bygones. But when our lips touched, I was horrified to recognize his smell and his taste. At least I never bothered spending time and money in therapy; all my work would have been undone in that brief moment. I knew I was blushing and was almost glad to have the heat as an excuse.

We sat down and I examined him as closely as I could without actually staring. He looked pretty much the same, I was disappointed to see. I'd kind of hoped for a softening middle or at least some grim lines around his mouth, resulting from his newfound unhappiness. But there he was: same wiry build, alert gray eyes, bony hands. The glasses were new, black-rimmed and rectangular. They made him seem artsy. "What happened to your contacts?" I asked. In college, he used to say that only the poor kids wore glasses. He traded in his aviator shades three months after graduation.

He shrugged. "I never really got used to sticking myself in the eye."

The waitress—a vacant-eyed, streaky-haired, nubile type in a khaki skirt that was too short to be tasteful—asked what we'd like to drink. I hoped Tim would order first so I could take his lead in the whole alcoholic/nonalcoholic game. But he nodded to me, and I boldly ordered a white wine, in the hope in would neutralize some of my adrenaline. Perhaps the nymphet waitress would card me and Tim could say something like, "You really do look amazing." But all the waitress said was, "We're out of chardonnay. White zinfandel okay?" She scratched her thigh with her pen in a way that I found inappropriate. I said yes to the wine even though I detest white zinfandel. Tim ordered a seltzer. I felt like a lush.

"How've you been?" he asked.

"Good," I answered. "Busy," I lied. I was clutching the sides of the wrought iron chair. I casually picked my cloth napkin off the table and smoothed it on my lap, wiping the sweat off my palms as I did so.

"You see Marcy much?" A busboy appeared to pour water, and Tim glanced up with an easy smile. Damn it—he looked genuinely calm.

"Pretty often. She's pregnant again."

"Wow." His eyebrows shot up. "How many does she have?"

"Two. Both boys. She's hoping for a girl."

He smiled and rolled his eyes as if to say, *Reproduction: yuck!* "And Dan? Still a workaholic?"

I grinned. In college and afterwards, we'd snickered at "straight-arrow Dan and his ten-year plan." Tim and I never had a plan, which I once thought was a good thing. "He's close to making partner," I said. "So he's working around the clock. Marcy never sees him."

"She's gotten pregnant three times, though," he said. "So I guess they're still having sex Tuesdays, Fridays, and alternate Sunday mornings."

"They had to drop the Sundays," I said. "The kids get up too early." I felt a twinge of guilt for ratting out my

best friend's secrets, but I'd always assumed Marcy and
Dan whispered about Tim and me, too. When Tim walked
out three years ago (a week after my twenty-ninth birthday), I called Marcy immediately, expecting her to be
shocked. I longed for her to tell me it was just a phase, that
he'd be back. Instead, she was quiet for a moment before
finally saying, "He's not good enough for you, honey. He
never was."

"Tell me about your job," Tim said, tantalizing me
with the possibility that maybe he did care, just a little.

"I'm the education editor," I said. He knew that already, but it sounded impressive, so I wanted to reiterate.
"The scope is daunting," I intoned, figuring that sounded
better than "paralyzing." "But I enjoy the challenge." A
total lie, of course, but I was working my way into Em-
powered Woman Mode, if only for the hour. I rattled on
about lowered educational standards and societal responsibility and the scope of my job.

I paused for a moment when I realized that even I was
no longer listening to my drivel. A drop of sweat slithered
down my back. I looked at Tim, his intense gaze, his stiff
shoulders. He was listening. For years, he had loved me—
at least in his own way—and he knew me as well as anyone. For an instant, I considered spilling it: how I didn't
give a damn about magnet schools or teacher testing or
corporate sponsorships for underprivileged students; how
my mind still wandered to tumbled-marble bathroom ac-
cents and gleaming maple floors.

But I waited too long, and he filled the silence with
proclamations about his own job and the social and politi-
cal force of *New Nation*. And then, after talking for a while
like a normal person, he said, "With the unprecedented

dissemination of information, society is being shaped by the media beyond its own will. So we have a choice. We can either help mold the collective consciousness or we can remain passive and allow our opinions to be shaped according to someone else's agenda." I experienced a rare flash of superiority, knowing full well that I had outscored Tim on the verbal SAT. Then I grew despondent. Somehow, it wasn't the time to start chattering about Ralph Lauren paints. Instead, I smirked in a way that I hoped was patronizing and said, "My, we've gotten deep."

He leaned back and laughed, sounding human at last. "You always could cut me down to size." We both knew the opposite was true but left it at that.

The slutty waitress brought our drinks. "Know what you want?" she asked.

"Excuse me?" I frowned, feeling violated.

"I think she wants to take our order, Kath." Tim grinned at the waitress. "Unless you're getting existential with us?" The waitress laughed, even though I'd bet money she didn't even know what "existential" means.

Between my nerves and the heat, I wasn't hungry, but I ordered grilled eggplant and goat cheese on focaccia. The portions here were oversized, and a sandwich would hold up better than a salad in a takeout container and save me from having to make dinner. Tim ordered a burger. Tim always orders a burger. He's one of those people who honest-to-God doesn't care about food, and a burger is something he doesn't have to think about.

When Tim and I lived together, I prepared pastas with sun-dried tomatoes and buttery sole with lemon. I was a freelancer then, writing for home and cooking magazines. On weekends, I'd invite other couples over for wine tastings

or "ethnic food experiences," and I'd spend entire days
tracking down obscure ingredients just so I could put aster-
isks on my recipes with a notation of, say, "available in east
African food markets." Tim didn't care much about the
food, of course, but he liked having people over, his cowork-
ers especially, but Marcy and Dan, too, and he liked seeing
how impressed they were by my creations.

Now, standing at my kitchen counter, I'd eat Triscuits
and port wine cheese spread until my stomach stopped
gurgling and call it dinner. Sometimes I'd invite friends
over not because I was feeling sociable but just so I'd have
an excuse to make real food. I'd double the recipe and fill
my fridge with Tupperware-encased leftovers. After four
straight nights of, say, lamb paprikash, I would usually
shove the rest down the disposal and nuke myself a Lean
Cuisine.

Tim gulped his seltzer. I gulped my wine—the heat
made me thirsty—and could practically feel my brain cells
keeling over from the shock. He cleared his throat. "After
our phone call, you're probably wondering why I came all
the way up here instead of just giving you the details on
the phone."

That's when it struck me: here I was, sitting across
from my first lover, the man I long assumed I would
marry, and we were having a business lunch. "I hadn't really thought about it," I said. And it was true: I'd been so
nervous about what it would be like to see him again that
I hadn't bothered to wonder about the story he'd alluded
to. "I figured you were just up here, anyway," I said. "Re-
searching that article you mentioned."

"It's bigger than that." He leaned forward. "I had to
see you in person." He lowered his voice. "This story is

huge. I know I don't have to tell you that this conversation is confidential."

"If you know you don't have to tell me, why are you telling me?"

"I know I can trust you," he said.

I resisted the twenty or so comebacks that jumped in my brain. "I'm listening," I said.

The story came from an intern who'd worked for Tim. Deirdre was a climber, he said, always looking for recognition, always expecting to be treated like one of the staff (who, if they were like Tim, had worked years to get to a position in which they could look down on interns). When Tim began covering a story about a politician's relationship with a call girl, Deirdre kept remarking how the same thing went on at her school, Mercer College. At first, Tim didn't think much of it. He assumed she was simply referring to the promiscuity and pig-like behavior so prevalent at institutions of higher learning. (He said this almost wistfully, undoubtedly thinking of how much he missed out on by having me as his steady girlfriend for his entire college career.) But when the call girl's fees came to light, Deirdre remarked, "Wow. That's a whole lot more than the girls at school make."

And this is when he started to listen. "How much do college call girls make these days?"

Deirdre plopped herself down in a chair and waited for a moment before finally asking, "Do you want to hear about it?"

He did.

The call girl operation was a longstanding Mercer College business, Deirdre said. Very entrepreneurial: student-founded, student-operated, student-owned. It was an open secret, winked at by the faculty and snickered at by non-participating students, who nevertheless were awed by the wicked glamour. No one knew exactly how big an operation it was; most guessed that there were ten or fifteen women on the roster.

Engrossed in the story, I was vaguely titillated, as if reading a tabloid headline while waiting to buy groceries. Then I remembered that Tim was not telling me this for my entertainment. "I don't see how—what good would I be on this story?" It was too much to hope that he'd ask me to write a feature on bordello décor.

"You've got the contacts."

I felt myself backtracking, trying to undo my bragging. "Just the dean of admissions. And he's easy to reach—listed in the college directory. I just did one interview. We're not close."

"And you've got this whole education thing working," he said. "You understand the system."

"I don't, though." I was speaking fast now, in a desperate bid to convey my incompetence. "I understand blind children taking their dogs to school, I understand replacing soda machines with juice dispensers. And anyway, I don't see how relevant all this is to education. This thing, it sounds like something you'd read in the *National Enquirer.*"

"These days, all the big news starts at the *National Enquirer*—the stuff everyone's too squeamish to print until it shows up in the grocery store checkout line. Besides, it's not like this story is without precedent. Don't you remember, back in the eighties, that big scandal about Ivy League prostitution? It was on the front page of the *New York Times.*"

Tim has had a subscription to the *Times* since he was in the sixth grade.

"The eighties?" I took a swig of my water. "If it wasn't in *Tiger Beat* magazine, I'd have missed it."

"Well, it was big, mainstream, national news." He leaned forward. "And it's happening again."

"I don't think I'm the right person for the job," I said.

He put his elbows on the table, leaned forward, closed his eyes and rubbed his temples. I recognized this gesture. It had always made me feel inadequate. He leaned back, opened his eyes. "You're perfectly positioned," he said. "You've got the title, you're affiliated with this"—he searched for an adjective that wouldn't annoy me—"non-threatening publication. People will be relaxed around you. Anyone you talk to will assume you're only going to say positive things about them because that's all *Salad* ever does."

He'd gone as far as he could on the Internet, he said, spending hours searching under "call girls," "prostitution," and "Mercer College." He was now on the e-mail lists of at least thirty porn sites, but he'd gotten no closer to breaking the story. "Deirdre says they keep it under wraps—it's all word of mouth."

He outlined his proposal: together, we would "blow this thing open." The story, under the byline, "Tim McAllister (with Kathy Hopkins, *Salad* magazine)," would break on-line in *New Nation*, and follow in print a day later in *Salad*. Any reprint or syndication fees would be split seventy-five/twenty-five in favor of *New Nation*. "I'll run it by my publisher," I said, wishing I could pitch a story on dorm decorating instead. ("Move over, plastic milk crates!") "He might not like it."

 five

"I love it," Richard said. "I LOVE IT."

"Is it really us, though?" I asked desperately. "We've got to keep our identity consistent."

"Sex in higher education." He walked to his window, looked out at the traffic, strode back to his desk. He was too excited to keep still. "This will get *Salad* the recognition we've been looking for. This will sell magazines. This will sell ad space!"

Sheila backed Richard up, of course. "Don't be afraid of a challenge, Kathy." She squeezed my arm in a show of sisterly support. This was what Sheila did every time she wanted to be convincing: she touched you and she inserted your name into conversation. "Kathy," she continued. "You've got to be willing to stretch sometimes, Kathy."

"It's not my ability I'm questioning," I hissed, suddenly wondering if I should have gone to law school like most of the other English majors I knew. "It's the magazine's reputation." Actually, *Salad* didn't have much of a reputation, good or bad, which was its real problem.

Only Jennifer was on my side. "Call girls? At college? That's, like, so *Inside Edition*." Jennifer, clad in a turquoise spandex mini dress and silver spike heels, was looking a bit like a professional herself today.

I tried every defensive tactic I could come up with. The advertisers might be put off by a story that revolved around illicit sex, I said. "Then why do advertisers pay so much to advertise in *People?*" Richard roared. "In *Cosmo?* In *U.S. News and World Report,* for Chrissakes? Because sex sells!"

I defended some of the important stories I had in the pipeline and expressed my concern that they might be neglected. "Nobody gives a rat's fuck about Shakespeare in the elementary schools!" he yelled. "What kind of a jackass really thinks a bunch of ten-year-olds are going to like *Hamlet?*"

"Richard, honey," Sheila murmured, rubbing his thigh. "You're a passionate man, and I love that about you, but think if this is the kind of language you really want to be using, Richard."

I couldn't talk my way out of it. It was settled: I was to make the coed call girls story my top priority, spending as much time in Western Massachusetts as needed. Richard's main concern revolved around Tim, whom I'd described as "an old friend from college," and the collaboration with his on-line publication. Richard said, "We don't want to get lost in this deal, leave all the credit to *New Nation*."

I didn't care about any of that, of course. "What about the stories I'm working on? I can't just abandon them." I was feeling very defensive on the bard's behalf.

"Jennifer can help with the filler pieces," Richard said, brushing the air.

"But I need her as my sec—" I caught myself just in time. "As my assistant."

"She's still your assistant," Richard said. "She'll do both."

"She's up to the challenge," Sheila chimed in.

Jennifer looked up from her nails, which appeared to have been decorated with glitter glue. "This is *so* going to cut into my novel," she muttered.

I called Tim to give him the good news. "I knew you wouldn't pass this up," he said. And I wondered, yet again, if he knew me at all.

Once I'd thought Tim knew me better than anyone else on the planet. After we met for the second time, in the lecture hall, he offered to buy me a cup of coffee, and I said yes even though I hadn't started drinking coffee yet. I said yes because he was sophisticated enough to "need a shot of caffeine." He drank his coffee black, which I found impossibly worldly.

I don't remember everything we talked about in the snack bar that day, but I remember how he looked at me, like there was no one else in the room. I'd had a couple of boyfriends in high school, gone to formal dances, made out in the back seat of a few station wagons. But no one had ever looked at me like that before. For years, he looked at me like that. Then, gradually, he didn't. Since Tim left, there have been days when I've wondered if anyone will ever look at me like that again.

For now, at least, Tim and I had something in common, a shared goal. My first task was to "feel out" my contacts. I spent maybe three minutes thinking of the best way of approaching the dean. "Oh! I forgot to ask in my interview the other day—do you have hookers at your school?" I headed to the library instead.

I love any excuse to leave the office, and a visit to the Boston Public Library, which just manages to be too far from the office to walk to, meant a trip on the T. To prepare for the journey, I popped into an Au Bon Pain for a croissant and an iced coffee. One must keep up one's strength. Then, because I'd need something to read while on public transportation, I bought a decorating magazine entitled, *Windows and Walls,* both of which I happen to have in my apartment.

At the library, I tried the computers first, but most of the information I sought was labeled "restricted"—meaning, I guess, that if you want to look at porn, you have to be a librarian. Instead, I hit the stacks. My first valuable piece of retail material: *Mayflower Madam*, by Sidney Biddle Barrows. I settled into a comfy chair and smirked at the thought that I was getting paid for this. Most people who make the kind of money that I do have to spend their days flipping burgers or punching cash registers. Thirty pages into the book, I was convinced I had chosen the wrong profession. As told by Barrows, prostitution was even better than being a lawyer, which, after all, involved endless briefs and gray suits with skirts that fell below the knee. Forty pages in, I realized that call girls had to do more than wear fabulous clothes and answer to a name like Camille. They actually had to have sex with the old farts.

The library was pleasant: noise and temperature-controlled. Maybe I should have been a librarian.

I leafed through some other books and clicked through some unrestricted on-line articles. By the end of the day,

I was an expert on all the things they don't teach you about in college: sexual role-playing, garter belts, and vaginal condoms. I developed a new appreciation for law-abiding madams who paid taxes. I discovered that most masseuses really aren't hookers and that dominatrixes rarely have sex with their clients. Finally, I confirmed what I'd always suspected: that everyone was having sex more than I was.

How I was supposed to apply all of this to Mercer College, I hadn't a clue. On Monday, I'd "poke around" at the campus. I didn't really know what that entailed, since my interviews had always been "soft," engaged with willing participants who often approved my final draft before it went to print.

Meanwhile, I had a weekend to endure.

 six

It could have been worse. I could have been eating Häagen-Dazs from a carton and watching cartoons when Dennis showed up at my door on Saturday morning. I use the term "morning" loosely. It was just past noon. And I was asleep.

I don't know why I even answered the door. A single woman living alone should know better. He could have been a rapist. Or a Mormon.

At least I was decent, clad in the bathrobe my mother had given me when I was in college and she thought I was still a virgin. High-necked, flowered and frilly, it would arouse any man whose first sexual fantasies had revolved around Laura Ingalls.

"Oh God. I should have called to confirm." Attired in an apricot polo shirt and white Bermuda shorts, he looked crisp and clean, like he'd risen with the sun and energized himself with yoga and a supplement-laden smoothie. "I just—I thought we had plans . . ."

I do not wake easily, especially after a mere twelve hours of shut-eye. "Uh," I said. "Nuh. S'okay. Jus' napping." I am one of those inflexible types who hates it when someone shows up without calling first, even when I'm awake and my apartment is clean. As it was, I had an empty bottle of wine on my coffee table (it had started half empty, but how was he to know?) and Oreo crumbs all over the floor. Against my better instincts, I had spent Friday night planted in front of the television, watching *Dirty Dancing* and *An Officer and a Gentleman* on cable. I hated myself for being such a girl—and a sloppy one at that. My kitchen counter, which overlooks the living room, hadn't been cleared in weeks, and it was buried under catalogues, candy wrappers and overdue bills. Had I been a "look on the bright side" sort, I would have appreciated this encounter in the hope that Dennis would lose interest in me, an obvious pig. Instead, I saw myself through his eyes and was repulsed.

"I thought we could go shopping," he said. "But I can come back."

"Nuh, nuh. I'll get dressed." I motioned him into my living room and attempted a smile, which probably reeked of morning mouth. "Coffee," I intoned. "Jus' need coffee."

Women are so much better than men. A woman would have sensed my discomfort immediately and done her utmost to diffuse it. "Oh! I'm so sorry I didn't call first! I love sleeping late, too," she would have confided, assuring me that the only reason she was up before lunch today was because those pesky neighbors next door—or that noisy truck or that high-strung dog—were making such a racket. Then she would have shrugged it off and gotten out of my way as quickly as possible. "You go back to sleep," she would have commanded. "I'll give you a buzz later and tell you about all the good shopping you missed out on."

But Dennis wasn't a woman. (Which was the problem, now, wasn't it?) He merely settled himself on my floral plum couch ("Nice pattern," he did have the decency to say) and told me he'd be there whenever I was ready.

He didn't even want to buy anything—that was the real kicker. All he'd put me through, and he merely wanted to browse. His company had just gotten a big account with Mission Accomplished, a yuppie furniture store, and he was the account executive.

"The creatives ran some ideas past me, and I'm just not satisfied. I'd like you to tell me what you think." He walked briskly through the warm city streets. I practically had to jog to keep up with him. Mission Accomplished was in Back Bay, normally a fifteen minute walk from my Beacon Hill apartment, but we reached it in only ten. My stomach gurgled, my head hurt, and I was sweating like a pig. I needed more coffee, preferably iced. I hoped the next guy who had a thing for me would be more into wining-and-dining me and less into furthering his career.

As its name implied, Mission Accomplished carried a lot of mission style furniture, along with other simple, complementary and equally inoffensive items. There were mid-priced Mission tables, ladder back chairs, oatmeal-colored couches. It was like Pottery Barn without the panache. I found it a little too dull, a little too safe—a good bet for yuppies who have no sense of style but want to show they have class.

We stood in the middle of the showroom, thinking, comfortable for once in our silence. "What do you think?" he finally asked. Soft jazz played in the background while young couples dressed in polo shirts and khakis tiptoed across the plush carpeting, hesitantly fingering the furniture.

I tried to think of a nice word for "boring." "It's inoffensive," I finally said. "Doesn't thrill me."

"It doesn't have to," he said. "How would you sell it?"

"I have no idea."

He squinted at me for a minute. "The creatives are fixating on understatement. 'Furniture shouldn't shout, it should whisper.' Or, 'For people who don't need to prove anything.' Is it just me, or is that ho-hum?" We stopped in front of an overstuffed beige-and-white-striped couch and sat down. The couch was really comfortable, actually. Surrounded by the right accent pieces, it could really make a room.

I grinned. "It's not just you."

He picked up a sage chenille pillow and pulled at the fringe. "But how else do you get the message across?"

I looked around again, searching without luck for a single eccentric, colorful piece. "Define it by what it's not."

"I don't follow."

"People shop here because they're afraid of making a mistake, because they'd rather be boring than risk looking tasteless."

"Catchy," he said. "But I don't think management would go for it."

"No," I laughed. "You don't actually say that. I'm just trying to understand why someone would shop here in the first place."

"How do we tap into that?"

"You tap into their fears . . . and then make light of them. Okay," I said, thinking as I spoke. "Say you have a picture of this really ugly, really fussy couch. Bad color, lots of flounces. And underneath you have a line that says—wait! I've got it! Right in the middle of the couch is this bumper sticker that says, 'My other couch is a Mission Accomplished.' " I actually clapped my hands and was immediately appalled at such reflexive corniness.

Dennis didn't say anything. He just smiled and gazed at me with far too much delight.

I settled back into the cushy couch. "Beginner's luck."

"You like this. Admit it."

"It's fun." Next to the couch was a vase that I actually liked: sandstone, spherical, simple in the best sense. "But I can't imagine doing it every day, getting paid to do it."

"Isn't that the ultimate goal? To get paid for something that seems too fun to be work?"

I picked up the vase and checked the tag: too expensive for a writer's budget. "You've been reading too many self-help books." I put the vase back on its glass and wrought iron pedestal.

We went to a fifties style diner for brunch. It was considerate of Dennis to suggest brunch, I thought, when the rest of the city was thinking about dinner. The restaurant's air-conditioning made me shiver. I hate that about summer: it's always too hot outside, too cold in. I warmed my hands on my chunky coffee mug and rubbed the goose-flesh on my arms. Dennis asked the waitress to adjust the temperature.

Dennis twisted his neck around to inspect the neon and chrome. "What do you think of this place? Too kitschy?"

I shrugged. "There's good kitsch and bad kitsch. You get a diner that no one's bothered to update since the fifties—that's good kitsch. But at least in a place like this, you know you won't get hepatitis."

Our banter felt easy, natural—just as it had before our dinner date. Maybe I was overthinking things. Maybe I should just relax and see what happened.

"What are you doing this evening?" he asked. "There's this new bar in Harvard Square I've been wanting to check out."

Whoa. Too much, too soon. So much for relaxing.

"Sounds fun, but I've got a million things to do," I said, suddenly anxious to return to my empty apartment.

 seven

Monday I headed to Mercer College. I made the mistake of leaving at the height of rush hour, and even the reverse commute on the Mass Pike put me into bumper-to-bumper traffic. Traffic started moving once I hit the suburbs, and I know it was mean-spirited to feel smug at the sight of the inbound traffic, which was still inching along, but hey: you grab your pleasures where you can. A short time later, the traffic cleared and the land opened up, green and even, and I would have driven eighty miles an hour but for my four-cylinder engine and my deeply in-grained fear of speeding tickets.

Shortly before I hit the Mercer, I stopped for fuel because I wasn't sure the town was big enough to support a gas station. My faded beige Civic got excellent mileage, but I kept the gas receipt anyway. Richard was famously lax about reimbursing expenses. If he ignored enough of mine, I could simply refuse to visit the college again, and he'd start giving me some more of the usual, boring but normal assignments.

Yeah, that might work.

Higher up on my list of worries was finding a parking spot when I returned home. I'd bought my car (used) when I'd turned thirty because I felt that being an adult meant owning a car. Growing up in the suburbs spawns some twisted thinking. I had a Beacon Hill resident sticker for on-street parking, but spots were still scarce, especially in the evening, when people drove home from work; although Beacon Hill is within walking distance of most Boston businesses, a surprising number of residents commute out of the city. If I returned too late tonight, I might have to pay to park my car in a garage only to reclaim it and repark in the morning, when the commuters had left.

At last I reached the "blink and you'll miss it" town of Mercer, Massachusetts. It was one of those villages where life revolves around the college for the simple reason that there isn't a heck of a lot else there. After driving past College Cleaners, College Liquors ("We check ID's") and College Drugs (Did no one else find that funny?), I stopped at a gas station (there was one, after all) to ask for directions, which turned out to be, "Keep going down the road. Can't miss it."

My first step as an investigative reporter was to visit the admissions office and acquire a course catalogue. "I'd like a catalogue," I told the middle-aged, soft-bodied secretary.

"Sure," she said, without looking up. I was definitely making progress.

My second step was to scope the place out. In other words, I walked around, using the map in the course catalogue as my guide. Mercer College was green, leafy, brick-abundant in an East Coast, almost-Ivy kind of way. The student center contained worn oak tables and endless bulletin boards. The drama center featured a large stage. The stadium was too far from campus to bother visiting, but I studied the catalogue's picture for long enough to feel I had been there.

Behind the green, an enormous, blocky building was under construction. Next to it, a heavyweight sign read:

COMING SOON:
MERCER COLLEGE FITNESS CENTER

Rock Climbing Wall
Nautilus
Racquetball
Jacuzzi and Sauna
Video Arcade
Smoothie Bar

"True enjoyment comes from activity of the mind and exercise of the body; the two are united."
—*Alexander von Humboldt*

So that explained the rising tuition costs. Low student-to-teacher ratio, my ass.

In the student lounge, I partook of a coffee with skim milk and a blueberry muffin and read the course catalogue. On the way out of the lounge I picked up a free copy of the *Mercer Bugle* and stuck it in my briefcase for later perusal.

Throughout the day, I took copious notes, including my muffin among the details because you never know what might be relevant. Since it was summer, there were no students to interview, but I spoke to every university

worker who crossed my path. "Nice day." "Sure is quiet."
"Must be tough to get those coffee stains out of the oak."
To an onlooker, these exchanges would seem insignificant.
But I was relationship-building. Finding sources.

Tim was unimpressed. "A muffin?"

"That wasn't the only thing! I was just being thorough.
There were eleven pages of notes, in case you missed it."
He'd called just as I had started painting my toenails silver. I knew he would think such vanity silly, especially for
someone who was too old for a color out of the red or pink
family, and it ruined the moment. I screwed the top back
on the bottle. I took the portable phone into the bathroom, where I retrieved nail polish remover and a tissue.

I could hear his mouse clicking as he scrolled through
my notes. "I just—it just—I can't . . . you say here—I'm
on page four—that the dormitory beds were maple but the
desks were oak. This is significant because . . . ?"

"It wasn't easy to get admitted to a dorm, you know.
They're all shut up for the season, you know." Actually, I'd
stumbled across a dormitory that had its main door
propped open. I tiptoed into the foyer, peeked into a room
and scurried out before anyone could see me.

I scrubbed the polish off my two completed toes with
unnecessary violence. My voice was getting high and tight
in a way Tim undoubtedly recognized from our past. ("I
was counting on you to pick up the eggplant for the
recipe, you know." Or, "We're supposed to be at the party
at six, you know, and it's already six-thirty.")

"I know," he said, slow and low. In my naïve youth, I had

taken this stock response to mean, "You are right; I am ir-
rational and mean and ever so lucky to have you in my life."
Older now, my interpretation skills had improved. A closer
reading: "Just shut up, already."

"I don't see any mention of the admissions guy," he
said. "What was his name?"

"Archer."

"Right. I kind of assumed you'd meet with him."

"I've already met with him. I didn't have any other
questions."

"You could have asked—" He stopped and sighed. "Oh,
never mind. I just thought you'd come up with a little
more than this."

Back in the living room, I found my shoulder bag and
dug around till I found my notebook. The *Mercer Bugle*,
that thin freebie newspaper, came out with it. I scanned
my handwritten notes, looking for any worthwhile tidbit
that I may have neglected in my e-mail to Tim. Nothing.
Trying to eliminate all traces of shrillness from my voice, I
said, "I can't just go up to a random someone—custodial
worker, dean—and ask if they know anything about a
prostitution ring. Maybe someone else could. Maybe I'm
just not right for this assignment."

"You're fine for this assignment," he cooed, assuming I
was looking for his assurances when, really, I just wanted
to be fired. "This is a change of direction for you, that's all.
You'll catch on."

I shoved the notebook back into my briefcase. The
newspaper was still in my hand. I was looking at the back
page, I realized, the classifieds. My eye fell on the ads
in the personals section. (I read newspaper personals more

often than I care to admit, though I've never gone so far as to answer one.)

And there it was: *Need some excitement in your life? Let a hot college girl show you a good time. Call Chantal . . .*

"Tim," I said slowly, "I think I've got something."

 eight

I wore a denim mini skirt to the airport. Tim had on jeans, so I figured I'd made the right call. I sensed some ambivalence on his part, though; he'd paired the denim with a white office shirt and tie. He probably thought that made him look journalistic. Instead, it showed just how deep his problems with commitment ran. He couldn't even commit to a look.

"You're wearing contacts again," I remarked when he climbed into my car.

"You made me self-conscious the other day," he said.

"I didn't mean to," I said, although I was pleased that I had.

On the drive out to Mercer, we didn't talk about the investigation at all. We didn't even talk about our jobs. Instead, we caught each other up on gossip: marriages, babies and divorces. It amazed me that so many of my contemporaries had seen marriages through to their ends. It made them seem older than me, somehow.

We brought each other up-to-date on our families. His parents were still in upstate New York, while mine had moved from Connecticut to Scottsdale, Arizona, a short plane ride away from my as-yet-childless but presumably fertile brother and sister-in-law in Colorado. Meanwhile, while they awaited grandparenthood, my parents entertained themselves with a succession of exotic tours. Last month it was the Great Wall of China. In the fall they were planning a barge trip down the Rhine.

We stopped for burgers on the road and arrived in the town of Mercer with an hour to kill before our appointment with Chantal. "College Drugs," Tim read as I drove down the main drag. "Is it just me, or is that funny?"

"I like that it's next door to College Liquors," I said. "So how's your dad? Still working at the deli?" Tim's parents worked at the largest grocery store in Endicott.

"Yup. And Barb is still checking." Barb was Tim's mom. Since she wore a name tag, Tim's friends had always called her by her first name, even as he had called his friends' parents Mrs. This or Mr. That. It had always bugged him.

Tim suggested we check out a Mercer bar. We found one easily enough. The Snake Pit was situated on the main street. A banner in the front window read, rather prematurely, "Welcome Incoming Freshmen!" Underneath, in itsy bitsy decals, a notice on the window informed us that The Snake Pit would not serve alcohol to anyone under the age of twenty-one.

We perched ourselves on stools. The bar was slick but sticky. Decades of stale cigarette smoke clung to the air.

It was early afternoon, but so little daylight filtered

through the heavy green curtains that it could have been any time at all. I ordered a soda. Tim ordered a beer. I considered changing my order but decided to just act confident, like I hadn't even noticed the discrepancy. Besides, there wasn't any fitting in to be done; aside from the bartender, we were the only ones there.

"So, what are we going to say to this girl?" In truth, I dreaded meeting Chantal.

Tim elbowed me in the ribs. I drew back and gawked at him. "What?" He held a finger up to his lips and tilted his head toward the bartender.

The bartender was about fifteen years past college age, with a thick body and frizzy brown hair. His mustache was bushy. Either he was growing a beard or he simply hadn't bothered shaving for the past few days. He wore a kelly green polo shirt and stained khakis.

Tim sipped his beer. "Sure is quiet here when the college is out."

The bartender glanced briefly away from the television, then back again. "Mmm." One of those antagonistic talk shows was on the set, the sound turned off. A sullen girl with permed yellow hair, red lipstick, painful-looking acne and an extremely short skirt stared at the camera. Next to her, an obese woman with equally unnatural blond hair gestured wildly. The tag line at the bottom read, "I found my daughter in bed with my boyfriend."

Tim sipped his beer, squinted at the television, and tried again. "Bet you see a lot of wild stuff around here." The bartender glanced at Tim. He retrieved a remote control from under the bar and flicked around the stations, finally settling on a soap opera, still with the sound off. He stared at the set. On the show, a skinny, long-haired brunette sat on a bed and sobbed. Refusing to take a hint, Tim tried again. "It's probably better than TV, the kind of stuff that goes on with those college kids."

The bartender wheeled around. "Are you from the ABC?" His accent was pure Boston: *Ah you frawm the ABC?*

Tim stared, open-mouthed. "Television?"

"This place is clean," the bartender snapped. "I'm sick of you guys sniffin' around like I'm runnin' a crack house. Okay, sure, there's no bouncer here today. It's July, for Chrissake! The eighteen-year-olds aren't here yet. I keep tellin' you guys we check ID's." He gestured to me. "When Polly Purebred over here gets around to ordering her Cape Codder, I'll ask for the license, okay? Then you can go away and write up a report saying we're playing nice."

"You think we're what? From ABC News?" Tim shook his head. "I did meet Peter Jennings at a cocktail party once, but we're not who you think we are."

I elbowed him in the ribs. "Alcohol Beverage Control," I muttered. "The ABC."

He stared at me for a minute, then his eyes widened. He stopped shaking his head and began to nod instead. "Okay—right." The head continued to bob. "No. No! We're not from the ABC, and we're not looking to make any trouble for you. You can serve sixteen-year-olds, for all we care."

"Ten-year-olds!" I added, just to be helpful.

Tim looked at the bartender and held his gaze. I wondered what story he would concoct, how he would hide the truth. Would we be spies from a competing college? Authors of a university guide? "We're reporters," he said.

The bartender squinted. "Like from a newspaper?"

"Internet publication," Tim corrected. "It's much more forward-thinking. But the same basic idea."

The bartender nodded and chewed his lip.

"We have a source says there's something funny going on around here." The bartender raised his eyebrows in confusion. "Sex," Tim clarified. "For sale. You be willing to tell us what you know?"

The bartender's eyes widened. "Hookers? Here? Get out. I don't know nothing about no hookers." He leaned over the bar, engrossed. Apparently, we were even better than the soaps.

Tim nodded at the bartender. "Maybe you could keep your eyes open for us, then."

The bartender tightened his lips and shook his head. "I think it's terrible what you people did to Princess Di."

"Those weren't reporters," I said. "It was the paparazzi. You know—photographers who chase celebrities."

He crossed his arms over his barrel chest. "I know what paparazzi are," he said.

"Of course you do. I just—"

"I went to college. Just 'cause I tend bar doesn't mean I didn't go to college. Three semesters at U Mass Boston. Then one here at Mercer. Course that was a long time ago."

"There's money in it," Tim interrupted.

That got him. "What do you want me to do?"

His name was Gerry. He'd been working at The Snake Pit since his college years, first as a bouncer, now as bartender and manager. "We do check ID's." But, he confided, "Some of 'em are fake and you know they're fake, but what the hell you gonna do? A kid shows you some laminated thing, says it's a license from, oh, hell, Nebraska or something, and you're going to say, what? We got closed down four, five years ago—some asshole served a fourteen-year-old. Me, I don't serve anyone looks under seventeen."

Tim began spouting. Twenty-one's too old for the drinking age. If kids want to drink, they're going to drink, and it's best if they do it in a bar, where the management can make sure things don't get out of hand. Why are we wasting our tax dollars on liquor agents when the public schools stink and there are criminals roaming the street?

Next thing you know, we have our first source. "I'll be in touch, man." Tim gave him a high five.

"How do you know he won't tell people we've been snooping around?"

He smiled at me. "Easy. He's outside the system. Resents the system. He'd love to help expose some spoiled rich kids."

"You're jumping to conclusions. Just because he's a bartender, you assume he resents college kids. Besides, he even went here for a while."

"Not that simple. His beef about the ABC? That's the system."

I stared at him for a minute. Suddenly, his tie didn't seem at all stupid with the jeans. He seemed hip and savvy, and terribly, terribly smart. "You're right. I didn't even make the connection."

He put his hand behind my neck and gave it a brief, electrifying rub. "You'll learn," he said.

"Thanks for helping, Professor Higgins," I scowled.

What did I expect? Red velvet and mirrors? False eyelashes and a bustier?

Her smile froze when she saw me standing there with

Tim. She shoved her hands in the pockets of her tight, faded jeans and stuck out a plump hip. She was trying to look casual and provocative, but I sensed anxiety. Her tank top, purple with spaghetti straps, was clingy. It outlined her generous breasts and revealed just a hint of cleavage. She had wide brown eyes and streaky blond hair that fell halfway down her back. She could almost pass for a college student. Almost. Her neck looked old—well, too old for college, anyway—and her red high-heeled pumps looked like they had come from Payless, and none too recently. I tried to picture her with a backpack slung over her shoulder, but the image didn't fit.

"Do you go to Mercer?" I asked, wondering if she'd lie.

She looked at me for a moment, then flicked her eyes back to Tim. "You didn't tell me there would be two of you," she said.

Okay, I couldn't pull up the backpack image, but without warning I pictured Tim and me and Chantal . . . "Eew!" I said. "I'm not, we're not—"

Tim stuck out his hand. "I'm Tim McAllister. And this is Kathy Hopkins. We spoke on the phone."

She eyed his hand. Ignored it. He let it drop. She hadn't moved from the doorway, so we were stuck outside her ground-floor apartment. The balcony from the unit above provided some shade, but heat radiated from the parking lot behind us.

"We're not here for, um, the usual," Tim said, with forced laughter. "We just wanted to talk. We'll pay you for your time, of course."

She crossed her arms in front of her chest. "Who said anything about money?"

"Can we come in?" Tim asked.

She hesitated, then stepped out of the way.

It was a small studio, dark and narrow, simply furnished with a double bed, love seat and coffee table. At the far end was a kitchenette and a small stocked bar. No kitchen table, but I doubt she threw a lot of dinner parties. It looked like a room in a residential motel.

"Do you live here?" I asked.

"No," she said. "It's just a place for . . . meeting friends."

I nodded and held in everything I wanted to say about the restorative power of paint, matted art, candlesticks and some oversized throw pillows.

"May we sit?" Tim asked. She shrugged with something that approached a nod, and he settled himself on the chocolate brown love seat. Dark colors were a practical choice, given how well they hide stains.

"I'll stand," I said.

"You want anything to drink?"

"Diet Coke," Tim said. Sure, he'd already had a beer. I could feel my nerves sizzling under my skin.

"Do you have a chard—um, a glass of white wine would be nice, thanks."

She strolled over to the minifridge in her kitchenette. "There's chardonnay and pinot grigio chilled," she said. "I've got some sauvignon blanc, but you'd have to drink it warm or stick ice cubes in it."

"You know, I think I'll try the pinot grigio," I said, perking up. "It always tastes so good on a hot day."

"It does." She smiled at me, holding my gaze for a moment, clearly perplexed by my presence.

"So." Tim cleared his throat. "How long have you been, uh, doing this?"

"Doing what?" Her brown eyes were wide. She handed

us our drinks (she'd poured herself a glass of wine, too) and
settled onto the brown love seat, though none too close
to Tim.

"We saw your ad," I said. "In the newspaper." When
she didn't respond, I added, "We got the impression you
went to Mercer. Do you?"

She paused. "Does it matter?"

"It does, actually," Tim said.

She sipped her wine. "I don't go to Mercer," she said,
crossing her legs. Her face looked calm, but the red shoe
on her upper foot jiggled relentlessly.

Tim let out a disappointed sigh. "Well, do you know
anyone who does go to Mercer? Prostitutes, I mean."

She uncrossed her legs and put both feet on the ground
for balance. "What makes you think I know any prostitutes?" she asked evenly.

Tim chuckled nervously. "Professional trade organiza-
tion?"

Chantal stood up. "I think you should go."

"Look," Tim said. "I didn't mean to offend you. Like I
said, we'll pay you for your time."

"I want you to go." She was by the door now, opening
it, and before we knew it, we were on the other side.

I was ready to leave after that: pack it in, admit defeat.
But Tim insisted we give it one more shot, so we headed
back to the college. In the middle of the college green, he
suddenly stopped. He put his hands on his hips and looked
around, pivoting slowly.

I finally surrendered to my curiosity. "Where are we
going?"

"I have no idea." He said it proudly, savoring the challenge. "Okay, let's think. Admissions office?"

I looked at the imposing brick building. "Everyone who works there is in the system."

"Student Union?"

"Staffed by kids, mostly. They might have information, but they'd be too likely to gab to their friends. Plus, there's hardly anyone there since it's summer."

"French Department? History Department?"

"What would be the point? Faculty's gone for the summer. There's no one there but the janitors." He smiled at me, waiting. "Right!" I sounded too girlish for my tastes. I lowered my voice. "They have to clean up after those scummy kids, probably make lousy money. I don't know how much the ones who clean the academic buildings would know, though. We'd probably learn more from the janitors who work in the dorms." For a brief moment, I basked in my genius. Then I looked at Tim's pleased, crinkly eyes. With a shock, I realized he was beginning to develop crow's feet. Then I realized that he'd been leading me through his own thought processes, teaching me against my will. For once, I was only one step behind him instead of the usual two. At the moment, that seemed like progress.

We picked Nickerson House because it was the closest. From the name, I expected something stately and lush. Instead, it was a looming brick box set on grass trimmed too short. "Why do institutional buildings always look so, well, institutional?" I asked Tim as we climbed the concrete steps. "You just know the halls are going to be painted puke green or dingy yellow." We'd reached the front door. It was enormous and painted a shiny brown. Tim pulled the handle. It was locked. I said, "A building like this, it's so impersonal. A kid away from home for the first time, he needs something that looks more like home. Doesn't have to be a house, necessarily, just something small, something unique and inviting. Someplace he can feel safe to become his own person." I peered inside. "Okay. The walls are white, but it's that really dingy white, with gray undertones. Depressing."

Tim started down the steps. "Let's try the side door."

Along the side of the dorm ran a makeshift dirt path worn into the grass by thousands of sneakers. Waist-high rectangular windows allowed convenient access to thieves and rapists.

At the end of the building, we came across an iron door painted the same dark brown as the front. It was heavy, but it opened. We stepped inside. The walls here were light yellow, after all. Tim neglected to mention my insight.

Tim nodded down the hall. "You go this way. I'll check upstairs."

"But what if I find someone? Should I call you?"

He gave me a look of strained patience. "Surely you can handle this."

I glared at him, turned and started down the corridor. I heard him shuffling up the stairs.

The doors were all open, the rooms being prepped for the new occupants. I slipped inside one to hide. Truly, I wanted Tim to track down a source before I did. I could strike up a conversation with anyone about paint (I was happy to see that the freshly painted rooms were bright white—uninspired, yes, but supremely inoffensive), but I had yet to master a Miss Manners–approved way of asking complete strangers about flesh-for-rent.

My strategy backfired. Just as I was examining the

wood laminate built-in desks, a voice behind me scolded. "Hey! What you doing in here? You're not allowed in yet."

I turned and faced my potential source: a squat woman of about fifty, with frizzy graying hair held back in no particular style with bobby pins. Deeply etched lines in her face indicated that pissed-off was her normal state. She wore janitorial green and held a bottle of disinfectant in a hand that was dried and cracked from too much exposure to harsh chemicals.

"I'm sorry," I began. "I didn't mean to intrude." Miss Manners would be impressed. Tim would not.

"You get the letter?"

"Letter?"

"They send it every year, tells you where you're living, who you're living with. Tells you when to show up. For freshmen, that'd be August twenty-eighth."

I stared at her. "Freshman? You think I'm a freshman?"

"Or sophomore or junior or whatever. You think I really care?"

I held up my hands, ready to spill all. After all, Tim felt it appropriate to reveal our true identity to Gerry the bartender. Surely it would be time for me to pull out my press badge if I had such a thing. "I guess I should explain myself. My name is—"

There was a knock on the already-open door: Tim. "The place is looking great," he informed Broomhilda. "You're obviously working very hard."

The lines in her face softened. I can't believe the kind of crap some people fall for. "It's a big job," she said. "Just gets harder"—she shot me any ugly look "—when the students try getting into their rooms early."

I grinned at Tim. "She thinks I'm a freshman."

He began to smirk, then froze. He stared at me. Something very, very bad had just happened but I didn't yet know what it was. A slow smile crept across his face. "You must admit—you do look young for a junior."

 nine

I said no. He said chance of a lifetime. I said forget it. He said national exposure. I said absolutely not and let's get on with things. He said my boss would be disappointed. I said Richard would never know.

"Wouldn't he?"

"You'd tell Richard I wouldn't go undercover?" I could feel my face growing hot. We were sitting on my couch. I clutched a throw pillow and pretended it was his neck.

"Of course not."

"Then let's talk about other ways to research this thing." I released the pillow and retrieved my pad and pen from the coffee table.

He stretched his arms up and folded them behind his head. He looked at the ceiling. "But it might creep into the conversation."

"I can't believe you would do that to me! I can't believe

you've become that nasty!" My voice was getting tight and borderline tearful.

"I was kidding."

"I don't think you were." I suggested we try Chantal again, but Tim was convinced she had nothing to do with the college—and might not even be a hooker. "Then what is she?" I asked.

"Sex addict?" he tried.

"Maybe that's why she couldn't keep her hands off you," I snapped, remembering the way Chantal had edged away from Tim on the couch.

It went on like this for days. Even after he returned to Washington, he would call me at odd hours. He wouldn't even bother to say hello, just start in with, "I'd kill for an opportunity like this. I'd do it in a minute if I looked young enough." He'd shame me. "For once in your life, live up to your potential." He'd flatter me. "You're a talented journalist. This is the perfect opportunity to showcase your talent." He even sent me a FedEx package; inside was my picture glued to a cover of *Time* magazine, with "Woman of the Year" printed on the bottom. Tim had always been a closet cheeseball.

I held strong. I pretended I didn't like him calling me every day. And Tim didn't share his plan with Richard. In the end, though, it was Richard himself who pushed me over the edge.

Richard called the staff into his office for a meeting. Richard and Sheila were the only ones at *Salad* with offices. The rest of us lived in second-hand cubicles picked up from an Italian food products company that was going out of business. On hot days, the office smelled like garlic.

Richard's huge office, on the other hand, perpetually stank of Polo cologne. He looked very much the pampered executive, sitting behind his oversized mahogany desk, the bounty of a trade for ad space. His desk chair was standard swivel. The remaining chairs—the ones we sat in—were of molded plastic and looked like they belonged in a high school cafeteria.

Richard had thin blond hair that I could swear was highlighted and a red, acne-scarred face prematurely wrinkled by sun, salt, wind and the other perils of the yachting life. Just short of fifty, he looked closer to sixty, albeit a fit sixty. Like his wife, he logged a lot of hours at the gym. Once he even turned up at our aerobics class, clad in a muscle shirt and royal blue spandex shorts, which yucked me out beyond belief. Mostly, he stuck to the weight room, working his delts, pecs, triceps and abs. His legs, he completely ignored. As such, he was so disproportionately muscular on top that when he stood up he always looked like he might fall over.

Once we, his staff (behind his back we referred to ourselves as his subjects), were perched on our plastic chairs, he gave us the news: "I'm sorry to announce that Kristen will be leaving us." We all made efforts to look both surprised and dismayed. In fact, it had been common knowledge that Kristen, head of advertising sales, had been offered twice her salary to work for a magazine geared toward kayakers. "I can't wait to tell that cheap-shit Richard how much I'll be making," she had commented. We fellow drones all hoped that Richard would increase our salaries to keep pace with the competition.

"I was shocked to hear what the going rate for ad sales-people has become," he intoned. This was a man who thought teachers were overpaid. "Quite frankly, I don't think we can afford to replace Kristen." Richard was talking in the corporate, not-my-fault, "we." That had to be bad. Our cross-the-board raises were fading fast. "Sheila and I—" He paused to give an adoring look to his wife, which she returned. "We discussed alternatives."

"We thought outside the box," she piped in.

Richard smiled. "Here's what we came up with . . ."

When he was done, we just sat there, staring. He had proposed—no, commanded—that the staff spend an hour a day selling ad space. He would handle the established accounts. We would make cold calls.

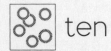 ten

I made two attempts to sell ad space. The first potential client hung up on me. The second screamed something about the Do Not Call registry. When she threatened a lawsuit, I hung up on her.

Tim could have sounded a little more surprised. But when I made my announcement—"I'll do it"—all he said was, "I knew you would." That, of course, made me want to change my mind all over again. But when he added, "You're too smart to turn down this kind of a story," I forgave his smugness.

He hopped on a plane almost immediately and called Richard from the airport to schedule a meeting. "I could have set the meeting," I said. "I work twenty feet from the guy."

"I just wanted him to know how committed to the story *New Nation* is," he assured me.

Perched on the edge of Richard's desk, he laid out his plan. I would call my old friend Dr. Archer, Mercer's dean of admissions, and say something along the lines of, "I've got an idea for the neatest article! I'll pretend to be a student so I can tell people what it's like to be in college today—the dreams of college students, the friendships, part-time work and volunteer efforts. It would be a real upbeat piece, super publicity for Mercer!"

I was aghast. "You want me to *lie?*"

"It's not lying," Tim said. "It's undercover investigating."

I crossed my arms. "You'd make a hell of a politician." Richard's Polo cologne was especially strong today. It was giving me a headache.

"Come on, Kath," Tim said. "If you can't step around the truth on this one little thing, how are you going to convince all those eighteen-year-olds that you're one of them?" He looked to Richard for backup. Richard merely frowned at one of his molded plastic chairs, as if willing Tim to move his butt to someplace other than the prized desk.

"Lying to the kids is different," I said. "I haven't met them before. They never bought me lunch."

Tim stared at me. "The time you interviewed this guy, you let him pick up the lunch tab?"

"Long story. At any rate, he's a nice man. He already knows me as the adult me. It's an ethics thing." I smirked at him. "If you can imagine it."

I stared at the familiar tableau behind Richard's desk: an assortment of his favorite *Salad* covers, expensively framed. Blurbs hinted at the crucial information within: "New England's Best B&B's," "Taking the Confusion out of Countertops," "What Your Child's Test Scores Really Mean."

Richard's enthusiasm for the story had already begun to

wane. Perhaps he didn't think we could pull it off. Or maybe, after his initial excitement, he just couldn't think of a single advertiser to woo with the story. Also, he was starting to wonder how he was going to fill an entire magazine without my contributions. "Kathy's going to have all that time at Mercer, pretending to write papers," Tim assured him. "She can be cranking out articles instead."

So much for my complete focus on the story.

"How much time are we talking about?" Richard asked. "A week? Two?"

"It will take significantly longer than that for Kathy to establish herself and turn up any meaningful leads," Tim said. "I think four months is a more reasonable time frame."

Richard gawked at him (as did I). "I guess we could get it done in three months. Though it would be tight."

"Four weeks," Richard said.

"Nine."

"Five."

"Eight."

"Six."

"Okay," Tim sighed, crossing his arms. "Seven."

Seven it was. But there was still the issue of talking Dr. Archer into the plan. I hoped he was made of stronger stuff than Richard, or at least than me.

Finally, Tim made the call. Passing himself off as the "assistant executive editor," he phoned Dr. Archer. The dean didn't like the idea; it seemed sneaky. He said no, and Tim hung up, looking defeated.

I enjoyed maybe three minutes of relative inner peace before Cara, Richard's assistant, buzzed him to say that there was a phone call for an assistant executive editor named Tim, and did Richard know what he was talking about, and if there were an editorial job opening, why hadn't Richard considered her because she'd been a journalism major in college and didn't intend to stay a secretary for the rest of her life.

Archer had changed his mind. Applications had been falling for years, and the free publicity was tantalizing. "Just between you and me" he told Tim (and the rest of us who were listening on the speaker phone), his job could be on the line if he didn't turn things around. Finally, he agreed to let me go undercover on the condition that no one know he was involved.

Tim proposed a plan involving forged transcripts and SAT records (white-out played a key role, as computer hacking was, you know, "unethical"), an exemplary personal essay (he offered to write it), and glowing fake letters of recommendation.

"That might work," Dr. Archer said. "Or, I could just send Kathy's name to the registrar."

It was the end of July. In a month, I would be entering college. I buried myself in an article about French language schools for preschoolers and tried not to think about it.

 eleven

Her name was Tiffany Weaver. She was an Aries from Buffalo, New York, who loved her collie (Mr. Big), cookie dough ice cream ("Sometimes I dig right around the ice cream and just scoop out the dough!"), and talking on the telephone ("So you might want to bring ear plugs!"). She had already bought her bedspread ("I hope you like pink! Because that's my favorite color!") but couldn't decide whether her milk crates should be just plain white or pink, too. ("Is that overdoing it?!")

Still clutching her rose-scented letter, I called Tim.

"Dead," I said when he answered.

"Excuse me?"

"We're playing *Jeopardy*. The answer to the question is, 'Dead.'"

"Okay, okay." He was quiet for a moment. "What does Elvis think the rest of us are?"

"Try this: What are you going to be if you don't get me a single room at Mercer College?"

"Ah."

"You can't expect me to live in a pink room with a girl named Tiffany."

"You know, Kathy," he cooed. "Some reporters sleep in tents and bombed-out buildings because that's where the story is."

"A bombed-out building can have a certain panache," I snapped. "The distressed look is very in."

"You're a freshman, and freshmen at Mercer have room-mates. You'd stick out if you had a single. We're talking about seven weeks of your life. Think of it as your bunker."

He was right, and I knew it. "But I hate pink!" I whimpered.

As recommended in my freshman packet, I called her. I didn't get past "Hi, Tiffany, this is Katie O'Connor" (I'd always wanted to be called Katie, which sounded so much hipper than Kathy; O'Connor is my mother's maiden name) when she started gushing. "I'm so excited that you called! Ever since I got my room assignment, I've been pic-turing you and wondering what you're like and hoping we'll be best friends. Since they used those living habits questionnaires for matching and all, you gotta think we're a lot alike. I mean, the computer can't be wrong, can it?"

"I don't think so," I said. "Modern technology is pretty impressive." I picked up a sponge and started working on a coffee stain on my counter.

"Did you read *1984?*"

"What? Oh—Orwell. Yes." I didn't add that I'd actually

read it in the eighties, when she was probably still chewing on board books.

"That's, like, so scary."

"It makes you think," I ventured.

"When you think about it, Big Brother is already out there. Like, the government knows so much about people."

"The government doesn't bother me so much," I said. "It's those telemarketers who call at dinner time." I paused, trying to bat the conversation back, then caught myself. "My mother hates the telemarketers."

"Mine does, too."

When Tiffany asked about my interests, I was prepared. I sang alto in my high school choir and in our a cappella group, the Roses (I was supposed to have graduated from Roosevelt High School). I was photo editor of the yearbook (as I said this, I realized I didn't have a yearbook, so I hoped Tiffany wouldn't pursue this part of my past). And, finally, I was president of the French Club.

"*Quelle choses accompli!*" Tiffany trilled.

"Yeah, uh—*merci.*"

Tiffany's resume was equally well-rounded (not to mention real). She played oboe in her school orchestra and hoped to join a choral group at Mercer. A member of the junior varsity swim team, she loved the sport but lacked the shoulders necessary to make her really good. She had been a member of the bulletin board committee, which, in her tenure, had introduced many novel lighting effects. But her real devotion lay outside of school.

"I was the secretary of our local CYC chapter."

"CYC?"

"Committed Young Christians. We go on retreats and talk about our faith and make pacts with God."

"What kind of pacts?"

"No drinking, no smoking, no premarital sex. But don't get the wrong idea about me—I love to have fun!"

I waited till after eleven to call Tim. It wasn't the low rates, so much—I just relished the idea of waking him up.

"I don't think my roommate is going to be much help in getting me to the hookers."

twelve

Sheila was thrilled about my upcoming project.

"It's all set," I told her. "I've got a dorm assignment, and—"

"Yes, yes, Richard told me all about it." She fluttered her French-manicured nails at my lips as if willing them sealed. "The timing is more perfect than perfect. My whole renovation project? I have been having the most impossible time management issues. But with you to help me out, I can do it all. This is fabulous!"

It seemed that Richard had taken one primary thing out of the meeting with Tim: that I would have plenty of time to write features. Sheila barely had to whimper about what a strain it was to work and pick out faucets at the same time and he'd assigned me as her slave.

I went immediately to Richard's office. "Perhaps there has been a misunderstanding." I tried to sound forceful, but my voice had taken on the "five-year-old girl about to cry" quiver it always gets when I feel defeated.

There was, of course, no misunderstanding—merely sub-jugation. When I told Richard that I couldn't possibly write all the lifestyle features while managing my own section, he shrugged. "So get Jennifer to write about education."

"But she doesn't know anything about it," I said.

He opened his mouth, then closed it again before he'd had a chance to say, "And you do?" But the sentiment hung there.

"Are you demoting me?" I immediately wished I hadn't asked; I was giving him the opportunity to say yes. But he smiled benevolently and shook his head and began to gush: you're such a valuable member of the team, you inspire others to do their best, your writing is so clean and crisp, blah, blah, blah. Early in his career, Richard had discovered that stroking egos was much cheaper than pay-ing decent wages. We all ridiculed his stroking (which only came when someone expressed displeasure) even as we craved it.

Richard said that since education pieces required more footwork than the lifestyle items, I could assign topics to Jennifer, have her do interviews and write drafts, then pol-ish the final version. At the same time, I could crank out a few articles about entertaining and decorating. "You're so good, you can write one of those in your sleep. Really, I'm just trying to free you up for the undercover piece because I know how much it means to you."

I smiled and nodded and finally agreed. It wasn't until I left his office that I realized that I'd been taken again.

* * *

I had two weeks before freshman orientation. If I could write, say, four articles, I'd be set for a while. I just couldn't see myself at the college, knocking out features about upholstery while pretending to write about Chaucer or Faulkner or whoever the hell eighteen-year-olds were forced to read these days.

I needed ideas and contact names. I'd been meaning to call Dennis, anyway; he'd left me a couple of messages that I'd felt guilty about not returning.

He was so happy to hear from me, so happy to be able to help me out. I wished once again that I could feel even a little bit attracted to him. Maybe it would come. At least he didn't repulse me; that was a definite plus.

"Actually, I've been meaning to call you," he said. "You remember your slogan idea for Mission Accomplished?"

"Uh—"

"The ugly sofa, the bumper sticker? My other couch is a Mission Accomplished?"

"Oh, right."

"They loved it."

"Who did?"

"The Mission Accomplished people. It's going to be all over the place in a couple of months: *The Globe, The Times, The New Yorker*—"

"Something I wrote is going to be in *The New Yorker?*"

"We'll pay you, of course. I didn't even have to push John. That's my boss. A really good guy. It won't be much, but we think you've more than earned it."

After he gave me the contact names and numbers I'd asked for, he asked me to go to an antiques fair on Saturday.

I told him honestly I'd be buried in work all weekend

and couldn't figure out whether I was disappointed or relieved.

Fittingly, the first article of the batch was a profile of
Mission Accomplished. They'd already agreed to a full-
page ad, so Richard was behind me "one hundred and ten
percent." Mitch Lambert, the owner, lit up when I walked
in the oversized glass front door. "Dennis told me you
came up with the ad idea! You're a genius!" I felt like
Maya Angelou.

Next, I wrote about tapas parties; do-it-yourself fram-
ing; and, finally, shopping on a budget (my conclusion:
"Often, it pays to spend a little more for quality"). I'd
hand in two of the articles now and hold out two more for
the next issue.

And with that completed, I was ready to pack up my
plastic milk crates and head for Mercer.

thirteen

Clay Aiken got to the room before I did. He was everywhere: on the walls, on the dresser, on the ceiling over Tiffany's pink bed. There were pictures cut from newspapers, magazine covers and posters purchased from God-knows-where. Clay, Clay, Clay: there was no escaping him. He made me long for the unicorns and rainbows I'd imagined Tiffany would favor. I dropped my suitcase and laundry bag, stuffed with linens, on the gray industrial carpet, sat on my bare mattress, and gawked at the room.

On the far wall, built-in brown laminate desks spanned the length of the aluminum-rimmed windows. Tiffany had claimed the desk near her window: it held a framed photograph of a collie and a closed laptop computer. On the opposite wall were our built-in bureaus, also of brown laminate. The beds, which ran along either side wall, were the only pieces not bolted-down—not that there was any place else to put them.

It wouldn't look much better once I'd unpacked. Richard had given me one hundred dollars with which to outfit my dorm room. Jennifer had come along on my shopping spree to lend her post-adolescent perspective. How my purchases broke down:

$25: Bedspread—a turquoise and pink striped monstrosity that would probably make me sweat, as synthetics always did

$9: Hello Kitty throw pillow

$8: towel; $3: washcloth—I wasn't convinced these would even absorb water

$4: lime green bath supply bucket

$9: toiletries, including lip balm, loofah, shower gel and a strawberry-scented shampoo (I'd have bees trying to pollinate my head)

$12: cheap makeup that would make my skin break out

$6: scrunchies

$10: white plastic milk crates

$14: "Green Day" CD

Richard refused to spring for a new wardrobe, so I brought along a bunch of jeans and T-shirts, some of which I'd owned since my (real) college days. I also packed my down pillow and 300-thread-count sheets because I didn't think I'd be able to sleep without them. I was tucking the too-big sheets around my lumpy twin mattress when I heard a voice.

"You settling in okay?" I jumped. I'd forgotten the door was open. Peering in was a beautiful boy with sparkling teeth and greenish gold eyes. He sported the kind of tan that you abandon forever once you join the world of nine-to-five. His wavy brown hair, tinged with blond, was about an inch too long for Wall Street. His gray T-shirt and black gym shorts didn't do much to cover a lean, muscled body.

"I'm fine," I said. "Just trying to adjust."

He scanned the walls. "You like that guy? What's his name?"

"Clay." I scrunched up my face. "I have nothing against him. He has a very nice voice. I just never imagined myself living with him."

He laughed. "Not a fan of pop music, huh? I'm Jeremy Dunbar. The Resident Assistant. I'm in room 322 if you need anything."

When I was in college, all the boys were named Jeff or John or Steve: nothing cute like Jeremy. Then again, I didn't have to put up with girls named Tiffany, so times weren't all bad.

She wasn't anything like I'd pictured. No poofy blond hair or fuzzy sweaters. She giggled, sure, but in a breathy, nervous way—not from an irrepressibly bubbly nature. She held her hands together as if hoping to build strength and smiled too wide with a naked need for acceptance. Her loose clothes were meant to hide a body that she probably considered obese but that, in reality, was only ten or fifteen pounds too heavy. She was the kind of girl who suffered the ironic self-consciousness of those who are rarely noticed. Her eyes were small and of an indiscriminate color. A plain elastic pulled her medium brown hair back from a round, pinkish face. Only her mouth was beautiful, full and red.

"Tiffany?" I asked, just to be sure. She had been misnamed. She would have had better luck trying to live up to a plain, strong name: Joan, maybe, or Ruth.

She nodded. "I hope it's okay that I took a bed. I was going to wait, didn't want to be all, you know, grabby. Not that the side I took is any better, I don't think, but my mother said that was silly and you wouldn't care and we should just get settled. Mothers!" She smiled.

I rolled my eyes. "Tell me about it." Too late I had realized I was the only freshman moving in without assistance. Where was my father, hauling crates? Where was my mother, fighting back tears and admonishing me not to stay up too late? Fortunately, my hallmates seemed too intent on their own boxes, posters and looming independence to sniff out imposters. I hoped Tiffany would assume my parents had already come and gone.

She motioned to her pink bed. "If you want, we can change."

"Don't worry about it," I said. Both beds were pushed against scratched, yellowed walls. Apparently, the paint crews had never made it this far. Of course, paint wouldn't have added much thickness, which I already realized was desperately lacking. In the room next door, I could hear parents offering to take their daughter to a nice restaurant. "Don't take this the wrong way," the girl replied. "But you always tell me to be honest. And I just, like, really want you to leave."

"Okay, then, honey." Her mother was trying to sound upbeat, but I could hear her open a zipper: probably getting a tissue out of her purse to surreptitiously wipe away tiny tears. I felt like knocking on the door and offering to go in the daughter's place. I could help buffer the parents' loneliness while sparing myself from whatever institutional atrocity the cafeteria was planning to serve. That's my idea of making good while doing good.

A skinny girl, her arms full of neon yellow flyers, knocked on our open door. She had long blond hair and a nose that turned up just a notch beyond cute. She wore one of those tiny tank tops with straps that can't possibly accommodate a bra, assuming a person wore a bra, which, apparently, she did not. She looked like a Tiffany.

"I'm Amber," she chirped. (I'd been close.) "Your R.A."

"I thought Jeremy was our R.A." As the very personification of a lie, I could only assume those around me were similarly disposed.

"You get both of us! Lucky you!" She thrust a yellow sheet in our direction. I stepped forward and took it. "This is the orientation week schedule. See you both at dinner!"

fourteen

Mercer felt more like camp than school. The materials I'd received in the mail informed me (and all those paying parents) that freshman orientation week "provides a time for transition and acclimation. Students can settle into dorms, meet classmates, and prepare for the rigorous academics that lie ahead." Apparently, the truth—"seven sleepless days and nights of beer swilling, junk-food munching and, for the lucky, virginity-losing"—didn't make good copy.

Our first night on campus, Amber's yellow sheet instructed us to "meet in dormitory hallways and proceed to dining hall" at six P.M. At 5:59, the heavy doors lining our narrow hall opened, almost in unison, and the new freshmen stepped out into the hall blinking, as if being exposed to daylight for the very first time. The shy ones crossed their arms and stared at the carpet, while the extroverts

laughed a touch too loud and called hellos to the friends
they had already made while carting up trunks and using the
communal bathrooms.

Amber and Jeremy worked their way to the middle of
the throng. "It looks like everyone's here," Jeremy said,
gazing out at the sea of heads. Everyone came to attention,
relieved to have something to focus on. The girls looked
especially pleased to have an excuse to stare at Jeremy's
flawless features.

"For those of you we haven't had a chance to meet, I'm
Jeremy and this is Amber." Amber gave a little wave. She
wore silver rings on each of her fingers, even the thumbs.
"We're both seniors, and we'll be your resident assistants
this year."

Someone snapped a piece of gum. It sounded unusually
loud in the close space. Jeremy halted his spiel to look at the
gum chewer, a tall, athletic-looking girl with blond hair
pulled back in a ponytail. "Anyone who chews gum will be
sent directly to the principal's office," he deadpanned.

The blond girl flushed red and reached up to remove
the gum without so much as a scrap of paper to stick it in.
"Sorry," she mumbled.

Jeremy's eyes widened. He held up his hand. "I was just
kidding. This isn't high school. You can chew gum whenever you want, even in class."

"You can chew gum in class?" someone asked, giddy
with freedom.

We walked to the dining hall in an orderly line and
took turns filling our plastic orange trays with cooked carrots, tater tots, and meat of an uncertain origin. There was
a salad bar, but I didn't trust the sneeze guard. A stainless
steel dispenser offered skim, low fat, whole and chocolate

milk. Most of the girls, myself included, bypassed it in favor of Diet Coke.

Since there was no table big enough to accommodate everyone, the larger boys pushed three tables together. We sat down, and, suddenly, everyone relaxed, perhaps because we had an instant topic of conversation.

"This meat looks nasty. What is it?"

"I think it's beef."

"Looks more like pork."

"It isn't veal, is it? I don't eat veal."

"I'm a vegetarian," a girl announced. "And the carrots are kind of nasty, too."

"Did anyone see what's for dessert?"

"This apple crumb thing. Smelled good."

"Maybe we could just skip dinner and eat dessert?"

"Hell, why not? Who's gonna stop us?"

"I might," Jeremy broke in.

Silence.

"I was *kidding*! *Geez*!"

After dinner, we strolled back to the dorm, in loose formation now. The air was warm with just the slightest hint of fall. Low in the sky, the sun cast a gold light on the brick buildings and made the grass glow so green it looked artificial.

Back at the dorm, we checked the downstairs lounge, only to see that the students from the third floor had already commandeered it. We trudged up to the second floor and lingered outside our rooms until someone finally plopped down on the floor and we all followed suit, our backs leaning against the hall's cold cinderblock walls.

An hour or so later, when Jeremy and Amber abandoned the group for their rooms, a tall, dark-haired boy in faded jeans nipped into his room and produced an enormous, shatter-proof bottle of vodka. "Anyone got orange juice?" Another boy, equally tall, volunteered to run to the convenience store, returning in an amazingly short time with a package of Dixie cups and a gallon of Tropicana.

By the time I stood up to go to bed (Tiffany, yawning, had left when Jeremy and Amber did), the same kids who had lined up so quietly and obediently a few hours before were lolling around on the floor, slurring words and laughing, a couple of girls sitting in boys' laps.

College had begun.

In time, I knew, jealousies would develop, boredom would fester, hierarchies would evolve. But for now, we were one big, happy, drunk, incestuous family. We traveled in packs. Those with cell phones programmed in each other's numbers; all day and all night, the phones rang, beeped, trilled and played music as hallmates summoned each other to dinner or down to the lounge. Foolishly, I had left my own phone at home, considering it a suspicious-looking luxury. If anything, I stood out for not having a perpetually ringing backpack.

We were an odd assortment. On paper, the student body was frighteningly homogenous: white, East Coast, reasonably bright and financially comfortable. Most of the students were exactly what you'd expect. For example, Mike and Jake—whom we all referred to as one entity, "Mike-n-Jake," from the first day—were big, affable jocks who set off their orthodontia-enhanced smiles with backwards baseball hats. They were rarely seen, that first week, without a beer. They were never seen without each other. But I was surprised and impressed at how accepting they were of Katherine's roommate, Amelia, who consistently introduced herself as "Amelia—I'm gay." Not like that was any surprise, given her spiky butch cut and her affinity for wearing men's cologne. Petite with huge brown eyes, she had a surprisingly delicate beauty that was only marred by her pierced tongue.

Frank and Cherie, the hall Goths, found each other right away and briefly formed a club of two. They had everything in common, it seemed: black clothes, black lipstick, black hair and pale makeup that didn't quite hide their equally virulent acne. Like Amelia, they had pierced tongues. In addition, Cherie had pierced her eyebrows, while Frank had too many piercings to count—at least without getting woozy. Within a couple of days, however, Cherie worked herself away from Frank and into the polo shirt–clad masses, muttering that Frank was "utterly humorless," while Frank wandered off to find some "real" Gothic life on campus.

Four days into the party, I called Tim. (Tiffany had brought along a cordless; mercifully, pink had been unavailable, so it was standard issue white.) "You can't believe the noise," I whispered. "Stereos, giggling, shouting—it goes on till two in the morning every goddamn night."

"So you're tired."

"Actually, no. I go to bed at two, get up at eleven. I figure I'm on California time."

"Any leads on the story?"

"Can't even work on it yet." I tried to sound disappointed, like I couldn't wait to start sleuthing. "It's just freshmen here now. Of course, the R.A.'s are upperclassmen, but if they were making big bucks as prostitutes, they wouldn't have to live with a bunch of freshmen just to cover their room bills."

"Talk to the R.A.'s. They might know something, heard some rumors."

In truth, the reason I'd waited four days to call was because I knew Tim would tell me to do something I didn't want to do. The imposter bit was turning out easier than I'd expected. The real eighteen-year-olds that surrounded me were so self-conscious, constantly worrying about their appearance, wondering what everyone thought of them, and obsessing over finding a significant other (the girls) or a truly meaningful one-night stand (the boys). As long as I kept conversations focused on them, they were happy. Getting information out of Jeremy and Amber might not be so easy.

I told Tim I needed a laptop computer.

"Isn't there some computer center you could use?"

"There is, but no one uses it. I'm the only person on the hall without a laptop. We're supposed to take them to class. It looks suspicious."

The first day, I had been dense enough to stick a memo board on our door, only to realize, too late, that e-mail and instant messaging had long since replaced the quaint traditions of my college years. I was all set to pull it down, when Katherine, the girl from next door, gave it an approving nod. "Cool. It's, like, retro."

The final event of orientation week was line dancing. Yes, line dancing. We arrived en masse at Andrews Hall, probably Mercer's grandest building. Situated at the end of the college green, it had all the pillars a grand building needs, and then some. Inside, the floors were wide-plank wood, the windows large and drafty, the ceilings sky-high.

It looked as though Andrews Hall had been standing since the American Revolution, or at least the Civil War, though in truth it was constructed during the nineteen-fifties.

The hall was already full of perspiring teenagers when we got there. It was dimly lit, although spots of light twirled around the floor. Some well-meaning entertainment chairman, ill-informed about country and western, had hung a disco ball. I sidled over to a long folding table, where paper cups of non-alcoholic punch were lined up like soldiers. The punch was red—perfect for staining all these hundreds of Abercrombie & Fitch T-shirts.

"Want to make the punch more interesting?" Katherine, the girl who lived next door, opened up her mini backpack to reveal a pint of vodka. While I hadn't met any other Katies yet, I'd come across two Katherines, one Catherine, three Kates and a Kat. As a kid, my official school name was "Kathy H.," meant to set me apart from the Kathies B., S., and T. None of the Katherines I met at Mercer went by Kathy. Apparently, the name had died from overuse.

At the sight of Katherine's vodka, I forgave her cruelty to her mother: I wasn't sure I could get through this night sober. I held out my half-empty cup. She filled it to the top.

Tiffany's eyes bugged out. "Where did you GET that?" She held her cup of virgin punch closely to her chest.

It hadn't even occurred to me to wonder how an eighteen-year-old had secured vodka. There'd been so much booze floating around the dorm, I'd all but forgotten about the drinking age.

Katherine reached into the pocket of her too-tight jeans and pulled out a laminated card. "North Dakota driver's license."

I studied the card. "Is this really what they look like?"

"Who the hell knows?" Katherine flipped her long hair over her shoulder. "Have you ever been to North Dakota? Have you ever even met anyone from North Dakota?"

I thought for a moment. "Actually, I've never even heard of anyone from North Dakota." I gulped the punch and smiled. "Maybe no one really lives in North Dakota."

"Why would they?" Katherine asked.

"Right. Especially when they can live in South Dakota instead." We both cackled. Katherine spilled punch on her jeans. We laughed even harder. Of course, the vodka hadn't had time to take effect yet, but we revelled in the knowledge that we would soon be woozy.

Tiffany's head darted back and forth between us. "But someone must live in North Dakota!" she squeaked. "They have senators from there!"

Katherine gave me a look and a smirk. She sipped her red cocktail and rolled her eyes to the ceiling, feigning interest in the disco ball. Democracy was crumbling. Really, Katherine wasn't any prettier than Tiffany: while lean, she was big-boned, and her long hair was a dull and kinky brown. But she knew what to wear (one of those belly-baring tops—never mind the chill) and she knew when to smirk.

Were I a real freshman, I would have taken her cue and ditched Tiffany as quickly as possible. Another drink, and Katherine would be doubled over by tales of my Clay-infested life. But somewhere along the way, while acquiring a job, car and apartment, I'd also acquired a conscience. I pretended to miss the message.

Jeremy picked a cup of punch off the table and joined

our circle. "How's it going?" He was wearing a green T-shirt, khakis and sneakers, probably trying to look like a benevolent camp counselor. It wasn't his fault that he looked more like a J. Crew model.

"No one's dancing," I said. It was true. "Achy Breaky Heart" was blasting, but all seemed immune to the rhythm.

"There's supposed to be some kind of lesson," Jeremy said.

"What? You need a lesson? Don't you line dance in— where are you from? Vermont?"

"New Hampshire. No, we try to stick to the really cool dances. Like the hustle."

Snickering, I drained my punch, wondering if our resident assistant would be upset to know it was spiked. I half expected Katherine to offer him vodka, but she had grown strangely quiet. "Do either of you know how to line dance?" I asked the girls.

Tiffany, mute, smiled in wonderment and fear. Jeremy grinned at her. "How about you, Tiffany?"

She emitted a giggle that was almost a wheeze then said, with some effort, "No. I've never learned." Sweat gleamed on her forehead.

Jeremy turned to Katherine. "You?"

She wrapped one arm around her waist and shook her head with what she probably meant to be nonchalance but which looked an awful lot like Parkinson's. Like Tiffany, she was looking at Jeremy a little too intently.

The music stopped, and an angular man-boy stepped on stage. He had greasy, shoulder-length brown hair and a soul patch—one of those tufts of beard-hair that sits marooned somewhere between the lip and chin of any guy who is foolish enough to think the seventies were cool. His T-shirt and jeans hung off his scrawny frame. Poorly fitting clothes were high-fashion, I'd noticed. The boys preferred pants that were two sizes too big, while the girls favored shirts three sizes too small.

He picked up a microphone that immediately assaulted our ears with an unbearably high pitch. "Can ya HEAR me?" The young man asked.

"Yes!" answered the crowd.

"Are ya SURE?"

"What an asshole," I muttered—too soft to hear, I thought, but Jeremy turned to me and grimaced.

"You have no idea."

The guy held up a Coke can in a toast and said, "Welcome to Mercer College, party capital of New England!" The crowd hooted and clapped with excessive enthusiasm. Apparently, Katherine wasn't the only one to smuggle in booze. I'd be willing to bet, too, that this kid's can held something other than cola. "I see you're havin' a *rockin'* time here at—what is this? Square dancing?" Laughter from the audience. "But if you're still in the mood to *partay* after you're done do-si-do-ing, then head on over to the party house!" At that, a pissed-off-looking college official appeared and snatched away the microphone. The guy yelled out a street address, but I missed it.

"Who was that jerk?" I asked.

"Troy," Jeremy said, grimacing.

The lady who'd taken the mike away from Troy was doing her best to pretend that things were going well. I'd been here less than a half hour, and already the crowd was thinning. "Now that you've all mastered line dancing," she piped, "it's time for learning the two-step!"

I saw my opportunity to interrogate Jeremy. "Care to dance?"

He grimaced. "I'm awful."

"So am I."

He looked at the floor. "I hope your feet aren't sensitive. Because they're going to get stepped on."

I looked him in the eye. "I don't even have feet. These are artificial. Bad frostbite incident on Everest—I don't like to talk about it." It was a dumb joke, really, but the booze was making me silly. Back when I really was eighteen, I wasn't silly nearly often enough.

Jeremy laughed and looked to Tiffany and Katherine to add to the joviality. Tiffany looked miserable. Katherine looked stunned. Guess she wouldn't be giving me any more vodka tonight

I shrieked when Jeremy stomped on my foot. He looked mortified. Remembering my fake foot story, I shouted, "Phantom limb! Phantom limb!"

His eyes crinkled in appreciation. "I told you I was bad."

"But I thought you were just saying that."

On stage, some guy in a cowboy hat was counting, "One! Two! One-and-two-and . . . !" We shuffled our way through the rest of the music. "I'm glad . . . I don't . . . make you . . . uncomfortable." He was trying to listen to the cowboy and talk at the same time.

"Why would you? Here. Just follow what I'm doing." I took the lead. Even tipsy, my rhythm was intact.

"The other girls on the hall . . ." He'd given up stepping and was now just swaying. "They clam up whenever I'm around. I don't know what I'm doing wrong, but that

happens to me all the time, not just in the dorm. I guess
it's me—I don't know how to relate to women. I don't
have any sisters. Maybe that's the problem."

Had I been sober, I would have spewed something sensi-
ble: in the dorm, he's in a position of authority, and that
makes some people nervous. Or, in college people are continually checking each other out; girls act unnatural around
all guys, not just him. But my single glass of punch had
contained as much vodka as you'd expect in three typical
drinks, so I did the unthinkable. I told the truth.

"Because you never had any sisters? Are you serious?" I
arched my neck to look up at him. The lights from the
disco ball made me blink.

His forehead was all scrunched up in thought. "Maybe
I'm getting a little too psychoanalytical."

"You don't know? You can't not know." I took two steps
back. We still held hands, making a little bridge between
us. "Jeremy." I gazed at him with mock seriousness.
"Here's the thing: you're hot."

"Oh, come on." He pulled me back to him and resumed
swaying almost in time to the music. Another couple col-
lided into us, and we all laughed.

"You're more than hot," I said, once the other couple
had galloped away. I craned my neck so I could see Jeremy's face. He had the cheekbones, the long straight
nose, the wide, well-defined mouth of every teenage girl's
fantasy. One of Jeremy's front teeth was just the tiniest bit
crooked and gleamed in the light. "You're smokin'," I announced. "The way girls act around you—it has nothing
to do with what you say or how you act. You could be
reciting sonnets or football stats. It wouldn't matter. Girls
can't get beyond your looks."

"That's ridiculous." He blushed underneath his tan. He'd all but stopped swaying and was having trouble looking at me. "I'm okay looking, I guess——"

"Okay looking! Jeremy, you look like Tom Cruise's more masculine younger brother." We'd stopped dancing entirely by now, two figures amid a sea of stomping adolescents. "Are you honestly saying that you don't know how handsome you are? Because that just makes you cuter." In truth, I liked making him squirm. Had he been my age—or I his—I would have been as mute as Tiffany. I was enjoying my new brazen self.

"Okay! I know I'm . . . okay looking. But so are lots of other guys on the hall. Mike, Jake——"

"Not in your league." I took his elbow and led him off the dance floor and to the punch table. It wasn't until I had my first sip of the sweet red liquid that I realized that I needed Katherine and her bottle if I wanted to keep feeling this happy.

Jeremy picked up a paper cup. "In high school, Mike was All-American in soccer."

"That impresses guys, not girls. Girls just go to soccer games so they can see who's got the best legs. Why do you think girls hate football so much? Bunch of fat guys with no necks. Where's the fun in that?"

"That's ridiculous!" He was laughing now. "If that's true, why aren't there more girls at swim meets?"

"We like a certain sense of mystery. Those Speedo's." I wrinkled my nose. "So Euro-trash."

He chugged his punch, crushed the cup and tossed it in an arc toward the garbage can. It missed.

"Nice shot," I said.

"I'm a natural athlete."

I grinned. He grinned.

He walked over to the garbage can and crouched down to retrieve his cup. He dropped it in the bin. "If this is true—about my looks, I mean—how come you don't get all weird around me?"

"You don't think I'm being weird?" I asked.

"Actually, you're off the charts. But you're certainly not clamming up."

I smiled with a drunk's honesty. "Let's just say I'm mature beyond my years."

 fifteen

At least I didn't throw up.

It had been years since I'd been truly drunk. But after dancing with Jeremy, Katherine didn't snub me, as expected. Instead, she cornered me with a fresh cup of spiked punch and pelted me with questions. Did Jeremy have a girlfriend? Was he interested in anyone? Would he consider dating anyone on the hall? Did I have designs on him?

I reported my honest ignorance of his romantic situation. Then I said I had no interest in dating him myself because I wouldn't be comfortable going out with someone so good-looking. She bought it, too, which just goes to show that people will believe anything if it's what they want to hear.

"So you like him?" I asked, guzzling the deadly punch.

She shrugged. "He's cute. But I'm not really looking to

get involved right now." Her eyes flickered around the room until she spotted Jeremy. She drank her punch, peering steadily over her cup.

My face was just starting to grow numb when Mike-n-Jake came over, looking antsy. "This party is lame," Mike said.

"Totally lame," echoed Jake.

"You girls goin' to the party?" Mike asked.

"Well, yeah," Katherine said with the slightest hint of an eye roll, as if only a loser would miss Troy's beer bash.

"Where is it?" I asked.

"Dunno," Mike said, shoving his hands into the front pockets of his faded and slightly frayed 501's. His worn blue T-shirt read BOB'S SURF SHOP. Jake's faded T-shirt was gray. It read COED NAKED LACROSSE. I know that's supposed to be funny, that it was supposed to be funny back when I was in college for real, but I've never figured out why. Jake's jeans were identical to Mike's save for a touch more fraying, his hands in the same front pockets, muscular shoulders curving forward. Mike was slightly taller, maybe six four to Jake's six two, and his hair was brown, while Jake's was blond. Without the hair color difference, I might never have been able to tell them apart.

"Maybe we should just go outside and hang. Then we can, like, see where everyone's going," Mike said.

"Or we can just ask," I said. I spotted Troy on the edge of the dance floor and strode boldly over. Booze makes me brave. "Hi," I said, smiling at his soul patch, which had a zit at its bottom corner.

He squinted at my face. Then he looked me up and down, far too slowly. Finally deciding I had leaped whatever minimum attractiveness barrier he had set up for all women, he smiled and pushed a strand of greasy hair from his face. "What can I do you for, baby?"

I steadied myself against an involuntary shudder and forced a smile. "My friends and I"—I looked over to Katherine and the boys, who had edged their way closer— "We wanted to go to your party. I mean, if that's okay."

He peered at the other three, paused and then nodded. "Right on. All are welcome at the House of Troy." He told me the address, made a peace sign, then disappeared into the crowd.

"That guy's a skank," Katherine said.

"Totally," I said. "Ready to go?"

In the cafeteria the next morning, Jeremy ambled over with a tray crowded with toaster pancakes, toaster waffles and a package of Pop-Tarts. I was sipping milky coffee, wondering if upping my stomach's acidity was worth the energy boost. My hair was unwashed, my face gray. I was eating alone; had anyone been looking for an overaged imposter, my solitary status would have given me away.

"You should have drunk a lot of water before bed," he said. "It keeps you from getting a hangover."

"I did. It didn't." I smeared cream cheese over a freezer bagel. "So you knew I'd been drinking."

He opened a packet of syrup and dumped it on his waffle. He smirked. "I had a hunch. I was kind of hoping you'd offer me some."

"I'd have thought you were above such illegal activity."

"Nothing illegal about it. I'm twenty-one."

"But you'd be encouraging illegal behavior in your— what are we, anyway?—your charges?"

He grimaced. "You make me sound like a nanny. I'm just there to help out in the dorm—answer questions, make sure things don't get out of hand. Once we're out of the dorm, I'm just another student."

Any other girl on the floor would kill to be having breakfast alone with Jeremy. Truly, I just wanted to be left in peace, but it was clear he wasn't leaving till he'd finished loading the carbs. As long as I was stuck, I figured I'd do some digging. "You missed quite a party last night."

"At Troy's? You went to that?"

I shrugged. "I didn't have anything better to do. Besides, isn't that what college is supposed to be about? Wild parties?"

"For some people it's about getting an education," he said primly.

"I was joking," I said, suddenly caring more about Jeremy's opinion than I did about investigating.

He looked at me carefully, little flecks of gold sparkling in his eyes. "I know you were," he said. "Well, at least I hoped you were. How was it, anyway? The party?"

I shrugged. "Okay. Loud." Actually, it had been awful. I'd had a vicious case of the spins, and the music was so loud that even today my hearing was slightly muffled. There were too many hot, sweaty, drunken, hormonal bodies crammed into a living room devoid of furniture, everyone jumping up and down to the pounding rhythm. Here and there, boys and girls clutched each other, exploring each other's mouths with their tongues. I felt like shaking them all and yelling, "For God's sake, use protection!"

As for research, it was useless. It was just another house party, indistinguishable from thousands of others in college towns across America. The girls on the dance floor weren't charging for sex. They were giving it away for free.

"I guess you're glad to have your classmates back," I said to Jeremy. It was the Saturday before classes began; upperclassmen were flooding the campus.

He speared an enormous, dripping chunk of waffle into his mouth and shrugged.

"So, what are the older students like? More wild partiers?"

He reached for one of his three glasses of milk. "There's all different types." The dining hall only offered one size of glass—small—so everyone helped themselves to at least two glasses of whatever they were drinking.

I tried again. "What are the different crowds like?"

He thought for a minute. "The jocks hang out together, give keg parties. A pretty easygoing group. The theater crowd is pretty much what you'd expect—black clothes, clove cigarettes. They tend to keep to themselves. There are a bunch of preppies here, kids with money who were supposed to go to Harvard like their fathers and grandfathers but couldn't get in. Not real studious," he said, laughing. I immediately had images of white convertibles and polo ponies. Plenty of room for debauchery but probably not the desperation needed to turn to prostitution. Unless it was done for thrills? Or if someone was trying to keep up with the Joneses—or the Cabots and the Lodges, as the case may be?

"Most people are pretty normal," he said. "They just hang out with their friends, do whatever interests them. What kind of stuff are you interested in?"

The table rattled next to Jeremy as someone set down a plastic tray: black coffee, water and Special K. I looked up just as Amber pulled out a chair and plunked down her skinny butt. "Thank God," she said. "Everyone in the hall left for breakfast at, like, sunrise. I thought I'd be sitting here alone." With her thumb and index finger, she made an L and held it up to her forehead. Without translation, I knew this signified "loser." One week as a freshman and I was already hip. I even knew enough not to use the word hip—unless, of course, I was talking about the part of my anatomy that would most greatly benefit from liposuction.

"Jeremy was just telling me about all the different crowds," I told Amber, hoping for more input.

"So what kind of stuff do you like to do?" Jeremy asked me again. Damn. I was hoping we'd skip over that part.

I tried to remember what I'd told Tiffany and drew a blank. Instead, I grasped back to my adolescence. "I like to sing. I was in a couple of groups in high school." For once, I wasn't lying.

"You mean, like in a band?"

"No, nothing that cool. Just choir. And some a cappella."

Amber guffawed. "Now that's a nice group of girls."

"Who?"

"The . . . I can't think of their name. The girls' singing group. What are they called? Jeremy, you'd know."

"Can't help you out," he said. "Be right back; I'm going to get some more milk." Good God: this would be his fourth glass. The boy's bones must be like iron.

"Tell me about this group of girls," I said to Amber, not really expecting much but hoping I could pass it on to Tim as research.

Amber rolled her eyes to the acoustic ceiling and shuddered dramatically. "I don't think they're in it for the singing, if you know what I mean. It just gives them an excuse to hang out together and get sent on trips around New England. They're known for being a little, like, adventurous."

"You mean—with guys?"

Amber smirked. "Bunch of whores."

I tried not to look too interested, although my heart was pounding. "Do you mean that literally?"

Amber's mouth twitched. She tore open her single-serving cereal box, poured half into her bowl and set the rest aside (probably for dinner). She spilled a little water in the bowl to dampen the cereal and stirred. "Nothing would surprise me," she finally said.

When Jeremy came back (the milk was chocolate this time), I tried to pry some information out of him. "Amber said the girls in that singing group are wild."

"That's a group you should stay away from," Jeremy said quietly. "That's all you need to know."

I didn't get to eat dinner alone, either. As lonely as I'd often felt eating in front of my television set, I longed for solitude. There was no place to be alone here. In my room, I had to make small talk with Tiffany. ("It must be really hard to live this far away from your dog." "I don't think Clay Aiken will ever do a concert in Mercer, but maybe he'll come to Boston some time." "No, those jeans don't make you look fat.") I had to make small talk every time I walked down the hall. ("Just going to the bookstore, hope the lines aren't too long." "Thanks, I like your scrunchy, too.") I even had to make small talk in the bathroom. ("I got my towels at Marshall's. I wanted to get fluffier ones, but my mother was too cheap to spring for them.")

At least tonight's food promised to be better than the swill they served in the cafeteria. Dr. Archer and his wife, Evelyn, had invited me to dinner. I didn't want to go. (Would he once again bug me about my marriage prospects?) I didn't think I should go. (What if someone saw me?) Still, I couldn't really say no. After all, I'd worked my way into the college by deceiving him and taking advantage of his good nature. In a few months, I would betray his trust and cast his school in a shameful light. In the meantime, didn't I at least owe him the pleasure of my company?

I tried to sneak out of the dorm unseen but ran into Amber at the front door. "Everyone's going to dinner at six. Don't you want to come with?"

"Ugh." I rolled my eyes. "I got so hungry this afternoon that I ate one of those gigantic cinnamon rolls from the convenience store. You know, the ones that are all hot and gooey."

Her hand flew to her mouth.

"I think it was, like, seven hundred calories. So, anyway, I figure I better skip dinner."

"Yeah, you'd better," she said somberly.

As for the dean's residence, I'd envisioned an old ivy-strewn house made of stone or brick and scented with pipe smoke. After walking a half mile from campus, though, I finally came upon a structure that I believe is called a raised ranch and which, in my opinion, represents the darkest hour in twentieth-century American architecture.

Evelyn Archer opened the door, accompanied by two enormous dogs. She grabbed the collar of a black one (it looked like a cross between a Labrador retriever and a tractor) and pulled back as she opened the door for me. As soon as I was in, she released the dog, which immediately reared up on its hind legs and threw its weight on my chest. I took a step back to keep from falling over and said, "Hey, big doggie!" in a manner meant to indicate a love of dogs.

"This is Bitty," Evelyn said. Bitty's tongue lolled out of the side of her mouth in a way that some people might consider cute. Saliva dripped from her mouth, just missing my arm. Instead, it landed on my shoe. "And this girl here"—she rubbed the head of a dull-eyed German shephard—"this is Cream Puff."

"Cute," I said. "And cute names, too."

Evelyn, an attractive, forty-ish woman with short, frosted hair, was smartly attired in brown slacks and a tan crewneck sweater, a clever combination that undoubtedly camouflaged the layers of dog dirt that accumulated during the course of a day. She slapped the German shepherd on the back in a way that looked overly aggressive but that the dog seemed to love. "Altoid is out back."

"Altoid?" I patted Bitty's head. She snapped at my face. I stumbled back in terror.

"Oh, sweet!" Evelyn chirped. "Bitty's trying to give you a kiss. She's always loved people. Altoid's . . . different. He needs to work on his social skills," she said. "He gets a teeny bit upset when he meets new people. He's very loyal, though."

"And an excellent watchdog," Dr. Archer said, entering the front hall with a scotch in one hand and a glass of white wine in the other. He held out the wine. "This is for you."

I took the glass. "Aren't you going to check my ID?"

"Oh, I'd say you're at least twenty-one." He held up his glass in a toast, and we both drank.

"There has been a string of break-ins around here, and we consider ourselves lucky to have Altoid on our side," Evelyn continued, deftly steering the conversation back to her dogs. Apparently, she and her husband heard Altoid barking wildly one night. "Altoid doesn't bark without a reason. Altoid is not a barker." They turned on the outside lights but didn't see anyone and went back to bed. The next morning, they learned of a robbery a couple of streets away.

They led me into the living room. I was still holding out for an enormous stone fireplace, mahogany paneling and shelves crammed with books. The books were there, but an awful lot of them were about dogs. Also, they were held in mismatched bookcases, most of which were laminate. And not white or black laminate, either, but brown, faux-wood laminate. Unforgivable. I read some of the books' titles, because, really, the written word matters so much more than the artificial trappings of a well-done house. Once again, I pretended to be interested in dogs. Evelyn offered to lend me some of her dog books, and I smiled without saying yes or no. I peered at the framed photographs arrayed among the books and was relieved to see that some were actually of people. "These your children?" I asked.

"Yes," Dr. Archer replied.

"They're Donald's children," Evelyn corrected, though not unhappily. "My children are all the four-legged kind." She rubbed Cream Puff's head with devotion.

"Oh," I said. "That's nice." The room fell silent just as I finally thought of the things I really wanted to ask: How long did the first marriage last? How do you get along with the children? Are previously married men "damaged goods," or are they better for having learned from their mistakes? After all, the older I got, the smaller my chances at first wifedom were becoming. I really did want to know what it would be like to be number two.

We didn't talk about that, of course. We talked about the guide dogs Evelyn was currently training and those she kept as pets. Bitty, Cream Puff and Altoid were all reject Seeing Eye dogs. "Bitty is too exuberant, Altoid is too aggressive, and my baby Cream Puff, well . . ."

"He's retarded," Dr. Archer laughed, draining his scotch and going to the freestanding bar to pour himself another. I didn't think people had bars in their living rooms anymore. I thought people worried that it would make them look like alcoholics.

"You know I don't like it when you use that word," Evelyn said.

Their eyes met and they glowed. Dr. Archer crossed the room with his full drink and plopped next to her on the couch. He rubbed her thigh and said, "Oh, my flower. You have such a sensitive soul." For a moment, they were the only two people in the room. And I decided that second wifedom might not be so awful, after all.

Dinner was, astonishingly enough, takeout Chinese. And not fresh takeout, either. Evelyn retrieved the cartons from the fridge and stuck them in the microwave. "I'm so busy with the dogs, I just can't be bothered to cook," she said without a trace of apology.

"Who can, these days?" I said nonchalantly, my inner child sobbing at the loss of a home-cooked dinner. I burned my tongue on the hot and sour soup (she should have only nuked it for about a minute and a half rather than three, I deduced). After that, I couldn't taste much, anyway.

Against my efforts, the dinner conversation revolved around my "research." I blabbed about how technology was changing student life and how today's students were more focused on future careers than in my day. It was a load of crap. From what I'd seen, college kids were still the idealistic screwups they had always been. They still drank too much and took off their clothes more often than they should. They had more toys than in my day—cell phones, televisions, computers, flashy cars—and their fashions were simultaneously uglier and more provocative. Above all, they took themselves too seriously and all too often forgot to seize the moment. Just as we had. Or I had, at any rate.

Unfortunately, Evelyn didn't forget about the dog books, although, mercifully, she only forced one on me. On my way out the door, she pressed a volume into my hands: *Soul Mates: Choosing the Perfect Dog*. "I sense there's something missing in your life," she said with a gentle pat on my head.

sixteen

When I told Tim what I had learned about the singing group, he said, "You're a genius!" I knew he meant it as a hyperbole, but I got all stupid and tingly nevertheless. I'd sent the details of my breakfast conversation with Jeremy and Amber over e-mail; with dorm walls this thin, I didn't dare say much over the phone. Since I still didn't have a laptop yet, I had to go to the computer center. The center was virtually empty, as all the parents who could afford to send their children to Mercer could afford to set them up with a whizzy laptop and color printer (which came in handy for advertising keggers). I coded the message in my best teen-speak:

Tim! College is fab! Like one big party! Real work starts this week (BUMMER!) and then I'm going to check out the extracurriculars. I wanted to join a singing group like

*in high school, but this one girl I talked to said the girls
in the group were "a bunch of whores." I can't believe the
language they use around here!*

I deleted the message right after sending it, of course,
but worried nonetheless that it would somehow be traced
back to me.

Tim called me right away. I was out, so Tiffany took a
message: my Uncle Tim had called. I waited till she went
to the bookstore and phoned him back. "Uncle Tim?"

"Think it's clever?"

"Brilliant. Like anybody's uncle really calls them at
college." I was whispering, worried that Katherine might
hear me.

"Her," he said.

"Excuse me?"

" 'Like anybody's uncle really calls *her* at college.' "

I ignored his correction. "Anyone more worldly than
Tiffany—which is basically anyone—would assume there's
something tawdry going on," I chastised him.

"Oh, right. They'd know you're an undercover journalist, just because you happen to have an unusually attentive
uncle."

"*She'd* know I'm an undercover journalist," I purred.

"Really?"

"Of course not," I hissed. "But you're not the only one
who can correct grammar. More likely, she'd just assume
that I'd been having an affair with my high school math
teacher, and we were staying in touch." I was sitting on the
floor by now, slouched against my bed.

"Actually," he chirped, "that kind of rumor might work

in our favor. Make you appealing to the right kind of people, if you know what I mean."

We went on like this for a little bit longer. Then he
called me a genius for having sleuthed so well, and I
melted. My e-mail had implied that I'd been digging relentlessly when I finally struck gold: no need for him to
know that everything had fallen into my lap after asking a
couple of vague questions.

I'd already figured out the obvious plan of attack and
how to implement it. In other words, I knew what Tim
was going to make me do, and even though I didn't want
to do it, I suggested it before he got the chance to present
it as his idea.

"The auditions are next week," I told him. "I think I'll
use 'You're Mean to Me' as my audition song." It had been
easy enough to track down the singing group, which was,
ironically, called the Wallflowers. There were audition
posters all over campus.

"Good thinking. I don't know that song, though."

"It's a torch song. Makes me think of our days together." Why did I always have to ruin my moments of
empowerment like this? "Just kidding—that's just the
first song that came to mind. Got any other ideas?"

"I leave it up to you. You're the musical one." When
Tim and I were college freshmen—real college freshmen—
I'd told him I was going to audition for one of Cornell's
prestigious a cappella groups. He shook his head in disap-
proval. "You've got to pick your priorities. If you focus
your energies and work really, really hard, you've got the
potential to be a great journalist. But let's face it. You're
never going to be a great singer." I skipped the audition,

telling myself that I probably wouldn't have made it, anyway. There were times—too many—when I wished I could re-embody my eighteen-year-old (twenty, twenty-four-year-old) self and shout back at Tim: Why must everything have a purpose? Why should I always be working toward a goal? Why can't we ever do things just for the hell of it, just for fun?

And here I was, eighteen again. And all I wished was that Tim was eighteen with me, lying on my bed, fully clothed, stroking my hair and telling me how great life would be when we finally grew up.

"I think we should set a time to meet," I whispered. "Away from here—at my office, maybe. Got any free time this week?" We agreed to meet at *Salad*'s office on Thursday afternoon.

When I was eighteen, I thought Tim was the most ambitious, focused person I had ever met. He was going to be a writer, he told me, that first day over coffee. A reporter. He seemed so much more mature than the other boys I had met at Cornell, who never seemed to think much beyond where their next beer was coming from.

When I asked him what dorm he lived in, he said, "I don't," and took a drink of his coffee. I waited. He set the cup down and told me he was a commuter student, a rarity at Cornell. He lived with his parents in Endicott, NY, an hour away.

"Why don't you just live on campus?" I asked, stupidly.

He raised his eyebrows. "What does your father do?"

"He's a banker."

"Your mother?"

"She was a housewife till a couple of years ago, but she got bored and got a job as an office manager."

He nodded. "My parents work at a grocery store. Dad's the deli manager, Mom's a checker."

"Oh," I said.

"But they're two of the smartest people I've ever met," he said, tipping up his chin. "Most of my friends' fathers work at IBM. There's a big plant in town. But they aren't any smarter than my parents. My mother does the *New York Times* crossword puzzle in pen."

I envisioned his parents as two professors in red grocery aprons, but when I met them at their tiny Cape-style house, about a month later, they surprised me. I stuck out my hand to greet his mother, as my mother had taught me, and said, "I'm pleased to meet you, Mrs. McAllister."

She ignored my hand and enfolded me in her bony arms. "I feel like I already know you, Kathy. Call me Barb. Everyone else does."

Meanwhile, Tim's father beamed at me. "You're just as beautiful as Tim said you were." I felt a flash of pure happiness. No boy had ever called me beautiful before. It didn't even occur to me to wish Tim had said it to me instead of to his parents.

When Tiffany came in, I went out. She wasn't so bad, really; her manic spurts, set to a Clay Aiken soundtrack, alternated with long silences during which she wrote letters on scented pink stationery or listened to defeatist music sung by wailing females. When I was lucky, she wore earphones. Perhaps she did this out of consideration for me, or maybe it was because, on one of my cranky hangover mornings, I'd remarked, "What is this—music to slit your writs by?"

Still, I'd been living alone three years, ever since Tim moved away. In my apartment on Beacon Hill, I left the bathroom door open, flipped on the television at two in the morning, strolled around with bleach cream under my nose. Partly, I needed to be alone to get away from the pressure of being found out. More fundamentally, however, I simply needed time by myself. As Sheila was fond of saying, I needed my space. Of course, her space tended toward the ten-thousand-square-foot range, while mine was more metaphoric.

"I'm heading to the bookstore," I told Tiffany. Her wounded look told me that I should have gone with her, that she was analyzing our pseudo-friendship and sensing a rift. "I can't believe I didn't think to go with you," I said, a bit too obviously. "I'm such an airhead—I mean, like, I need books, right?" I wondered whether anyone still said "airhead." Surely "space cadet" was out by now. I should really avoid slang altogether. "What time were you thinking about dinner?" I asked as I picked up my faux leather backpack.

"Whenever you want," Tiffany chirped, sitting up a little straighter on her bed. The night before, I'd left the dorm—in a group, of course—while Tiffany was in the bathroom. From her immersion into the aforementioned desperate wailing music, I gathered that she thought I'd done it on purpose.

The bookstore was mobbed. So much for getting a little space. I shoved my way to the textbooks, which were

arranged according to the classes for which they were assigned. I'd kept my course load as interesting as possible
without it being too demanding: photography, women's
studies, film, and, my personal favorite, a course entitled
"Ethics in Journalism." I began loading my basket, but before my arm even had a chance to start aching, I realized
that I didn't need all these books; I'd be leaving Mercer
before most of the reading came due. With some regret, I
returned most of the books to the shelf, reserving only a
photography reference and *Primary Colors*, the reading pre-
assigned for my first journalism class. I'd read the book a
few years back, even had it in hardback at my apartment,
but the standard class copy was necessary to avoid suspicion. The rest of the books could wait; I'd buy them as
they were assigned.

I picked out a Matisse poster—hardly original, but our
room was begging for a non-Clay element—and joined an
absurdly long line at the cash register. The skinny student
in front of me had oily, shoulder-length brown hair and
wore tight jeans and a ribbed T-shirt. I busied my brain
trying to decide whether it was male or female. I had finally decided on female when "she" craned her head
around to scan a blonde in a tube top and bell bottoms. I
marveled at the reemergence of such unlikely fashions,
then returned my bored attention to the student in front
of me. It was male, after all. It wasn't the girl-watching
that gave him away; I'd already learned that lesbianism
was suddenly chic, perhaps even more than tube tops. No,
it was the facial hair that tipped me off—a soul patch, to
be exact. My skills as an investigative journalist were
growing every day.

Troy scanned the room without pausing when he saw

me. Apparently, I hadn't made much of an impression at his party. Good.

A chubby, shaggy boy wearing oversized everything swaggered over and gave him a soulful handshake. "Troy, my man!"

"Hey, Homie!" Troy crowed. In a week, I had grown increasingly weary of suburban white boys trying to sound like they were from Harlem. Had there been any black students at Mercer, they would have been similarly exasperated.

Ever-so-casually, Baggy Boy plopped his plastic basket, overflowing with books, on the floor next to Troy. "No cutting!" I wanted to yell, but I didn't think it was wise to draw attention to myself. Besides, I never did get around to taking one of those assertiveness training classes.

"How's business, Bro?" the cutter asked. He began gliding his head from side to side as if listening to his own drummer. I think it was meant as a conversation filler.

Troy swirled his head around to make sure no one had heard. My heart raced. I set my face in the mask of perpetual boredom mastered by every eighteen-year-old I'd encountered. "What's your problem, Sean?" he hissed. "You trying to fuck me up?"

Sean reverted to a jittery white boy, struck by the realization that, in his attempt to be cool, he had revealed himself as the most despicable low-life imaginable: the dork. "I'm sorry—I didn't mean—I was just joking around."

His deference softened Troy. "Business is profitable," he murmured. "Didn't mean to snap, my man. It's just that—maybe you haven't heard—but it isn't exactly what you'd call legal."

Sean laughed. His shoulders loosened. He was in the groove again. "Fucking uptight society we live in."

Troy grinned. I half expected broken teeth or prominent fangs to appear about his soul patch, but no: clearly, his parents had sprung for orthodontia. "Who can blame us for breaking a few rules?"

Jeremy's door was open a crack. I rapped twice and poked my head in. He was sitting on his single bed, surrounded by books and papers. His bedspread was forest green, I noticed with approval, and he had painted his walls a cozy toast color. He looked up. When he saw it was me, he smiled.

I pointed to his books. "You're not doing work already?"

"I've got a neurology test the first day of class. Instructor wants to see what we know."

I raised my eyebrows. "Nervous?"

He shrugged. "Bored is more like it. I'm just not that into physiology."

"Actually, I was making a joke." I tried to be gentle. "You know, neurology—nervous."

He held my gaze. "I know you were. But it just wasn't that funny."

I gawked at him. "Maybe this is the real reason girls get so uncomfortable around you! Maybe it has nothing to do with your looks at all!"

He softened and looked away. With a sly grin, he said, "No, I think you were right the first time. I'm just such an Adonis."

"Yeah, that must be it," I said, as if I didn't believe him at all. "So why are you taking neurology if you find it so boring?"

"I'm pre-med."

"Oh!" Okay, I admit it: I was impressed. "I didn't know Mercer had a pre-med program."

"They don't, I mean, not technically. But I'm a bio major, and I'll have taken every physiology class they offer by the time I graduate." He folded his arms behind his head and leaned against the wall. Very Calvin Klein, I thought, except his eyes weren't vacant enough.

"Why do you want to be a doctor?"

"It's about the most important job you can have, right?"

I thought about it. "Right."

"And impressive."

"Extremely impressive." I waited for more arguments. They didn't come. "But what makes you want to do it—to survive med school, put up with the sleep deprivation, cut up all those cadavers. What drives you?"

Suddenly sober, he reached for his books, started shuffling through the papers on his bed. Finally, unexpectedly, the truth: "My father. It's what he always wanted to do, except his family couldn't afford to send him to college. I guess he planted it in my brain pretty young, because I've always just figured I'd be a doctor some day."

I feigned interest in an Ansel Adams poster, which I considered unoriginal but a big step up from the Jessica Simpson shot that presided over so many college boys' rooms. "I have an older brother," I said. "He's a doctor. Well, an ophthalmologist—I mean, that is a doctor, just not what you normally think of. I've always thought he chose that specialty because by the time he realized he didn't really like dealing with the human body, he was too far gone to back out. This way, he gets to do laser surgery all day long without ever needing to touch anyone." This was the first true thing I'd said in so long, it jarred me a bit. I was afraid that one truth would lead to a multitude of others.

"Does he live nearby?" Jeremy asked.

"Denver."

I searched for a way to change topics and suddenly realized why I'd come in the first place. "I just got back from the bookstore. What a zoo. I'm already starting to recognize faces, though. Like that guy—what was his name? The one who had the party."

"Troy," he said flatly.

"Right." I knew that of course. I was just being crafty. "Sounds like you don't like him much."

"Not particularly."

I paused, waiting for him to continue. Most people can't bear silence and will start blabbing just to fill it. Unfortunately, Jeremy was the exception. "I don't see why," I continued. "Yeah, okay, he's fake and sleazy and a major poseur, but beyond that he's probably a very nice person."

Jeremy smiled. "He's what my mother would call a bad influence. So tell me more about your brother. Did your parents pressure him to go into medicine?"

There was a rap at the door. It was Katherine. She was wearing her usual tank top, which looked just like the undershirts my mother used to make me wear in grade school. "Um, hi." She giggled. I wouldn't have pegged Katherine as the giggling type, but Jeremy was so cute, he probably could have made a mime giggle.

Katherine's eyes flitted to me. I detected something: disappointment, irritation, envy—something unfriendly, at any rate. "I was just, I was, you know, thinking. Jeremy, maybe you could give me some advice." Katherine smiled at him and leaned against the door jamb. "I'm just, like, so totally confused about notebooks. I was going to go loose-leaf, that's what I used in high school, but now I see all these people buying spiral, and, ohmigod, I, like, hate making decisions!"

I slipped out, and Katherine's giggle became noticeably louder.

Tiffany was dressed and ready for dinner at 4:30, perhaps so she wouldn't risk me leaving without her. She wore bell-bottom pants. If we were truly friends instead of just pretending, I would have found a nice way to tell her that bell-bottoms are a no-no for anyone larger than a size four—which is to say most of us—and that they actually look pretty stupid on the skinny chicks, too. Her shirt was oversized, shapeless and pink: no, no and no. She wore bright pink lipstick and black eyeliner that had already begun to smudge. I longed to drive her to the nearest Clinique counter.

Since she'd gotten dressed up, such as it was, I felt I had to follow suit. That meant changing into clean jeans and a long-sleeved powder blue Gap shirt that said "Snow Angel." I brushed my hair and used my pink tube of Maybelline mascara before remembering that I'd neglected to pack eye makeup remover.

Since we were virtually the first ones at dinner, we had our pick of tables. Tiffany, first off the food line, chose a windowless spot next to the garbage cans. "This okay?" She anxiously clutched her tray.

"Perfect!" I soothed. The garbage clearly hadn't been emptied since lunch—there was a soiled napkin sticking out of the flapping door—and I detected a faint odor of old fried chicken.

We placed our orange plastic trays across from each other on a table meant for ten. Tiffany had bravely heaped a glutinous white mound of turkey tetrazzini on her heavy white plate. I'd stuck with the salad bar, figuring the iceberg lettuce hadn't been out long enough to be coughed or sneezed on.

Stories of dining hall horrors abound, but I'd never understood them before now. Because Cornell boasted a top hotel and restaurant mangement school, the food there was excellent. The sundae bar alone was worth an extra pants size. Mercer was another story. Casseroles reigned supreme, many of them bathed in a watery, garlic-free tomato sauce that stained the plates a suspicious orange color. Ground meat—beef, I think, though I never wanted to press the issue—was also popular, with or without the orange sauce.

Tiffany had barely finished chewing her first bite of tetrazzini when she said, "So what do you think of Katherine? Pretty slutty, huh?"

"Well, I don't know," I said.

"I don't think she's a virgin."

I attempted an expression of shocked contemplation. Tiffany shoved some more pasta into her mouth. "And she doesn't even mind living with Amelia," she said. She scrunched her nose and, mercifully, swallowed. "If I'd gotten Amelia for a roommate, I would have made my mother call Housing Services to switch me. She'd probably switch me now if she even knew I was on the same hall with her."

I stirred my lettuce around, trying to coat each tasteless leaf with ranch dressing. "Amelia seems to keep her private life pretty much to herself."

"The Bible says homosexuality is a sin," Tiffany said as forcefully as I'd ever heard her say anything.

I almost chirped, "Hate the sin, love the sinner!" But I didn't think it was fair to call Amelia, one of the nicest people I'd met at Mercer, a sinner. "How's the tetrazzini?" I said instead.

"Pretty good." She nodded and chewed. Amazingly, her plate was almost empty. And then: "I think Cherie might be queer, too." I blinked at her. At Troy's party, I'd seen Cherie, clad in her usual black on black, piercings sparkling, sucking face with a tall, skinny guy in a rugby shirt. Cherie might be having trouble deciding whether or not she wanted to remain a Goth, but her sexual identity seemed pretty clear-cut.

By the time we got around to dessert (Boston cream pie—and not bad, actually), Tiffany had dissected every girl on the hall (and a couple of the less attractive boys). Finally, she licked the last of the custard off her fork and put it on her tray. "Well, I'm off to my fellowship group," she announced. "We're talking about Mary Magdalene today. Want to come with?"

I mumbled something about wanting to get my things organized before classes started the next day and skulked off in search of another piece of pie.

 seventeen

Meeting with Tim on Thursday meant skipping my "Ethics in Journalism" class. The irony was not lost on me.

It was only the second class and I was sorry to be missing it. Tuesday's session had focused on *Primary Colors*. The instructor and I had had a spirited discussion about *Newsweek*'s decision to fire Joe Klein. After about fifteen minutes, a squinting girl raised her hand and asked, "Who is Joe Klein?" Of course, I was the only person in class who'd read the book before Anonymous's identity was revealed, then followed the resulting controversy after a computer program that analyzed writing styles pinpointed Klein. I felt like an absolute relic and tried to cover my tracks with liberal allusions to "my sixth-grade current events studies."

Today's class, we were to talk about the press's treatment

of the British royal family. As a decade-long subscriber to *People* magazine, I felt I had much to offer the discussion. I feared that the instructor, a stodgy, humorless man, would probably dwell far too long on Diana's death, neglecting not only Squidgygate but also Fergie's toe-sucking episode and Charles's professed wish to be reincarnated as Camilla's tampon.

On my way into the city, I stopped at Marcy's house for coffee. I called her from my room right before I'd left and told her I was "out in the field" doing some research. "I wasn't sure you'd be home," I said.

"I'm always home," she moaned. Tim had forbidden me from telling anyone—"even Marcy, *especially* Marcy"—about my undercover life, and I didn't want to lie to her. But she'd left a message on my answering machine ("Just me. Nothing important. Guess you're out doing something fun. Call me if you—*Jacob! Stop that! Jacob! No!*—Gotta go, Kathy. *JACOB!*") which was such a rare event these days that I couldn't just ignore her. Besides, pregnancy made Marcy so self-involved that I figured I was safe. If she questioned my casual attire, I'd tell her that I was just going to the library to do a little research, which wasn't technically a lie since I had two papers due this week.

"There are five Jacobs in Jacob's preschool," Marcy announced as she opened the door of her colonial house. She was wearing a green and white striped maternity shirt over black stretch pants. "Five!"

The Rubinsteins live on a tree-lined street in Newton, in the kind of house I'd like to live in when I grow up. I entered the house and stepped over a plastic airplane. When Jacob entered toddlerhood, trips to Marcy's house inevitably meant twisting an ankle over some primary-colored plastic thing. Once, in bare feet, I landed squarely on a flimsy red fire truck with spectacularly sharp edges. The force broke a ladder off the truck. The pain shot all the way up my calf. Still, I held my tears. Jacob was less stoic. "It was his favorite truck," Marcy informed me without apology while her son wailed in her arms. It took me about three months to forgive her insensitivity. Now I look before I step. Also, I keep my shoes on, no matter how hard they pinch.

"How many kids in the preschool?" I asked, heading for the kitchen.

"Sixty. The list came today." She retrieved mugs from her cherry cabinet with Mission-style hardware. I had more than a little input when Marcy and Dan redesigned their kitchen last year. Marcy pulled out my favorite mug, a gift from her sister-in-law, Pamela. It said, "You're my sister-in-law by marriage but my friend by choice." As Marcy despised Pamela almost as much as Pamela despised her, we could only assume the mug had been marked way, way down. Marcy had tried to bury the mug far back in her cabinet, but I always insisted she pull it out for me.

"Five kids out of sixty isn't so bad," I said as we headed to the playroom.

She glared at me. "Half of the sixty are girls."

"I was hoping you wouldn't pick up on that." On our way to the playroom, she popped into a bathroom, opened the medicine cabinet and retrieved baby oil and a Q-tip. "Not to be rude, but . . ." she said.

"I ran out of eye makeup remover," I replied, accepting the offering.

We settled ourselves on the pouffy leather sectional with the built-in recliners (which Marcy and Dan had purchased without consulting me). I winced as a LEGO cut into my butt, then silently swept it to the ground. Jacob sat cross-legged on the floor, his glazed eyes staring at the primary-color clad young men who bounded around on the big screen TV (also purchased without my input), flapping their arms and singing "Cock-a-doodle! Cock-a-doodly-do!"

"Say hi to Kathy, Jacob." Marcy said.

"Hi to Kathy, Jacob." Jacob twisted his neck and gave me a sly grin. I winked at him. We had long since made our peace about the fire truck. "You look like a raccoon," he added.

"Yeah, yeah," I said. I put my mug on a marble coaster and squirted some baby oil on the Q-tip. A drop of oil hit my blue jeans. Damn. There were only three washers in the dorm's dank basement. I'd avoided them until now, but this had been my last pair of clean jeans. Time to start saving quarters.

"And Joshuas?" Marcy said, continuing her rant. "Three. I told Dan it was too trendy."

I looked around. "Where is Joshua, anyway? Usually, I've tripped over him by now." Joshua was sixteen months old. He got stepped on a lot, usually by his older brother, who always insisted it was an accident.

"Napping. Thank God he sleeps."

Jacob looked up at his mother. "I think Joshy's crying."

Marcy shook her head reflexively. "That isn't crying, honey. Those are just the noises he makes in his sleep." Now that Jacob mentioned it, I, too, detected a faint wailing.

Marcy sipped her coffee. I knew better than to ask about restrictions on caffeine in pregnancy. The woman hadn't had a decent night's sleep in four years. "There are two other mothers coming to my shower that have Jacobs," she said.

"I thought your shower was supposed to be a surprise."

"Alex's mom let it slip. The Alex from the Mommy-and-Me group. The other Alex's mom—the girl Alex—was really ticked. She's the one throwing it."

"I know. I got an invitation."

"You're coming, aren't you?"

I had spent the two weeks since receiving the invitation trying to come up with a decent excuse. Every time I mixed with Marcy's mommy friends, the conversation inevitably turned to breast-feeding and episiotomies. I felt simultaneously bored, left out, envious and repulsed. "To the shower? Wouldn't miss it for the world."

Marcy picked up a stapled packet of blue pages and shook her head. "Out of thirty boys, there are five Jacobs. One-sixth of the boys are named Jacob!"

"You were always really good at math."

"Thank you."

We sipped.

During Marcy's first pregnancy, we used to meet for lunch downtown. She was a banker then, with French-manicured nails and a navy blue maternity suit that cost two hundred dollars. Over flavored iced teas, we mulled over countless boy names, trying to find the perfect one: masculine, yet sensitive; intelligent, yet fun; recognizable but not overused. She'd come up with Jacob. "I've never even known a Jacob," she'd said, and I'd concurred.

"I should have called him Isaac," she now muttered. "There isn't a single Isaac in the preschool."

"Jacob is much cuter," I assured her.

She squinted at the class list and flipped a few pages. "I can't believe some of these names," she said, some measure of self-confidence returning to her voice. "I mean, Nixon? Who would name their kid Nixon?"

"Someone born after the Ford administration?" I ventured.

Before I left, Marcy asked, "How's your job?" I knew she was just being polite.

"Okay," I shrugged. And that was the end of that. I never even had to lie.

eighteen

It was good to be the real me again, if only for the day. I stopped at my apartment before heading into the office. I swapped the scrunchy in my hair for a tortoiseshell barrette. My jeans I traded for a cotton dress. There was a new message on my answering machine (I'd been calling in for messages every few days). My parents were calling to say good-bye before heading off on their trip down the Rhine.

I hummed as I set off on my half hour walk to the office, that damned cock-a-doodle song thoroughly lodged in my brain.

The office elevator was broken again. I wasn't thrilled about walking the four flights of stairs, but at least I hadn't been in the damn thing when it had halted. Much of *Salad*'s staff boasted well-muscled calves. When the elevator wasn't broken, those burned by experience or merely cautious chose the stairs. I took my chances. After all, the

longest anyone ever got stuck was three hours, and they
had Cheetos and beer being passed down the whole time.
That didn't sound so bad, although Kristen called it the
most traumatic experience of your life. "You try drinking
four beers then not knowing when you'll get to the john!"

Jennifer wasn't at her desk, which sat just outside my
cubicle. Instead, she was at mine, her empty Starbucks cup
indicating that she'd been there since morning (in the afternoon, she drank Diet Coke).

Tim, wearing a soft denim shirt with khakis (a combo I
had always liked), sat on my desk, leaning against the canvas partition. Jennifer looked awfully comfy in my gray
swivel chair, which wasn't, quite frankly, all that comfy
but was a step up from hers. My "to file" basket, which had
always been overflowing, waiting for Jennifer's attention,
was finally empty.

"You filed," I said. I suppose I should have said hello first.

"My mind turns to total mush when I work in a clut-
tered space."

I gave Tim a look, as if to say, "Can you believe this
chick?"

"How's the world's oldest coed?" he asked.

"There's a sixty-two-year-old in my women's studies
class," I shot back. "And she's got more to say than all
those teenagers combined."

"Touché," he said.

I dropped my Coach bag on the desk. "Jennifer, would
you mind sitting somewhere else?"

A scowl flickered across her face. She stood up and
smoothed her fuchsia mini skirt. Never one to forfeit the
last word, she said, "It's just been nice to have a computer
that, like, works." At this, I was supposed to scurry down

to the nearest computer superstore, flash my Visa, and equip the little pumpkin with a Pentium processor and CD-ROM drive.

"I didn't mean to sound so territorial," I muttered. "But I feel like I've been away for a year, and there's stuff I need to get done." In my women's studies class, we'd touched on women's reflexive tendency to apologize. One red-faced freshman, convinced that she'd been liberated by grrrrrl power, found the premise infuriating. "I'm sorry, but I just don't agree!" Jennifer, of course, was a glaring exception to this gender rule. For a delightfully nasty moment it occurred to me that Jennifer might be a man in drag. But the idea was ludicrous. Given the amount of skin and curves her wardrobe revealed, her body could only be the real thing.

Jennifer flipped her hair (it was looking oddly maroon today) over her shoulder. "No big deal," she said to me. "And Tim, thanks for letting me bounce those ideas off you." She strode regally away in the direction of the vending machine.

"What ideas?" I asked Tim, trying not to sound panicked. I envisioned brilliant article proposals on education reform, mainstreaming, school vouchers and all those other touchy topics I'd been too cowardly to address. I settled into my chair and noticed a black canvas bag on the ground.

"Nothing," he said. "She was just talking to me about her novel."

"Ah," I said, relieved. I recognized that the sense of superiority washing over me was ignoble, but I enjoyed it just the same. "The famous novel-in-waiting. Since when do you know anything about fiction?" Unlike some journalists, Tim was no frustrated novelist. He didn't see the point of making things up when there was so much real stuff to write about.

He grinned. "Hey, I studied *Catcher in the Rye* in the ninth grade."

"So you're pretty much an expert."

"Pretty much."

Tim reached into the black bag and retrieved a dark gray laptop. I stared at it. I looked up at him beseechingly. "Is it? Could it be?"

He handed it over. "Don't get too attached. It's a loaner from my office."

We met with Richard and briefed him on my progress. "Is that all you've found out?" he asked when I told him about the Wallflowers, my voice breathy with excitement.

"Kathy's going to infiltrate the group," Tim said. "Tryouts are coming up, and she's a shoo-in. After that, everything should fall into place pretty quickly."

I handed over the articles I'd held in reserve ("Tapas Take Center Stage" and "You've Been Framed: A Do-It Yourself Guide"). Neither was going to win any awards, but they'd fill the necessary inches.

Tim and I spent the afternoon huddled at my desk, with me at the laptop's keyboard. Tim sat so close, I could feel his breath against my cheek. We outlined everything we knew: the initial tip from Tim's intern; Mercer's cost and admissions standards; the college's social structure; the suspected ringleader; the odd role of the singing group. We formulated our plan of attack. I would infiltrate the singing group; Tim, posing as my older brother (hey, I'd already told Jeremy I had one) would visit once or twice and maybe even get "drunk" and look for action.

At six o'clock, we shut down the computer. We walked to a dimly lit Chinese restaurant around the corner that specialized in red vinyl booths and scorpion bowls. We reminisced about the first time we had drunk from a scorpion bowl—graduation week, our senior year—and how we'd spent the rest of the night taking turns puking into the toilet of the off-campus apartment I shared with Marcy (and Tim, most nights). The memory seemed sweet now. We ordered a small bowl from our non-English speaking waiter.

The vast bowl—the small wasn't so small—sat on the table between us, fruit floating inside. With long straws, we sipped the deadly concoction, which tasted remarkably like that ancient Shanghai drink, Kool-Aid. I'd expected the taste to make me nauseous, as Scorpion Bowls always did after that fateful night, but it didn't. That seemed significant. It didn't even occur to me that this restaurant might just use a different flavor of Kool-Aid.

I recalled my recent hangover. "Less than a week ago, I swore I'd never drink again, and now look at me."

Tim took the straw out of his mouth and twirled it between his fingers. "This is for professional purposes only. We've got to loosen you up for your rehearsal." After dinner, Tim was going to help me practice my audition song. My nerves were more fraught from the thought of performing for Tim than they were for the actual auditions.

"In that case, we might need another bowl after this one." I sucked on my straw. I was starting to glow.

Tim fished a maraschino out of the bowl. He stuck the cherry between his teeth and pulled it off the stem. "It's hard to rehearse when you're getting your stomach pumped."

"But think of all of those nice medical personnel who

would be on hand to give me feedback. Doctors tend to be very musically inclined."

We ate egg rolls and dumplings and moo shu pork. We drank the entire scorpion bowl and sucked on alcohol-soaked orange slices. We were the only people in the place, which relied on the business lunch crowd. Our fortune cookies came with the bill. We broke them in half. As I tried to read my fortune—not easy, considering the bad lighting and my drunken vision, which made me see triple—I put half the cookie in my mouth. It was too chewy and vaguely lemony. I held my fortune near the stubby candle, encased in a knobby red glass globe. "Love comes to those who wait," it said, unbelievably.

I handed it to Tim. He peered at the slip of paper and smiled. "Mine's better." He handed me his slip: "A man who wears a clean shirt is respected by his neighbors."

We stumbled two blocks before hailing a cab to take us back to my apartment. The driver, who, his cab permit told us, was named Fazel, listened to my address and nodded without a word. The cab stank of stale cigarette smoke. NPR hummed in the background. I nuzzled Tim's shoulder. His denim shirt smelled like Chinese food. He put his arm around me, and I leaned against his chest, bouncing as the cab jostled through potholes.

It took me awhile to open the front door to my building. That was probably because I was trying to open it with my mailbox key. Once inside, I clutched Tim's arm as we climbed the two flights to my apartment. The stairs seemed to alternately lurch up and fall away. I stumbled but maintained my balance by clutching the thick wooden bannister. Tim was marginally more steady.

Once inside, Tim slipped off his shoes and set them by

the door. For once, the apartment was immaculate; I'd known Tim was coming back to hear me sing, after all. After all those years of living together, it seemed unlikely that he'd believe I'd changed my evil ways and become tidy, but you never know. It didn't much matter. He wasn't looking around for dust and year-old magazines. He was too busy pulling me toward him and kissing me.

My lips—indeed, my entire face—felt numb from the alcohol, but I recognized his taste, his touch. How had I forgotten how he'd rub the small of my back when we embraced? And even in that blurry state, I was conscious enough to decide that I wanted a small wedding in a country inn and not the blow-out affair that I'd envisioned in my twenties.

Tim nibbled my earlobe in a gerbil-like way that I'd once found vaguely annoying but now seemed so sensual. "Can I have some water?"

"Sure." I stepped back, alarmed, and checked his face for signs of regret or repulsion. I saw neither, merely thirst.

I poured two glasses from a filtration pitcher. To keep my balance, I focused on a sticker on the pitcher's side. The filter was due to be changed last February. I dumped out the water and refilled from the tap, clutching the cold faucet. I knew I should put ice in the glasses, but I worried that the extra minute would give Tim just enough time to realize that the woman he had just been kissing was not some exciting stranger but just me.

When I returned to the living room, he was sitting on the couch, a small smile on his lips. I handed him the glass. He took a long drink and put the glass on the coffee table, carefully positioning it in the middle of a coaster. I sat next to him, somewhat nervously, and placed my glass on the floor. He put his hands on my shoulders and looked at me. "I've missed you."

"I've missed you too." For a moment, the room stopped spinning. He brushed my hair behind my ears with his fingers, put his hand on the back of my head, and kissed me gently. Then he leaned against me, and we sank back into the couch. He kissed my cheeks and eyelids. He parted my lips with his tongue. It was just like I'd always dreamed it would be.

Until I threw up.

 nineteen

Life circles back on itself. Here I was, once again, mooning over Tim. Was he thinking about me right now? Did he like me as much as I liked him? Where was this going to lead? At least my virginity was no longer an issue—not that either of us had removed a single article of clothing before I upchucked.

He'd had an early flight back to Washington. When I woke up, he was gone. I didn't get to see his reaction to me in the sober light of day. I didn't know whether he felt sorry or relieved to be leaving my apartment. He left a note, at least: "Never did get to hear you sing. We'll have to reschedule. Take two aspirin and drink lots of water. If that doesn't work, try a Bloody Mary." He signed it, "L., T." What, exactly, did the "L" stand for, I wondered. Love? Like? Left you again?

I missed my morning classes but made it back to Mercer

in time for lunch. The cafeteria offered a choice of boiled hot dogs or rectangular pizza so greasy that it would take a fistful of napkins to blot the excess oil. Since both options made my stomach churn, I made my way over to the all-day breakfast bar, where I retrieved yogurt, an English muffin and coffee.

Once again, I was breaking the "never eat alone" rule. And, once again, Jeremy stepped in to relieve me of my solitary state.

He looked solemn. "You had us worried."

I squinted at him. "Why? Who?"

"Tiffany and me. She said you were going into the city to have dinner with your brother but that you'd be back around eleven."

"It got late. I stayed over. What are you, my mother?" I tried to sound amused, but it came out snippy. All I really wanted was to be left to suffer in silence.

"You told me your brother lives in Denver."

I stared at him. He stared back. I shifted my gaze down to the table. It was dark brown and bore a thick wax coating from decades of use. "I wasn't with my brother. It was—an old friend. We got talking and it got late and I just, you know, crashed at his place."

"Talking."

"Excuse me?"

"That's all you were doing."

He didn't sound like my mother, after all. My mother had never been this invasive. "You know, Jeremy, I like you and you're a great R.A., but I don't think this is any of your business." I was in no mood to listen to a speech about the importance of condoms in the age of communicable diseases.

He closed his eyes for a moment and rubbed his fingers over his eyelids. When he looked at me again, he said, "I don't mean to butt in. But it's part of my job. R.A.'s are trained to recognize substance abuse problems."

I gawked at him. "You think I'm doing drugs?" It seemed funny all of a sudden, and I cackled. Had I not been so nauseous, I would have let out a belly laugh.

"Alcohol is a drug," he said. He wasn't laughing.

"Oh, that," I sighed. "Okay, I'm hung over. Jeremy, let's get real. It's the first week of classes. Half the campus is hungover."

"It's your second hangover of the week. And your drinking is already causing you to miss classes."

"I know," I said. "It was stupid. And I didn't mean to—last night, things just got out of hand. I don't have a drinking problem, I swear. Aside from these two times, it's been years since I've had a hangover."

When I realized what I'd said, my first thought was of Tim and how disappointed he'd be that I'd slipped up so easily. My second thought was that I needed to cover my ass—quickly. "Well, a year, at least," I said. "My friends and I, we had this schnapps phase junior year, but last year I stuck pretty much to Coke." Jeremy looked horrified. "What?" I asked.

"You were doing coke in high school?"

I dropped my face in my hands and took a deep breath. Finally, I leaned toward him. "Not coke—Coke! Big C! You know, as in, 'I'd like to give the world a Coke,' 'It's the real thing,' 'Give yourself a break today.'"

"That last one would be McDonald's."

"You watch too much television," I snapped.

He placed his tray carefully on the table and sat

down. His chair shrieked as he scooted closer to the table.

"Ow," I yelped at the sound. We locked eyes. "I am not an alcoholic."

He shrugged and took a long drink of milk. He looked at the ceiling. "If you say so."

I looked at his plate: three hot dogs on doughy buns. "A little alcohol is good for the heart," I said. "Nitrates can kill you."

He tore open a package of mustard, and it squirted his T-shirt. I smirked through my pain. He swiped at his chest with a napkin. "And what should I have instead?" he asked. "An English muffin and coffee? What kind of a lunch is that—the anorexic special?"

"Now I'm an anorexic?" I laughed, all hostility gone. Come to think of it, my pants were getting a little loose. Next time I went back to my apartment, I'd pull out that box of clothes that I never really believed I'd fit into again but couldn't bear to give away.

He rolled his eyes. "No, I don't think you're an anorexic." He needn't have sounded like it was such a pre-posterous idea. "Listen," he said, his voice softening. "A group of us were thinking about going out for burgers to-night. You want to come?"

"Thanks, but I've got a, um, study thing tonight. Maybe some other time." In truth, I had my singing audition. I knew what Jeremy thought of that crowd; I didn't want him to launch into a speech about why I should steer clear.

Eager to avoid another lecture on the evils of alco-hol, I had my story prepared for Tiffany. "What a night," I said as I walked into our room. "My brother and I ate dinner at this Chinese place. I think I've got food poisoning." It was fairly safe to assume that Tiffany and Jeremy wouldn't compare notes on my alibi. I dropped my backpack on the floor and placed the laptop beside it. I collapsed onto the pink and turquoise bedspread, which still carried the stench of artificial materials. "My brother had an old laptop he wasn't using."

Tiffany barely looked up from her textbook. "Jeremy was worried about you."

"Yeah. I saw him in the dining hall."

"He thought something might have happened."

"Nothing happened. I stayed at my brother's. I'm sorry." I tried to sound genuinely contrite but sounded about as annoyed as I was. "I should have called," I continued. "It never occurred to me that you might be so worried that you'd report my absence."

She wrinkled her nose. "I didn't report anything. Jeremy came looking for you, then he got all—weird."

"Oh," I said. "Sorry."

She closed the textbook, ran her finger along the cover. "If I disappeared, no one would worry. No one."

I rubbed my temples. "Of course they would," I said with the patience usually reserved for an exasperating but well-meaning child. "Jeremy would worry about you just like he did about me."

She crossed her arms over her chest. "No way."

My head hurt more by the moment. "Of course he would. Jeremy's a really nice person. And so are you," I added quickly and unconvincingly.

She leaned forward, tantalized by the possibility of bonding through gossip. "He is *so* fat."

I squinted at her. "I don't follow."

"You know. FAT!"

"I, um, I don't know. Jeremy's a lot of things, but fat is not one of them."

She slumped back on her pink bedspread, deflated. "Fat with a P."

"Pat?"

"No! P-H-A-T. *Phat*."

"Oh, right! Like, cool or something. *Phat*. Yes. Jeremy is phat." I squinted at my Matisse poster. It really was very pretty.

"I am such a geek," Tiffany whined. "If anyone else said *phat*, you'd know right away they meant *phat* and not *fat*."

"I wouldn't," I said slowly. "It's not you. It's me. Let's just say I'm not as tuned in to popular culture as the average eighteen-year-old."

twenty

These girls did not look like hookers. The leader, Vanessa, looked like my high school French teacher, a skinny, lank-haired, twittery woman named Mademoiselle Shlott. One day, in the middle of conjugating the verb *rire,* Mademoiselle grabbed her shrunken cheeks and yelled, "Why can't you pay attention to me for five goddamn minutes!" In shock, we halted our note passing and whispering. Her shoulders began to shake and her face grew wet with tears. "How do you think it feels to be standing up here, day after day? Don't you think I know what you say about me? DON'T YOU THINK I KNOW?" She ran out of the room, and we never saw here again. (For the rest of the year, the softball coach, who confessed that *escargot* was the only French word he knew, supervised the class.) In retrospect, perhaps the saddest thing was that Mademoiselle Shlott had it all wrong: we never said anything about her. In fact, until her breakdown, we never thought about her at all.

But Vanessa possessed something that Mademoiselle Shlott did not: a voice like Ella Fitzgerald. It was astonishing to hear a voice that big coming out of a body that skinny. Vanessa sounded like she weighed two hundred pounds. Also, she didn't dress like Mademoiselle Shlott, who favored knee-length skirts and cardigans. Vanessa wore frayed jeans and a pale pink baby doll top that offered a peak at the hoop in her navel.

Penny was Costello to Vanessa's Abbott. All bulges and curves, she probably did weigh two hundred pounds. She had big blue eyes, a tiny bow mouth, and a sweet baby-girl voice. She was quite striking, in a sixteenth-century kind of way, but I was surprised that the local johns were so enlightened. Unlike a lot of heavy girls, she dressed to accentuate her curves and possessed the self-confidence to wear thigh high boots over her generous legs.

There were six more girls in the group, none of them especially beautiful. I wondered if the less attractive girls were drawn to prostitution because they longed to feel desirable. Briefly I worried that I was on the wrong track, that these girls were just here to, well, sing. But I'd mentioned the audition to Amber—"That girls' singing group we talked about? I'm auditioning. I know you said they're a little, well, wild, but I really love to sing."

She gawked as if I'd just confessed to eating a dozen Krispy Kreme donuts. "Those girls are bad news, Katie. Seriously."

The auditions were being held in a dorm common room that appeared to have been decorated in the seventies: orange vinyl cushions, brown industrial carpet, the very same molded plastic chairs that Richard had in his office. Then again, given the popularity of anything "retro," the room could have been decorated in the last year, eradicating all traces of late-millennium mauve. The chairs were arranged in a horseshoe. Following a couple of songs intended to give us an idea of "what we, ya know, do," the existing Wallflowers had taken up residence on the couches. There were openings for four new members—a soprano, two altos and a tenor. That was good news for me, an alto.

They had us fill out index cards with our name, graduating year, phone number and experience. (Mine: "Lead alto in my high school's a capella group; member, choir; first runner-up, All State Choir." I wondered briefly whether there was any such thing as All State Choir. I figured I was pretty safe as long as I left out which state it was in.)

We handed in the cards. There was a lot of throat clearing and paper shuffling. Some of the girls had brought along class work. I figured they'd be automatically excluded for their poor prostitute potential. The Wallflowers sifted through the index cards and sorted them. I wondered if the sorting served any real purpose or if they were just enjoying the power gained from making twenty-five girls test the staying power of their Teen Spirit antiperspirant, a sample of which we had all received on our first day of school.

One by one, the Wallflowers called up the hopeful girls. In sync with the demonstration, they sang the forties: "Someone to Watch over Me," "My Funny Valentine." Some of these girls could actually sing. My chances were looking dim.

Tiffany sang before me. She had come on a whim. During our dinner the other night I had stupidly mentioned the audition. She'd said, "Oh, fun! I'll do it, too!" I didn't know how to discourage her without sounding like I didn't want to spend time together, which I knew from experience would send her into a depression, complete with a wailing-women soundtrack. I just hoped she couldn't sing. Leading her to a life of prostitution was even worse than making her feel unpopular.

She stood in the middle of the horseshoe. She wore black leggings and a long red cable sweater. When she'd gotten dressed, she'd asked, "Does this make me look even fatter than I really am?"

To this, I had no reasonable answer save the obligatory, "You're not fat!"

Doing her makeup (which was far too heavy), she'd remarked, "I wish my eyes were green. Or blue, even. Anything but brown."

I'd come back with, "But your eyes are such a pretty shade—almost gold."

Then, predictably, came the hair. "I wish my hair were curly."

It took every ounce of strength to say, "Isn't it funny how everyone with straight hair wishes it were curly, and everyone with curly hair wishes it were straight?" when I really wanted to advise her to get tinted contacts, a perm and a membership to Weight Watchers.

Vanessa glanced up and said, "Okay . . . Tiffany? Go ahead." Tiffany began to sing. A few notes in, I gasped. It wasn't that Tiffany's voice was especially good or bad—it was breathy but tuneful. It was that she was singing my song, "You're Mean to Me," a song she had never even heard of until I sang it for her two nights ago. She'd told me she was going to sing a show tune, something from

"My Fair Lady" or "The Music Man." Imitation may be the purest form of flattery, but I hadn't sung yet. It was going to look like I was imitating her.

As Tiffany sang, the girls on the couches smiled. They could all be called Mona, so complete was their collective mastery of the don't-you-wonder-what-I'm-thinking? smirk. I'd been checking them continually, hoping to catch even one of them in the act of eyeball rolling or eyebrow raising. As yet, they had given not the slightest clue of whom they did or didn't like.

When Tiffany finished, she flushed with pleasure and, eyes to the ground, scurried back to the seat next to mine. "Do you think they liked me?" she whispered.

"That was my song," I hissed.

"I didn't think you'd mind." Not only didn't she sound sorry, she was actually smiling a little. Another Mona: she'd fit right in.

"Katie? O'Connor? Is Katie here?" It took me a minute to remember that that was supposed to be my name.

"Here!" I popped up.

"You ready?" skinny Vanessa asked.

"To sing, you mean?" I asked stupidly.

"Yes. To sing." At last—a raised eyebrow. Goody.

I walked to the middle of the horseshoe. During Tiffany's solo, I'd been so busy thinking venomous thoughts that I hadn't had time to think of another song to sing. I'd have to pull an instant replay, I thought miserably. There simply wasn't another song I knew well enough to perform, unless you counted "I Will Survive," that silly song from the seventies. After Tim dumped me, Marcy bought me a tape of the song and forced me to drink vodka and cranberry juice until I stood on my bed and belted it out. From then on, every time I got depressed about Tim, she made me perform. I sang the song a lot. Marcy was really supportive during that time. She gave me endless pep talks about how men are scum and how I didn't need a man. Of course, she was already married to Dan, which didn't do a hell of a lot for her credibility.

Still, no matter how many times I had sung that song, I never quite pulled it off. I needed something easier, catchy and simple and not too challenging. Only one song came to mind. I tried desperately to think of something else, but time had run out. What the hell. At least I could say I tried. I put my hands on my hips and flapped my elbows back and forth. "Cock-a-doodle," I began. "Cock-a-doodly-doo . . ."

As I sang, some of the Mona's mouths began to twitch, then they revealed, miraculously—teeth! They were smiling! There was even a little finger snapping. When I finished, I grinned at them. They grinned back. As I walked back to my seat, I looked at the girls on the folding chairs and knew that, for that one glorious moment, every one of them hated me.

After that, I couldn't face another dinner with Tiffany—I couldn't face another minute with Tiffany—but I feared the repercussions of slipping out with any fellow hall mates. So, rather than heading back to the dorm after the auditions, I walked in the opposite direction, to where my forlorn Civic sat in a vast lot, and drove to the A&P on the edge of town. In Mercer, the service and retail hot spots—the A&P, the Jiffy Lube, the Denny's—had all been banished to the border. As such, there was surprisingly heavy traffic for such a small town.

The A&P was old, scruffy and underheated. The fruit was underripe; the lettuce was wilted. There was no organic milk or fat-free cream cheese. It was the only grocery store in town, though, so it was packed.

I filled my handheld basket with a bag of Hawaiian sweet rolls, an apple and a rotisserie chicken so hot that steam coated the inside of its hard plastic container. I was well within acceptable express line limits: "12 Items or Less." (It should be "12 Items or Fewer," a detail that never fails to annoy me, although I know I should get over it.) In front of me, a little girl with carefully styled corkscrew curls and perfectly straight blond bangs turned around and smiled. She had pale blue eyes fringed with eyelashes so light they were almost invisible. Her lavender T-shirt read PRINCESS. I smiled back.

Her blond mother gently stroked the girl's silky head. The girl leaned against her instinctively. The mother turned just enough for me to see her face. I stepped back in shock, knocking into the man behind me. "Sorry," I murmured as I scurried off to join another line before Chantal could see me.

twenty-one

Prostitution simply wasn't in Tiffany's future. The Monday after the auditions, the Wallflowers posted a list of new members, and her name wasn't there. It was through no fault of mine, but she subjected me to acoustic guitar and wailing women, anyway. Since I was still pissed at her for stealing my song, I was a little short on sympathy. Besides, she could have been gracious enough to congratulate me for getting into the group rather than remarking, "Your song didn't seem like what they mostly sing."

I was sitting on the floor outside my door, highlighting a textbook, when Jeremy came down the hall. "You locked out? Or did Clay Aiken stop by to perform unspeakable acts with Tiffany?"

"Neither. She's just listening to really bad, really loud music. By the way, Clay is on the outs ever since Katherine told Tiffany he was so last Thursday or last year or, God, could have been last millenium."

"Harsh."

"How do you think Clay feels?"

He sat down next to me. He wore gray gym shorts and a gray T-shirt and glistened with sweat. He looked like an ad for men's cologne although, quite frankly, he didn't smell like one. "What's she got up her butt today?" he asked. By now it was common knowledge that Tiffany was passive aggressive. I remembered Jeremy warning me about the singing group. I wasn't in a mood for another one of his lectures but figured he'd find out about it sooner or later. "We both auditioned for the Wallflowers. I got in. She didn't."

I waited for him to react with shock or disappointment. Instead, he smiled. "Awesome. I didn't know you could sing."

"I can't, but don't tell anyone." I checked his face. Where was the condemnation? Perhaps he figured this was a done deal: no point acting all self-righteous. Or maybe these girls weren't evil en masse; rather, there were one or two high-profile floozies. On consideration, that made sense. Granted, I hadn't spent much time with them yet, but I couldn't believe they were all on the game.

"Listen," Jeremy said. "About yesterday? The things I said? Can we just, you know—"

"Forget it ever happened?" I finished. I was learning to talk in questionese.

"Exactly." He grinned. I beamed back, so pleased to hear a declarative statement for a change.

It was almost ten o'clock. Had I been back in my old adult life, I would have been in my pajamas. But it felt early, even though it was a weeknight. I was restless. Also, I didn't want to spend too much time sitting in the hall with Jeremy lest it spark any rumors.

I made up something about having a paper due tomorrow and headed outside without saying good-bye to Tiffany. I had my key: I figured I could do without my coat. It was colder out than I'd expected. If I were still thirty-two, I would have gone back up for my coat. But tonight I was eighteen, so I clutched my arms and dared the night to chill me.

There were two barely-used pay phones at the library. Tiffany and Amber were the only other students I knew of without cell phones, but Tiffany was getting one for Christmas, while Amber was a Resident Assistant on financial aid. It was bad enough that it had taken me this long to get my own computer. The other kids probably assumed I was really, really poor.

I dialed Tim's number, putting the charges on a phone card that I'd bought in the bookstore. My heart was pounding. It had been four days since our kiss, and I hadn't heard from him. I'd fought the impulse to run to the phone the minute the Wallflowers list had been posted. I didn't want to seem too eager; Tim had never responded well to pressure.

He wasn't home. "You must be working late, Uncle Tim," I chirped, trying not to sound disappointed. "I just wanted to share my great news with you. I got into the group I told you about. Maybe you can make it to one of my concerts."

I thought about doing some research for my Ethics in Journalism class but realized my reading list was in the room with Tiffany. Oh, well. It's not like I was going to be here long enough to get a grade. Besides, I did have some experience in journalism, after all—and I'm not just talking about *Salad*. I figured I could wing it.

I spent the first few years after college as a freelancer. My specialty was women's issues—or, more specifically, women victim's issues. I did it all: the glass ceiling, sexual harassment, domestic violence, anorexia. I had a hard time getting beyond the yuck factor: so much seemed like none of my damn business. How much money do you make? Did you just not eat, or did you scarf a dozen donuts and then stick a finger down your throat? Did your boyfriend rape you after he beat you up? I split my time between waiting for the phone to ring and finding excuses not to write.

My income that year was something like $4000. I didn't write for the *Globe*. I didn't write for anything anyone had ever heard of. Tim said that was okay, that all that mattered was amassing clippings.

I managed to avoid living in squalor since Tim made five times my salary—hardly a fortune, but he was already building a name covering Massachusetts politics for the *Globe*. That's what brought us to Boston in the first place. I was happy to go, since Marcy, who had grown up in the area, had just moved to Cambridge; Dan was in his second year at Harvard Law School. As for my contribution to the household, that was the year I learned to cook. It provided three activities—cookbook reading, grocery shopping and meal preparation—that I could undertake in lieu of writing, all the while feeling I was doing something useful. I told myself I was being selfless, making these great meals as a special treat for Tim. In truth, Tim's tastebuds were just as insensitive as the rest of him. He could have lived on peanut butter sandwiches and been perfectly happy.

When I wasn't cooking I was painting the walls Dutch blue or turning old lace tablecloths into romantic curtains. Our apartment was in a crumbling old row house in Charlestown. My mother referred to it as "the firetrap," ranting about everything from the purple claw foot bathtub (which I liked) to the vent-transported odor of our downstairs neighbor's cigarette smoke (which I didn't). I didn't mind, really; she couldn't complain about the house and ask when Tim and I were getting married at the same time.

I didn't tell Tim when I sent my query letter to *Northshore Living*. Judging from my extensive history of rejections, they wouldn't want me writing for them, anyway. I called the proposed article, "A Tablecloth's Reincarnation." It presented ways to give an old, stained lace tablecloth new life. Bunched and hung from two hooks, it became the kind of elegant swags that graced my living room (I included a blurry snapshot). Cut and hemmed, it worked as a dresser scarf, runner or doily. A simple tacking job could transform cheap, solid-colored pillows or placemats into faux heirlooms, while lace scraps cut into strips became elegant ribbons, and squares became gift basket liners.

They loved it at *Northshore Living*. They said it married Yankee thrift with contemporary elegance. To my astonishment, they asked me to do a monthly column, which they called "Everything Old is New Again." Month after month, I suggested ways to give new life to old, cherished pieces—"that family heirloom you can't bear to part with or a cracked coffee mug from the earliest days of your marriage." Mismatched teacups became herb planters. Cut-glass dishes found their way into the bathroom to hold soap and candles. Gilt frames salvaged from ugly pictures surrounded new, dining room—worthy mirrors.

The column didn't pay particularly well—*Northshore Living*'s readers weren't the only ones who exercised Yankee thrift—but it thickened my clippings folder and gave me confidence. With Tim, I tried to shrug it off. "At least it'll help pay the bills until I get going with my real writing." But the truth was, I loved it. It required no prying questions, no confrontations with ex-husbands or ex-bosses. It gave me an excuse to poke around in thrift shops and consignment stores. It allowed me to focus on such noncontroversial topics as milk glass and braided rugs.

The column provided such exposure that a chain of suburban Boston newspapers asked me to do a column for them, too—weekly, this time. This one I called "Other People's Junk." Each week, I presented an item I had uncovered at a yard sale or thrift shop. I'd typically hunt down a similar item and tell my readers what they would pay for it at retail. I bought a framed poster for $3, say, and chucked the poster. Then I found an identical frame at Pier One for $22. When you took into account the hunting, the research and the writing, I spent perhaps twelve hours a week on the column, which paid $35 a pop. Take away the money I spent on my purchases, and I was left with an hourly rate that Tim described as being "what people cross borders in the middle of night to escape from." I told him he shouldn't end a sentence with a preposition. He told me I should limit my junk work to assignments that paid well. "It's okay to write for free, but you should at least be spending your time on something that matters to you." My dirty secret, of course, was that I already was.

By the time I'd joined *Salad*, things with Tim had deteriorated almost completely. The job offer was tantalizing:

paid vacation, sick days, health insurance—even a dental plan! When I told Tim I was going to accept the job, I expected outrage and disgust. How could I sell out like that? Instead, he just remarked, "It sounds like a good fit." I took that to mean that he thought I lacked depth, although, in retrospect, perhaps he was simply relieved that he could finally leave without worrying that I'd end up on the street.

Walking back to the dorm at Mercer, I suddenly felt thirty-two again. I had an alternate life vision. I imagined—as I did far too often—that in a parallel universe, Tim had never left. Or, rather, he did leave for Washington, but he'd taken me along, sporting a diamond, of course (one carat, flanked by sapphires and set in platinum). By now we would have left Georgetown: we needed more space when the baby came along. Now that she was two (I'd always had a hunch our first child would be a girl), we were thinking about trying for a second.

I took a shortcut behind a block of dorms. The walkway was well lit, but there were too many shady spots beneath trees, too many bushes. I heard some rustling, and a rush of adrenaline made my chest constrict, my face tingle. I began to walk faster. All those rape prevention talks had gotten to me. I rounded a corner and came across a cluster of preppies sitting on a bench, chatting. We exchanged smiles. My courage returned. I took a few steps back and peered around the building, back into the shadows. A girl emerged from behind a tree. She had beautiful hair, dark and long. She turned back and reached out. A much older man, wearing khakis and a dark golf sweater, leaned forward and gave her a lingering kiss. They parted. Keys jingling, she scurried up her concrete dorm steps.

Before I could get a good look at his face, he got back in

his car, turned on the engine and sped away. I scurried along the sidewalk, trying unsuccessfully to read the license plate. If only I were better with cars. People on detective shows always come out with observations like, "1992 Pontiac Seville, silver, with a dent on the passenger door." The best I could do was: gold or tan four-door sedan. Or maybe two-door. I wasn't actually counting. But I'm pretty sure it was a sedan.

Taking a deep breath, I pulled on the dorm door the girl had disappeared behind, but it was locked. No matter: she'd be in her room by now, anyway.

twenty-two

She was setting herself up for rejection, practically begging for it, but if Tiffany had asked me to attend her Christian fellowship meeting on any other day, I would have considered it. I was that desperate for roommate harmony. "And after the meeting, we're all going out to dinner at Denny's." Her cheeks flushed with the pride of a person in possession of a social life. The kids I had met from her fellowship group would make perfectly nice dinner companions. They were, for the most part, wholesome and friendly and good-hearted (anyone who would voluntarily socialize with Tiffany was made of stronger stuff than I).

But the meeting coincided with my first Wallflowers rehearsal. "I can't," I said. She glared at me, waiting for an explanation. Since I didn't want to open any old wounds, I dug at a fresh one. "I'm not—you know."

"What?" She was challenging me.

"That kind of a Christian." It came out all wrong, but I didn't know how else to say it.

Her mouth tightened. "The group welcomes Christians of all denominations."

"That's nice, but—" I took a deep breath. How was I going to get out of this? And then it came to me. "I'm Jewish." I tried to remember if I had shared any Christmas or Easter stories.

She stared at me. "Your last name is O'Connor."

I stared back. Score one for the Tiffster. I almost said the name had been changed from Cohen but managed to stifle any excessively creative impulses. "My mother's Irish," I said before quickly correcting myself. "I mean, my father." I've always been a lousy liar. "My mother's not at all religious, so she always let my father have his Christmas trees and Easter baskets, but I've always thought of myself as Jewish." That was good: covering my bases. Maybe I wasn't so bad at lying, after all. Of course, I had been getting a lot of practice.

So Tiffany went her way (after telling me that Judaism is a beautiful religion and that maybe in time I would learn to welcome the love of Jesus into my life), and I went mine.

Perhaps it was the guilt from lying about my religion, but when I walked into the dorm lounge for my Wallflowers rehearsal, I thought for one paralyzing minute that the nuns from my parochial school had come to get me. Knee-length navy blue skirts, plain white blouses: habits were the only thing missing.

"This has been the Wallflowers' standard attire since its

founding in 1952," Vanessa explained once we were all as-
sembled. "I think we all like its classic look and sense of
tradition." I peered around. Thankfully, mine wasn't the
only nose wrinkled in distaste. One girl, with spiky black
hair and a spectacular array of facial hardware, looked especially unimpressed. "But there's also a feeling that we
could use a little updating," Vanessa continued.

Another new recruit raised her hand half way. "Maybe
we could shorten the skirts a little? Like maybe an inch?"
Her voice was so soft, I wondered how anyone would ever
hear her singing. "And we could wear, like, short-sleeve
shirts?"

"No short skirts," piped in a chubby redhead attired in
the nun garb. "No short anything."

The soft-spoken girl fluttered her hands. "Jeans? And
T-shirts? Like, really cool and casual?"

"No jeans," said the redhead. "I look awful in jeans."

"Jeans might work, Shelby," Vanessa said, clearly unimpressed. "Thanks for your input. And, Gigi." She smiled at
the redhead. "You are not fat." Everyone giggled in sympathy. "But we've talked about really revamping our image." She exchanged a meaningful glance with Penny.
"Possibly even changing the name."

There was a collective gasp. "We will still be Mercer's
oldest singing group," Penny trilled, a reassuring smile on
her round face. "We just need a little updating."

I considered raising my hand and suggesting we call
the group, "Penny and the Novitiates," but I sensed no
one would laugh. Another new girl, skinny with buck-
teeth (most Wallflowers were at least ten pounds under-
weight or twenty pounds overweight), cleared her throat.
"The new outfits? Like you mentioned? I was in this

singing group, you know, in high school? We wore black cocktail dresses—you know, real classy and kind of old-fashioned. So maybe we could do that?"

Vanessa's lips tightened. Penny's nostrils flared. "The Red Hots have already laid claim to the black cocktail dress look," Vanessa hissed. "And we most definitely want to set ourselves apart from them."

The Red Hots? Why had I never heard of the Red Hots? Should I be troubled? And, perhaps even more crucially: after life among the eighteen year olds, would I ever stop thinking in questions?

"I so hate the Red Hots," said the redhead. "I am so pissed that they've, like, totally claimed the color black. Everyone knows it's the most slimming."

"We could wear white," the bucktoothed girl said with a shrug. She really did stand out as the only student at Mercer not enhanced by adolescent orthodontia.

I laughed. "And call ourselves the Sacrificial Virgins."

They all smiled politely but, aside from the spiky haired girl, who snorted, looked mildly hurt. Someone actually sighed. I had hit a nerve. Perhaps they were collectively ashamed of their famed promiscuity. Yeah. That was it. Surely I wasn't so stupid that I'd gotten myself into the wrong singing group.

Soft-spoken Shelby offered another idea. "We could just wear our old prom dresses. Mine was a Jessica McClintock. It was really pretty." She smiled, revealing a mouth full of braces. I'd bet money Shelby was one of those students who treated every class as if it were a personal conversation between herself and the professor. Maybe she just spoke quietly so people would strain to listen to her.

The spiky-haired girl shook her head. The chain that

connected her nose ring to her earring swayed gently. "Nuh-uh. The only way I'm putting myself into lace is if I get to accessorize with Doc Martens and biker gloves."

I nodded. "I like it. Really. Taffeta with high-tops, a little leather here and there. It's . . . ironic." I nodded at my own choice of words. Irony was very big with this generation.

Penny shook her head. "People would laugh at us."

I shook my head. "No, they wouldn't. We'd be laughing at ourselves first."

"The Red Hots might get away with a stunt like that," Penny said. I sensed quiet hissing. "But we have traditionally been more conservative." There were two singing groups. I had joined the conservative one. This was bad. Bad, bad, bad. I tried to convince myself that Gigi, Shelby and all the other gawky girls were closet tramps. They were so brimming with self doubts and poor body images, they were positively ripe for meaningless sexual encounters.

"I think Katie's got a point," Vanessa said. "It's like we're saying we're so above that corny high school crap. And we are, aren't we? I am, anyway."

Before we began to sing, Shelby spoke again. "There's just this other thing I wanted to ask? Our meetings? Are they always at this time? Because my Christian fellowship group meets now, and I'd really like to be able to do both."

I was toast.

Jeremy poked his head out of his door as I walked past. "Hey, Katie. How'd the rehearsal go?"

"Okay." I tried to sound nonchalant. He followed me to my room. I sat on my bed, leaving the maple desk chair for him. He perched on the edge, then sprang up, too antsy to sit still. He looked like he had something to say, but he didn't say it. I spoke to fill an increasingly awkward pause. "We're changing our name. The Wall-flowers, I mean."

"Oh?" He looked confused, as if I'd changed the subject, when, in fact, I had not. "To what?" He stuck his hands into the front pockets of his soft blue jeans. His forearms were brown and ropy with muscles.

"The Alternative Prom Queens."

His eyebrows shot up. "I like it." And then, "Tiffany told me you're Jewish," he said abruptly. Oh, God—he was here for another talk: it's bad enough that you're a lush, but this lying has got to stop.

"I'm not really," I said, ready to come clean. I pulled my backpack onto my lap and opened the front pocket. I rummaged around the pens before realizing I wasn't actually looking for anything. I was just trying to expend some of my nervous energy.

"Oh, I know." He shook his head. "You're just half, and you've barely even been to Temple, and you love lobster." He smiled. "You're like me."

"No. I'm not." I looked into his eyes. How could I lie to him? "I've never been to Temple," I said.

He shrugged. "I've only been once. My grandmother took me, and I was so young, I barely even remember it. My mother had a fit." He snorted. "All those Jewish mother jokes—my mother's nothing like that. Which is the point, I guess. Growing up, she didn't dream of being a teacher or a nurse or even a housewife. She just dreamed of being Presbyterian."

"That's awfully specific," I said.

"Okay, she would have preferred Episcopalian, but this was close enough."

He told me everything. How his mother made him take tennis lessons and dance classes ("You saw what good those did"). How she developed a passion for sailing and shrimp cocktail. How she tried to keep him from making friends with children of dubious ethnicity ("Anyone whose name began or ended with an *o* was automatically out"). How his mother, Sylvia, once told she looked French, started calling herself Sylvie. This after a phase where she tried to head off any ethnic connotations by saying her name was "Sylvia—like Sylvia Plath the poet." As Jeremy remarked, "The suicide bit didn't faze her. Sylvia Plath was a pure-bred WASP who went to a Seven Sisters school, and that was good enough."

As for his father: "He sells life insurance, which explains a lot, I guess—everything's very big picture, like how much are you going to have when it's all over. Also, he's a big believer in the American dream; anybody can work their way up, and all that. So he doesn't care if someone's Jewish or black or Chinese, as long as they're not poor. He has no patience for poor people. He believes welfare shouldn't be reformed, it should be abolished. His father was a roofer—my mother doesn't like to talk about that—and he figures if he could make it to the middle class, why can't everyone else?"

"And he thinks you should be a doctor."

"No, he's *decided* I'm going to be a doctor."

"Why?"

"My second-grade teacher said I had this incredible aptitude for science. That pretty much sealed it for my dad.

That's what I get for being able to name all the planets."
As he talked, he walked idly around the room, examining
the posters before settling on my bed, close enough to
talk, but not awkwardly so.

I'd never heard Jeremy talk so much about himself. He
told me that he wanted to travel after graduation, that he
wanted adventure. He told me he wanted to "get more in
touch with myself." Then he laughed and said, "I can't believe I just said something so trite." But after all those
years about not thinking about religion ("Officially, we be-
long to the local Presbyterian church, but we didn't actually show up except for the occasional Easter"), he'd been
wondering about his Jewish side. He told me about his
mother's parents, and about his cousins—how warm they
were, how funny and open. How they made him feel he
should explore his heritage.

This was so not the time to say, "The thing about me
being Jewish? It was a total lie to avoid spending time
with Tiffany." Instead, I allowed a long, full pause into the
one-sided soul-bearing discussion. "So, what's your Jewish
mother like?" he finally asked.

I tried to skirt the question. "It's not my mother who's
Jewish, it's my father."

He wrinkled his eyebrows. "O'Connor?"

I couldn't believe I'd made that mistake twice.

"Changed from Cohen."

He nodded. Then he put his hand on my cheek and held
it there. For a wild, incredibly stupid second, I thought he
was giving me a Hebrew blessing. But then he leaned forward and kissed me. My lips tingled. My stomach warmed.
Then I realized who and where I was, and I lurched away.

"Oh, my God," I said. "Oh, my God, oh, my God." I put my hand over my lips in a bizarre gesture of modesty. I felt like a child molester.

"I'm sorry," he said. "I thought . . . I don't know. We seemed to connect and—"

"Just because I'm—Jewish?" I asked.

"No, of course not. I've liked you from the beginning." He stood up and tugged at his golden brown curls. He looked about sixteen years old. "I guess I thought it was mutual, but it's not, I guess, and . . . and . . ." He let out a huge, agonized sigh. "I feel like such a jerk."

"It's not you," I said. "It's me." And that was true, perhaps for the first of all the millions of times that line has been uttered.

"Right," he said glumly. Good God, he looked like he was going to cry. I wondered if he'd ever said those same words to any of the leagues of girls who'd fallen in love with his J. Crew looks.

"No, really." I put my hand on his arm, but when I realized I wanted to keep it there, I took it away. "I have this thing, this problem with men. I'm not sure how I feel about them." Once again, I was allowing a speck of honesty to float up above the lies.

He blinked at me. "You mean you're . . . gay?"

I opened my mouth to speak, and then I shut it. I could hardly explain that the love of my life had dumped me on my butt a week after my twenty-ninth birthday. I could hardly say that I'd vowed to only date men who I could conceivably end up marrying some day. I could hardly say that he'd be perfect if I were ten years younger—except that if I were ten years younger, he'd be eleven. I looked at the floor. "I'm not sure yet," I whispered.

He stroked my hair, much of his confidence clearly re-gained: it really *was* me and not him. "When you spent the night in Boston, I just assumed it was with a man." He gazed at me, oozing sympathy. "I guess you've got a lot to work out."

"I guess I do."

Tim answered his phone on the first ring. "What's new, Kath?" he asked. By now, I knew he had Caller ID, so I wasn't surprised that he knew it was me.

I'd planned to make it all funny, and I didn't know what to do about that catch in my throat. "I'm a Jewish lesbian," I blurted out.

twenty-three

Okay, so I should have come clean to Tim about my screwup with the Wallflowers (which were, as I'd told Jeremy, henceforth to be known as the Alternative Prom Queens). I could have slipped it in: "The group that I thought were hookers? The funniest thing—they're just a bunch of girls who like to sing!" But Tim was so sympathetic about my new identity crisis ("I'm sure there are plenty of Jewish lesbians who live happy, full lives") that I didn't want to ruin the moment, especially after he said, "Great work—I'm really impressed" when I told him about the incident I'd witnessed the night before. I was even dumb enough to feel all warm and tingly when he said he'd come up for my first concert. Maybe then we could talk about our kiss—and what it meant for our future. It wasn't until I got off the phone that I realized what a disaster that would be. One look and he'd know what I should have figured out from the beginning: that I'd hooked myself up with a bunch of virgins.

I tried not to think about it. I was so busy with classes and rehearsals, I barely had time to think about why I was at Mercer in the first place. I began to envision a new kind of article, a human interest piece not unlike the one we had proposed to Dr. Archer: thirty-something career gal infiltrates freshman hall and tells all—how college kids have changed over the years, their priorities and their goals. I floated it by Tim, who said, "I hate those gimmicky pieces." Then, to smooth my ruffled feathers, he added, "Though I'm sure you'd do a great job on it."

The Alternative Prom Queens had scheduled a concert already, so we were rehearsing constantly. Add to that time for shopping and alterations, and I was hardly ever in the dorm. Our new look was a radical departure from the novitiate garb. We were to dress as, well, alternative prom queens. Taffeta was *de riguer*, but creative alterations and accessories were encouraged. After a night at my apartment, I claimed to have hit the jackpot at a thrift store and presented the group with three frilly monstrosities. "Can you believe anyone would actually wear these?"

In truth, they were former bridesmaid dresses. I don't care how pretty something is at first glance (not that any of these were); once you've seen the exact same dress on three to ten other women (not to mention the occasional flower girl), it's hard to love it. I unloaded a shiny turquoise tent, worn for my cousin Sharon's wedding, and the purple velvet thing I'd worn as a bridesmaid for this girl called Celine. When Celine worked—briefly—in *Salad*'s advertising department, we went out for drinks two or three times. I was astonished when she asked me to be in her wedding—and had no prepared excuse for why I couldn't do it since I never, ever could have seen it coming. She had ten bridesmaids at her wedding, though, and I, too, would have been hard-pressed to come up with ten really close friends. Still, I kept wondering if any of the others had ever seen her through a bad breakup or a death in the family or even a bad case of the flu, or whether she'd chosen us all because she thought we'd look good in purple velvet.

As for the third frilly dress, it came from Marcy's wedding. That one I kept for myself. I was her maid of honor, after all. The dress was peach lace, and it looked down-right fetching when I cut it to mini length and paired it with red high-tops.

Relations with Tiffany were becoming even more strained. She had a boyfriend—her first, as far as I knew—but instead of growing giggly and elated, she had become even more morose and nervous. Ethan and Tiffany had met in a study group, but from what I'd walked in on one afternoon, it appeared that they were engaging in some highly un-studious behavior. After that time, I jiggled my key in the lock for a while before entering. I never caught them again, however; he wasn't around much. Tiffany, on the other hand, was almost always in the room, engaged in the age-old pursuit of waiting by the phone. When she did go out, to classes, mostly, the first thing she'd ask upon her return was, "Did I get any calls?"

Once, I replied, "Yeah, your mom." Her face lit up and then fell in such quick succession that I wondered if she didn't detest her mother for the instant's heartbreak.

A couple of girls from her fellowship group stopped by one day to ask Tiffany to join them for ice cream, but she turned them down.

"Why didn't you go with your friends?" I asked after they left. I could have had the room to myself for an hour. A whole hour!

"They aren't really my friends," she said. "They hardly even know me."

When Ethan did call, Tiffany's voice became breathy and giggly. She'd take the cordless phone to her bed, where she'd sit with her knees to her forehead, seeking privacy in the darkness between her thighs and chest. Then she'd hang up, lunge into her closet and grab some clothes that were no more flattering than the ones she was wearing. She had lost weight. I wasn't sure whether love diminished her appetite or whether she was unwilling to sacrifice valuable phone-sitting time for a meal. For Ethan had informed her, early on, that he didn't leave messages. "I don't like machines," he'd said. Tiffany believed him, but I was inclined to think he wanted to see or talk to her when and only when it suited him; otherwise, he couldn't be bothered.

It was driving me crazy. I wanted to be annoyed or vaguely amused. Instead, I was worried. "Want to see a movie tonight?" I asked one Wednesday evening. She was sitting on her bed with her arms around her knees, staring into space. "What?" She looked surprised. She shook her head. "I've got too much to do. You know, reading."

"You might want to think about playing hard to get," I blurted. "Some guys like you better when you seem less available."

She glared at me, and I realized with a shock that Tiffany no longer wanted to be my best friend. Quite the contrary. "Mind your own beeswax," she said, and it would have been laughable had it been said without such venom.

As for Jeremy, he was the other friend I'd lost. It was different, of course. I didn't feel sorry for him; I just missed him. He was the only student I'd met here who resembled an adult. Now I felt uncomfortable every time I ran into him, so I avoided him as much as possible. If I was about to leave my room and heard him outside, I'd stall until he was gone. A month in a dorm, and I was acting eighteen.

After my fight with Tiffany, there was nothing to do but leave. It was three o'clock on a Tuesday, but the sky was so black it looked like early evening. I sat in my Civic and waited for the deluge. When most people think of fall in New England, they picture red and orange leaves flaming against a sharp blue sky, but that's just part of it. Late September brings violent weather shifts, seventy and sunny one day, forty-five and pounding rain the next. There's nothing like a good storm to rip those pretty leaves off the trees and catapult us prematurely into winter. September is hurricane season. Headache season. The low pressure from the incoming storm made my brain expand. My head hurt like hell, and I'd forgotten to stop by College Drugs for a bottle of Aleve.

It was the kind of day when all I wanted was to read a good book beside a roaring fire, a cat on my lap, a mug of sweet tea on my table. But I don't have a fireplace. Or a cat. And without those, the whole tea ritual seems kind of empty.

Right now, I'd settle for being back in my apartment. I'd been here for four weeks already, and I'd learned nothing. I'd retraced my walk to the library on several evenings and hung around that dorm looking for the girl with the long, shiny hair and had come up empty. I wasn't sure I could stand three more weeks—especially if it meant admitting defeat at the end. As such, I was doing the only thing I could think of to get the damned story finished in time for my deadline, if not before. I was stalking a source.

Okay, Tim had written off Chantal as being a dead end, just a small-time hooker in a small town, but I wasn't so sure. It is hard to keep a secret in a small town. Maybe she'd heard or seen something. Or maybe not. I'd run out of ideas, and Chantal was my last hope.

Her blinds were drawn. With the front window being positioned under the upstairs apartment's landing, there wasn't much light to be let in, even on a clear day.

It was 2:30 and five minutes after the sky had begun to unload when I saw a man scurry to her door, head down, and knock. He wore a jean jacket that looked to be highly effective at absorbing rain. He was fortyish, with a large rear end and no neck to speak of. The door opened briefly and he slipped inside. I tried not to think about what was going on in there, but it was hard not to. I shuddered. Really, what did I expect—Richard Gere? At least this guy looked clean. Well, cleanish. I hoped he was nice to her.

At 2:50, the door opened again, and the man slipped out. I looked away, although of course he was fully dressed. Once I saw his pickup truck leaving the parking lot, I got out of my car and sprinted for Chantal's front door. Fortunately, I'd brought a slicker to Mercer. It wasn't very warm, but at least it kept me dry. She opened the door immediately, probably expecting the big butt guy to have come back for seconds. She wore a bathrobe: red and black flannel, not exactly what I would have pictured, but it does get cold here. She stared at me.

"I was hoping to catch you before your three o'clock," I said, as if stopping by my hairdresser's for a bang trim.

"My three o'clock what?" she said carefully. For at least a half a second I considered that maybe she was just having an affair with the guy in the pickup, but surely an affair demands a little foreplay and after play, not to mention a nice meal. Twenty minutes wouldn't cut it.

"You probably don't remember me," I said. "My name is Katie. I came here a couple of months ago."

She narrowed her eyes. "July twenty-seventh. Three o'clock. Except your name was Kathy then."

I blinked at her. "You have an amazing memory."

"I can't exactly keep written records." She crossed her arms and hugged herself, providing a kind of flannel armor. "Look. If you're going to take me in, just take me in."

"I don't follow."

"You got nothin' on me," she said. "But if you're going to book me anyway, I gotta call my lawyer to bail me out. My daughter gets out of after-school care at six, and they get really pissed if you're late."

I couldn't believe I once thought Chantal could be a college student. She was almost young enough, but her teeth were too crooked, her eyes too weary. Only her hands bespoke a woman of leisure. Her fingers were long and smooth, her oval nails painted a delicate shell pink.

"I'm not a cop," I told her. "I'm a reporter."

She raised her eyebrows. "And that guy you were with? The nerdy one—Tim?"

"He's a reporter, too." We stared at each other for a moment. "Do you really think he's nerdy?"

She laughed, a surprisingly girlish sound. "That's not

necessarily a bad thing. Nerds usually have the biggest dicks."

I was speechless for a moment—I don't discuss penises very often, even (or especially) Penises I Have Known—but then I stuck a hand on my hip and tilted my head in a world-weary way. "Actually, it's pretty average."

We ate at the Denny's just off the highway. It smelled of disinfectant and grease. I'd suggested the restaurant because I was reasonably sure I wouldn't run into anyone I knew there. I assumed Chantal would share the same desire for anonymity, but when the hostess greeted her with a warm, "Hey, Cheryl," she smiled back. As the hostess seated us in a window booth (which boasted a view of the highway off-ramp), she said to Chantal, "You're cuttin' out of work early," to which Chantal shrugged and said, "Business is slow today. The rain."

We slid into a slippery brown booth. She pulled a laminated menu from behind the sugar shaker and began to read. I stared at her. "Cheryl?"

"Mmm?" She looked up.

"I thought your name was Chantal."

"I thought your name was Kathy." She went back to the menu.

"How do you know the hostess?" I finally asked.

"Our daughters are in the same class. First grade."

"And she knows about your, um, business?" Chantal—Cheryl—had finally admitted to being a pro—her preferred term—after she'd taken me into her apartment and checked me for a listening device. Then she'd changed into jeans and a gray sweatshirt and stuck her tangled blond hair into a messy ponytail.

She looked up from her menu. "Some parents at the school, the accountants and professors, people like that, don't think much of me being a palm reader, but they don't say nothin'."

"A palm reader? But what if someone shows up and actually wants a palm read?"

"Then I read it." She shrugged. "I'm good, too. This one lady, I looked at her hand for a long time then said, now don't be upset or nothin', but I think your husband's steppin' out on you. So she goes home and confronts him, and sure enough, he's got a little cupcake on the side."

"And you could tell that from her palm?"

She tightened her mouth, considered lying, then decided to tell the truth. "Nah. Her husband had been a client for years, then he suddenly stopped showing up. Figured he must be getting it for free."

"So what happened?"

"He cried a lot, told her he never loved anyone else and broke off the affair."

"So you saved their marriage!"

"Sure. Plus I got one of my best clients back." She grinned slyly.

The waitress brought us ice water in cloudy glasses. I almost didn't order anything since it was too late for lunch and too early for dinner, but even Denny's food had to be better than whatever cornstarch-thickened mess they were preparing at the dining hall. I ordered a club sandwich, while Cheryl chose a grand slam breakfast. "I never get to eat breakfast," she said once the waitress had gone. "Too many early clients."

"I would have thought you'd be busier at night."

She shook her head. "They like to catch me on their way

into work. The lunch hour's pretty busy, too. I'd get a lot of after-work business, but I've got to pick up Destiny. When I had her, I swore I'd always put family ahead of work, and I've stuck to it."

"Is Destiny—was Destiny—from, um, working?"

"I don't follow." She took a gulp of water.

"Do you know who the father is?" I asked, hoping I wasn't being offensive.

"Oh! You mean was I on the game. Nah, that came later. I had this boyfriend, Brent, we went out all through high school, then the summer after we graduate I get pregnant and he splits." She shrugged. "It don't matter. Destiny and I, we do okay. It was rough the first three years, before I got in the game. All these dumb-shit minimum-wage jobs. Every time Destiny got sick and I had to take off work, I got fired. Now I make my own hours, make good money. We do okay."

The waitress brought our plates. Cheryl dumped syrup over her pancakes, bacon and sausage, careful to leave the scrambled eggs unsoaked. I glanced at the other diners— not many at this odd hour, but there were a few, nonetheless. We were the only ones who weren't either dangerously obese or wearing trucker hats or both. My club sandwich could have fed me for the next two days, if only I had a fridge.

"What about competition?" I asked, extracting a frilly toothpick from a towering triangle of my sandwich. "Are you the only game in town?" I took a bite. A tomato slice slid out of the sandwich and onto my plate, followed by a piece of bacon. I never have mastered the multi-decker sandwich.

She shoveled some scrambled egg into her mouth. Still

chewing, she speared a piece of bacon and a wad of pancakes. She lifted her shoulders at my question then gob-
bled the next bite before pausing to wipe her mouth with
a paper napkin. "Sorry," she said. "I'm hungrier than I
thought. I've heard there are other girls around, but we
don't exactly get together for coffee."

"Any chance"—I checked to make sure no one was
listening—"could any of them be from Mercer?"

I expected her to look shocked, but she merely
shrugged. Cheryl was a big shrugger. "Could be."

"That wouldn't surprise you?"

"Nothing surprises me anymore."

I nodded. "But you haven't heard any rumors?"

"No. But that doesn't mean anything. Give me your
number, and I'll call if I hear anything."

twenty-four

I discouraged Tim from coming to the concert by saying it was too risky. He wanted to ask Gerry, the bartender at The Snake Pit, about the encounter I'd seen by the bushes, but I urged him to do it some other evening. I'd played that scene over in my head so many times that I'd started to wonder if there wasn't an innocent explanation. Maybe the man was just saying good night to his daughter. His favorite daughter. Who he really, really, really liked.

Still, I had the jitters. It was stage fright, pure and simple. Backstage, I plucked at the chrysanthemums in my hair (this being fall, mums were plentiful and cheap). I smoothed my peach lace and scuffed the floor with my high-tops. I tried to tell myself that this was just another night in the life of an investigative reporter, that I would spend my time scanning the audience for any potential johns who were dumb enough to confuse us with the Red

Hots. But I knew, of course, that I had no good reason to be here. The Alternative Prom Queens were a bunch of nice girls who liked to harmonize. They took up too much time and provided no clues about the elusive prostitution ring, which I was starting to suspect was a fiction anyway. But I was enjoying myself. Singing in a college a cappella group, I was doing something I'd always regretted missing out on. It was one of the points on my mental grievance list against Tim. I was reclaiming a college experience I'd never had: one that had nothing whatsoever to do with my future—as either a reporter or Tim's lucky wife—and everything to do with having a good time and making the most of my youth, which was more fleeting than anyone around me could suspect. I would never cut a record, I would never belt out tunes on Broadway. Even if I had the ambition, I lacked the talent. A college concert was the pinnacle of my singing achievement. It made my head buzz with excitement and my stomach churn with fear.

There were forty-two people in the audience. I should have lost myself in the music and passed on the counting, but I couldn't help it. Anyway, it didn't take long. Thirty-one female, eleven male (two of whom appeared to be faculty). The auditorium seated five hundred.

I desperately wished for latecomers until the forty-third audience member slipped in: Tim.

Perspiration dampened the polyester lining of my dress. My throat constricted (good thing I didn't have a solo). I couldn't put a label on what I was feeling, but it was much, much worse than stage fright.

The concert was a success—at least as successful as it could be without much of an audience. But no one screwed up, and the forty-five people in the audience (there had been three latecomers) applauded enthusiastically. Okay, forty-four did, anyway.

After our last number, we walked in a line backstage, taking turns pushing the curtain aside (we'd been unable to find someone to actually open and close the curtain for us). There were giggles, squeals and something that resembled a group hug. "People were actually smiling!" Vanessa gushed. "Did you see?"

Eventually, I trudged up the long, now-empty aisle to Tim, who leaned against the back wall, his arms crossed casually in front of him. Only his tight-lipped smile betrayed any tension.

I was trying to figure out the best way to break the news about the Prom Queens, but he did it for me. "Those girls aren't hookers." He didn't sound angry or even irritated. Rather, his voice was controlled, slow and patient, as if he were telling an especially dim child, "First put on your underpants, *then* the trousers."

"I was just about to tell you," I said, as if this were a piece of late-breaking news.

I heard a giggle behind me. Relieved at the interruption, I turned to Shelby, who squeezed my arm and did a little jump. Her smile was quite literally blinding, as her braces reflected the stage lights. She wore a studded leather jacket over turquoise satin, and her brown hair hung in ringlets. She looked like a child who had raided her trampy teenage sister's closet. "I am so pumped!" she said. "I am so jazzed! This is, like, the best day of my life!"

"You ought to get out more," Tim purred.

Shelby shot him a look of purest disdain and turned her attention back to me. "Mother's boyfriend?" she whispered in my ear.

"Mmm," I replied, vaguely.

"Mine's always trying to act cool, too. Just ignore him—it works for me."

"I was Kathy's high school music teacher," Tim said casually. "It was so nice of her to invite me to her concert."

Shelby looked at him strangely. "I'll see you at practice," she said as she left.

I tried to look at Tim but couldn't stand it. Instead, I examined my high-tops. What had appeared fun and quirky an hour ago suddenly seemed trite and regressive.

"I'm called Katie here," I said finally.

"I wish you had mentioned that." We were quiet for another moment, until he asked, "Want to go for a drink?"

"You have no idea."

The Snake Pit was packed and noisy. We claimed a corner near the bar so we could grab the first available stools. I was relieved at the crowd, as we couldn't possibly discuss my incompetence among so many potential eavesdroppers. I felt a little ridiculous in my reconstructed prom outfit, but no one seemed to notice. "You still a wine drinker?" Tim asked with much more practicality than sentiment.

"As long as it's not white zin," I said. "They guzzle that stuff by the caseload around here."

Tim ordered a beer for himself—some obscure import—and the wine for me. The bartender—not Gerry, our informant—jerked his head in my direction. "She got ID?"

Tim stared at him for a moment, smirked briefly, then looked over to me with mock concern. "You *are* twenty-one, right?"

"Of course," I said. For a moment, I longed for my license,

which was hidden in the glove compartment of my car, but I knew I could never pull it out and blow my cover. "I just, um, left my ID at home."

"Lotta that goin' around," the bartender sneered.

"How about we go back to your room and get it, then," Tim suggested.

The bartender guffawed. "Better make sure she's eighteen before you take her home. Don't want to be getting into any trouble." Tim leaned back to the bartender, and they exchanged words I couldn't hear.

"It's not funny," I said, once we were out on the street.

"Actually, it is," Tim said, as he walked briskly to the liquor store two doors down. "Your roommate around?"

"I doubt it. Her boyfriend's speaking to her this week, and his roommate usually goes home weekends."

The door of College Liquors jingled as Tim opened it. "Wait here," he instructed.

Back in my room, he opened the brown bag. He took out a six-pack of dark brown beer and set it on the floor. Then he reached back in. "For you," he said, presenting a bottle of very pink wine.

"My favorite," I sneered.

"You were expecting an oaky chardonnay with vanilla undertones? You're supposed to be eighteen. Consider yourself lucky. I almost bought you peach wine."

I grabbed the bottle of white zinfandel and reached for the corkscrew that I kept in the top drawer of my desk. "You won't be needing that," Tim said. He took the bottle from me, and with one quick turn of the wrist, it was open. I retrieved the single wine glass that I left out on my desk and held it out to be filled. Then, I settled onto my bed. Tim sat on my chair, even though it was much harder than my bed and much farther away from me. Perhaps that was the point. "You could just drink wine out of your mug like all the other freshman," he suggested.

I snorted. "College isn't quite the same as in our day. Kid down the hall? Very into his port—tawny, not ruby. Has to be at least twenty years old."

"The kid?"

"The port." I gulped my wine. It tasted much better than I'd expected it to. "But I think it's because of all those years in France."

"The port?"

"No, the kid. He went to high school in Paris. Port's from Portugal."

"I know that." He smiled, or softened, at least.

I drank some more. Maybe Jeremy was right; I was getting a bit too attached to my booze. "As for my sophisticated tastes, I've got it covered." I held my glass up in a mock toast. "Ever since my parents' separation—this was sophomore year of high school—my mother, who's a borderline lush but not really an alcoholic, has taken me on three wine tasting vacations. Two in Napa, one in the south of France."

"This would be your Jewish mother."

"The very same."

"And how did she get a fifteen-year-old on these tours?"

"She was sleeping with the tour coordinator."

"Male or female?"

"Oh, male. I'm the only lesbian in my family. And even that may be just a phase." I smiled, and so did he, although he still didn't move over to my bed. I drained my glass. It was actually kind of tasty if you thought of it as juice.

Tim took a swig of beer and squinted at my Matisse

poster. "You know, Kathy, you don't have to be quite so—creative. Your father can be a banker. Your mother can be a part-time office manager. Home can be a brick colonial in Connecticut. Sound familiar?"

"Vaguely. But then tell me this: why don't my parents ever call? Why aren't they coming up for Parents Weekend? Why am I the only girl on the hall who doesn't want to sleep with our Greek god of an R.A., who, by the way, thinks I'm quite the hot little number." I looked for signs of jealousy and came up empty. "Because I come from a dysfunctional family, that's why! Mine's not even the weirdest around, judging from the stories I've heard."

"Look." He put his beer on my desk. "I just think that the less you say, the better. And borrowing from your real life may not be such a bad idea. Half-truths are generally more believable than total lies."

"Are you speaking from personal experience?" I snapped. Our reconciliation was sliding further and further away.

"Let's just—oh, Christ." He ran his hand through his hair. "Can we just talk about the investigation?" Thus he steered the conversation away from my relationship screwups and back to my career screwups, where it belonged.

"I joined the wrong singing group," I announced.

"So I gathered."

"But it still gives me an inside perspective." I yapped for a bit about the microcosm of college singing groups. He bought the argument for the same reason I thought of it in the first place; at Cornell, a cappella groups were an elite, trendy group. At Mercer, there were only two girls' groups, one of which had nothing better to do on Saturday nights, the other of which had too much. (They had yet to give any kind of performance.) "There will be tours to other colleges, joint events"—this I claimed because Penny had said that the Red Hots sometimes sing at nearby schools—"and if they ever get invited to something like that again, maybe we can ask to be included."

Tim went along with it. As he drained his beer, he nodded through a gulp and wiped a touch of froth from the corner of his mouth. If only I'd joined the Red Hots, maybe I would have had the nerve to lick it off before he got to it. That's the kind of behavior that would come naturally to that set. "Okay," he said. "Whatever. I guess it's a done deal, anyway—it would look suspicious if you backed out now. Just try to find out something worthwhile. Time's running out." He stood up and reached for his jacket, which he'd thrown next to me on the bed. "Enjoy your wine."

"You're not staying?" My voice cracked. Whenever I get upset, I acquire the voice of a fourteen-year-old boy. I lowered it an octave. "I thought we might work on our notes, plot strategy. Something." I paused. "We didn't get very far the other night."

"Yeah. Sorry about that."

"No need to apologize." I tried to catch his eye. He focused on finding his car keys. "I thought we were having—fun."

He put his hand on the doorknob. "The bartender at The Snake Pit said Gerry would be coming in around now. I'm going to check back with him, see if he's heard anything. I'll be back in D.C. on Monday. You can e-mail me. Plus I'll be in Boston again next weekend in case you want to meet face-to-face. I shouldn't hang around the college too much. People might get suspicious."

There was a knock on the door. Tim dropped the knob

and looked at me. I shrugged. I knew I should panic, but I was much too romantically depressed. In short, I was beginning to feel like a real college freshman.

Tim waited about a minute for the knocker to leave, then he opened the door. The knocker was still there: Jeremy. "Hi," he said, seeing Tim, except it came out more like a question: "Hi?"

Tim held up his hand in a lazy wave directed back to me. "Thanks for inviting me to your concert." He nodded at Jeremy and strolled through the door.

"Tim—wait," I said, far too desperately. He turned around slowly and gave me a warning look. I wouldn't call a teacher by his first name.

"Thanks," I said. "For coming to the performance." He smiled with utter falseness. He was an even worse actor than I.

"Wouldn't have missed it for the world," he said, walking away.

Jeremy still stood in the doorway. I swallowed hard. I didn't want to say anything, too afraid I would cry. I held the wine glass to my lips and, realizing it was empty, poured myself another glass. I held the bottle up to Jeremy as a silent offering. He shook his head. Noticing Tim's remaining five bottles of beer on the floor, he pulled one out of the carton and wrenched it open.

"My old music teacher," I said, as brightly as I could manage. "It was our first concert tonight, and he was in the area."

Jeremy nodded. "You were good. I was there." He took a long drink of the beer.

"Really? I didn't see you. I counted heads but I couldn't see faces very well."

He shrugged. "It's easy to get lost in the crowd. Anyway, it's why I'm here—to tell you, you know, that you were great." We held each other's eyes for a moment. But I couldn't help it. My eyes wandered to the door, as if it might still project a fading image of Tim. Jeremy looked at the door. He looked back at me. "You're not really a lesbian, are you?"

twenty-five

I told Jeremy everything. I really had no choice. He knew something was up. So I told him how ashamed I was of the lies and deception, how terrified I was of being found out. He swore he wouldn't tell a soul. "And stop feeling guilty," he admonished, stroking my hand. "You are so completely blameless. He's the one who should have known better."

"It's just as much my fault as his," I wailed. "Because I was so stupid. I *am* so stupid!"

Jeremy shook his head. "A teacher should never get involved with a student—never. He should be fired."

I shook my head in return. "He didn't pursue me. It wasn't like that. I'm the one who kept coming in after hours to practice *The Hallelujah Chorus*. I'm the one who insisted on taking up the cello when, really, I have no aptitude for strings at all."

"He's older," Jeremy said, pressing my hand. "He's the adult, and it was up to him to keep things at a proper distance. He got to you at an especially vulnerable time. You were probably looking for a father figure."

"What makes you think that?" I asked blankly.

He shrugged. "It's pretty common after a divorce."

I nodded. "Oh, right! The divorce. It was hard on me." Then the tears started again. My emotions were real, even if my story was manufactured. "I thought he loved me," I sobbed.

"This teacher—is he married?" Jeremy asked.

I barked a bitter laugh through my tears. "No way. He's got a total fear of commitment."

Unlike Tim, Jeremy had no qualms about sitting next to me on the bed. He put his arm around me and smoothed his cheek against my hair. All along, I'd seen him as this really nice, spectacular-looking kid, albeit the most mature of all the kids who surrounded me. Now I wasn't thinking about his age. I was thinking about how rotten it was for me to be telling him all these lies. And about how good he smelled.

I rested my head on his chest for a moment and then stood up. "I think I need some time alone. But thank you. Really."

He stood up slowly and looked down with the most gentle expression I'd ever seen on a man. He nodded once and ran an index finger along my wet cheek.

Once he was gone, I curled up on my bed. All that crying had worn me out.

*　*　*

The next day, the red sheets were posted all over campus. "GET RED HOT WITH THE RED HOTS! TONIGHT! 7:00! McCALL AUDITORIUM! BE THERE!!!!!" They lacked subtlety, I thought.

But then again, what did I think—that the entire college would be atwitter because some pretty girls in little black dresses would be singing torch songs?

"You going to the Red Hots concert?" I asked Amber.

"And miss *Celebrity Fear Factor?*" she snorted. "I think not."

Katherine said she hoped she would never be that desperate for entertainment. "Not that I, like, think singing's dorky or anything. I'm sure your group's, you know, totally fab. And your next concert? You gotta tell me about it way ahead of time and then keep reminding me, like, every day because I am *so* not organized."

Only Jeremy showed something approaching interest: "I'll go with you, if you want." I told him I was meeting my singing group friends there, but that it would be nice to have him along.

I'm not sure what I expected—standing room only, perhaps, or at least a pack of people sitting at least figuratively and possibly literally on the edge of their seats. Like I said, when I was in college, singing groups were a big, big deal. Obviously, membership in the Alternative Prom Queens did not convey instant coolness status, but I just assumed the Red Hots had the kind of celebrity aura that we lacked.

The Red Hots drew a bigger crowd than the Prom Queens, but not by much; I counted fifty-one attendees before the lights went down. Troy was there, as were a fair number of other guys who didn't look like they typically went in for this kind of thing. Still, they looked more like boyfriends than johns or pimps. Then again, what did a john or pimp look like, exactly? Did I really expect some hairy guy laden with twenty pounds of gold chains to cruise around Mercer?

I felt emotionally flooded by one of my habitual flashes of self-doubt. Face it: I didn't have a clue what I was doing. Someone—practically anyone—could do a better job than I. Jennifer could investigate circles around me. I already knew her education articles would be better than anything I had managed to crank out. She'd sent me some e-mails outlining her ideas: a profile of an inner city child currently being bused to the suburbs; a story about a parochial school that opened its facilities to a class of autistic kids; a comparison between two kids from the same working-class high school, one of whom was now a Harvard freshman, the other a Costco clerk. I could practically see the finished articles, provocative and informative, all the pieces fitting together and building to some insightful epiphany in the final paragraph. She said she'd send me the finished product today, but I hadn't checked my e-mail yet. Too busy, I told myself, but really, I wasn't feeling strong enough to be shown up by a maroon-haired chick with a butterfly tattoo.

In the auditorium, Jeremy caused a stir. The other girls in my group stared at him and blushed. Then they looked at me with newfound awe. "This is Jeremy," I said, and they nodded and said, "Yes. Hi." He was one of those campus hunks that girls like Vanessa, Penny and Shelby—and myself, when I was their age—always assume they can only admire from afar.

I sat next to Vanessa. She leaned over and whispered, "I can't believe you know Jeremy."

I shrugged. "He's my R.A.," I murmured.

She leaned back, checked my face and squinted. Then she put her mouth next to my ear again. "Are you and Jeremy a thing? Or is he here to see Brynn?"

Now it was my turn to be surprised. "Who?" I mouthed.

"Ex-girlfriend," she whispered, her breath warm in my hair. "One of the Red Hots."

I turned to Jeremy. He smiled at me. I smiled back, but my mouth felt tight. Was I jealous? Or worried? I felt oddly deceived, like he should have told me about his former squeeze, although, really, it was none of my business.

The lights dimmed, and several spotlights swooped and played along the darkened stage. Very, very hokey—and it got worse. "Ladies and gentleman," a deep voice intoned. "Put your hands together and welcome the Red Hots!"

There were whoops and whistles and polite clapping as a bunch of girls in high heels clicked across the stage to form a line.

They kicked off the set with "Mr. Sandman," then, unbelievably, moved on to "You're Mean to Me." Aha! I thought. No wonder Tiffany didn't get to be an Alternative Prom Queen. Her audition song—that is, my would-be audition song—was a standard Red Hots number. For a brief moment, I felt the fates were on my side. After all, if Tiffany hadn't come to the audition and stolen my song, I never would have made it into the group. Then I remembered that, really, I had no reason to be in the singing group, aside from chasing a few adolescent fantasies of fame and coolness.

The girls on stage were uniformly attractive and fairly interchangeable: mostly blond hair parted in the middle,

falling halfway down the back; black eyeliner, red lipstick—
and, of course, the trademark little black dresses with
heels. (A few girls wore panty hose with open-toed san-
dals, I noticed, mentally tsk-tsking.) One girl stood out as
the prettiest. She had natural waves cascading through un-
naturally blond hair and bee-stung lips that, were she ten
years older, I'd assume were collagen-enhanced. Her nose
was pert and just avoided showing too much nostril. Her
eyes were huge and should have been blue but appeared to
be brown. Oh, well: nothing that contacts couldn't fix.
Were Hugh Hefner here, she'd be his hands-down number
one pick, but I held out hope for Jeremy. Surely his taste
wasn't so, well, obvious. I glanced at Jeremy, tried to see if
he was watching anyone in particular. Then I looked back
at the girls, only to see Miss October sending me some serious hate vibes.

I leaned over to Jeremy's ear. "Who's the blond?" As if
that narrowed things down.

"Just somebody I used to . . . date."

"Was it serious?" I asked on our walk back to the
dorm.

"What?" He tried to look confused.

"You and Loni Anderson."

"Huh?" Now he was genuinely confused. I had to
watch myself on the references.

"I mean you and, um, Pamela Anderson. The blond
chick. Brynn."

"How do you know her name?"

"I read it in *Us* magazine." He cocked an eyebrow at me,
looking a little too pleased. I rolled my eyes. "Vanessa told

me. I didn't ask her. She just told me. So—how long did you go out?"

He shrugged. "I don't know. Six months, a year."

"Which was it?"

"Two years and three months."

"Oh!" I felt an odd pang. "So it *was* serious."

He ran a hand over his face. "It was fun at times, exhausting most of the time. We were eighteen. It wasn't serious."

"What, you can't be serious if you're only eighteen? There are some states where you can get married at fourteen. Maybe even twelve. Anyway, if things between you and Brynn lasted that long, you must've turned nineteen and twenty at some point."

"I didn't mean to put down eighteen-year-olds." I looked at him quizzically. He continued, "You're different. Like you've got an old soul or something."

I'd momentarily forgotten that I was supposed to be eighteen. "Or something. So what happened? With you and Brynn."

"You're jealous."

"I'm nosy."

He exhaled. "We went in different directions. She got into some stuff. I just—it wasn't for me." He looked me straight in the eye. "She wasn't who I thought she was."

I looked at my hands, picked at a cuticle. "I guess that could be a real shock."

Katherine and Amelia, laden with brown bags, got back to the dorm just as Jeremy and I did. After Jeremy left us in the hall, Katherine raised her eyebrows and smirked. "What?" I snapped.

"Nothing. We're having a PMS binge if you want to join us."

"Great," I said. "I'm PMSing, too."

I took the smaller, sloshing brown bag from her while she pulled out her key. I peaked inside. There were two bottles of wine, both of which appeared colorful. An oversized package of cheese puffs bulged out of Amelia's bag.

Amber walked by wearing tight jeans and a baby doll shirt. How did someone that thin find tight-fitting clothes? Do jeans come in negative sizes?

"Hey, Amber, we're bingeing," Katherine said. "You in?"

"You don't actually have to eat anything," Amelia clarified.

"Thanks, but I'm going out," she said, flipping open a shiny new cell phone. Oh, man. Now I was the only girl around without one of those things. Okay, Tiffany didn't have a cell phone, either, but she didn't need it as much as I did. Besides, she said she was getting one for Christmas. I'd have to talk to Tim about it.

Katherine and Amelia's room possessed just the college panache that mine lacked. Their beds were covered in Indian-print bedspreads and piled with pillows. Near the bead-covered window, a steamer trunk surrounded by still more pillows provided a sitting area. Instead of posters, old album covers adorned their purple walls. It was nothing short of groovy.

Katherine retrieved a pink light bulb from her desk and screwed it into her desk lamp. Then she turned off the overhead lights and lit two chunky candles. "Wanna see my belly button?" she asked. She pulled up her spandex T-shirt, which already revealed about an inch of skin, and displayed her navel, newly adorned with a gold ring.

"Ouch!" I said. "Didn't that hurt?"

"No pain, no gain," Amelia said. "I talked her into it."

"I've always wanted one," Katherine said, looking fondly at her tummy. "It's so sexy."

"You didn't go to the Human Canvas, did you?" I asked. "That place looks scary."

"That was half the fun," Amelia said. "Thor—he's the owner—has tattoos everywhere, even on his face. He barely looks human."

"So what's going on with you and Jeremy?" Katherine asked after I'd gotten all the details of her adventures in body jewelry.

"Nothing!" I said, perhaps a bit too emphatically. "We're just friends."

"Mm hmm." She pulled out the two bottles of wine and twisted off the top. "Zinfandel or peach?" she asked.

"Zinfandel," I said, while Amelia requested peach. "He just wanted to see his old girlfriend sing tonight," I explained, "and I wanted to see the Red Hots."

Katherine pulled an ice tray out of her minifridge, cracked it and dropped large cubes into three lined-up wineglasses. "She pretty?"

"No, Jeremy goes in for ugly girls. Of course she's pretty. In a slutty sort of way." I felt disloyal to Jeremy for saying that (although it was true), but I wanted to avert any rumors about us. Katherine handed me my glass. I took a long, sweet swallow. "It's been over for a while, though, so the coast is clear for you."

"Me!" Katherine looked shocked—shocked!

"Well?" I said.

"Oh, I gave up on him long ago. He's just not my type."

I cackled. "What is your type?"

"A guy who goes for me when I throw myself at him. Jeremy's a lost cause." She kicked off her clogs and settled herself on a heap of pillows. "Now, Mike—he's looking good. Nice butt, ya know. Not the sharpest crayon in the box, but he's cute. Give me a month, and I'll have him worshipping at my feet—not to mention doing my laundry."

Amelia was laying out a feast on the trunk. In addition to the cheese puffs, there was canned cheese, butter crackers, chocolate kisses, Ring Dings and Twinkies. "No," Katherine said, "*I'm* not the one who's hot for Jeremy . . ."

Amelia's delicate face turned red. "This is so embarrassing," she muttered.

I gasped. "But you're gay!"

Amelia stared at her hands. "I'm having a crisis," she whimpered. Her pierced tongue gave her a slight lisp: "I'm having a crithith."

"So you're coming out of the closet?" I asked. "Or, wait—going back into the closet?"

"There is no closet!" Katherine exclaimed. "There was never a closet! She's never even had sex!"

"With a man or a woman?"

"With anyone! She's a big V!" Katherine made the victory sign on her forehead, although it was clear that she didn't consider virginity to be anyone's victory.

"I don't think you have to have sex to know your sexual orientation," I said. Katherine raised her eyebrows. I plowed ahead to avert any discussion of my own sexual history, which I hadn't quite worked out yet. Also, I hoped the myth of my own homosexuality had never made it past Jeremy. He wasn't a gossip, but living in such close quarters, things can get around. "Sex is the least of it. It's more an issue of magnetism. Who do you like to look at? Who would you like to kiss?"

"Having sex can give you some idea, though," Katherine said, lounging on the pillows. "I mean, none of the guys I've done ever called me a dyke." She looked at Amelia. "No offense," she said quickly.

I stuck a cheese puff in my mouth and sucked it until it became mushy. The saltiness provided a nice foil for the wine's sugar. "Katherine," I asked, "How many guys have you, you know—"

"Fucked?"

"I was trying to find a more delicate term."

She looked at the ceiling and began ticking off her fingers. Amelia and I waited silently. "I'm not sure," she said finally. "I can only think of seventeen, but I know there's been more." Seventeen! I gawked at her. I'd always suspected everybody else was having more sex than I was. Now it had been confirmed. I felt like lecturing Katherine on the dangers of unwanted pregnancies and sexually transmitted diseases, but I suspected her mother had slipped her a pamphlet or two over the years.

"And you?" Katherine asked.

"Three," I answered honestly. "But the last two were short-term rebound things." Katherine nodded. Amelia seemed nonplussed. Apparently, three was a respectable number for a college freshman. "But, honestly, I think I rushed into things. You're smart to have waited, Amelia. Not wanting to screw a guy in high school doesn't mean you're gay, you know."

"I know." Amelia sighed. "I just don't know how I'm going to tell my mother."

"She wants you to be gay?" I asked. "That's really open-minded of her."

Amelia laughed grimly. "When I told her I was gay, she shut herself in her room for five hours. Then she asked me not to tell anybody. Did I ever mention that I founded a gay student association at my school?"

"Did your mother know?"

"She did when I showed her the picture in the yearbook. I never liked any of the boys in high school," Amelia sighed. "So I figured I must dig girls."

"But did you?" I asked. "Like girls, I mean."

Amelia nodded vigorously, then paused for a minute and shrugged. "I had this friend in high school? Clarissa? We were best friends, and one day we, you know, kissed. And it felt good." She stuck up her chin for emphasis. "But then she got all weirded out, said she didn't want to be queer, and started going out with this total skank. When I thought about what it must be like kissing him, it made me feel all yucky, you know? And Clarissa and me, we weren't friends anymore, and that made me feel all bad. And I couldn't stop thinking about her. So I figured I must be in love." She reached for a Twinkie and ripped open the wrapper. "I told my mother," she said with a satisfied smile. "She hit the roof."

"That doesn't mean you're gay, though," I said. "Maybe you were just sad about losing your friend." Amelia looked so depressed at the thought of life as a straight woman that I changed course. "Then again, maybe you are gay, but just a little bisexual, too. That's nothing to be ashamed of." I'd read an article recently about the prevalence of bisexuality. It sounded downright exhausting to me, but I understood that it was a valid and hip choice—especially if, like Amelia, you sport spiky hair and a pierced tongue. "So what if you noticed that Jeremy's a hunk? Jeremy is a hunk. That doesn't mean you want to have sex with him."

"But I do!" Amelia exclaimed.

"Oh," I said.

She thought for a moment, flicking her tongue at the Twinkie and licking off little bits of cream. "I want to peel off his shirt with my teeth," she murmured. More Twinkie. More cream. "And run my tongue inside his navel. I want to suck on his toes and sit on his face—"

"Okay!" I said, laughing and pretending not to be embarrassed. "I get the picture."

Katherine squirted cheese on her thumb and sucked it off with a loud pop. "Amelia, babe," she said. "You are so not gay."

"Damn it," Amelia said, finally taking a big bite out of the Twinkie. "My mother is going to be so fucking happy."

Brynn lived off campus, on the top floor of a brick apartment building with cheap, oversized windows. I'd gotten her address from the campus directory. I wondered how many boys had tracked her down just as I had, although for an entirely different purpose. The first night I parked across from the building, I saw her hunched over her computer, which cast a ghostly glow. The next night, she leaned out of her window, smoking a cigarette. Day three, she sat on her bed, knees up, highlighting a text book. She had roommates, I assumed, but she always seemed to be alone. The fourth day, she finally left the building. Her car was a sporty silver Audi, far nicer than anything I ever hoped to own. She left the city limits, and I tailed her carefully.

She pulled off the highway two towns away and drove down a quiet road before turning into the lot of the Gray Gull restaurant. I'd heard of it—after all, there aren't many restaurants in the middle of nowhere—but it wasn't the kind of spot generally favored by college kids. It had gray weathered shingles and a lobster pot out front. After Brynn, dressed conservatively in khakis and a jean jacket, went inside, I lingered by the front door, pretending to study the menu: clam chowder, onion soup, fried clams, fried scallops, broiled haddock, Indian pudding . . . The clams would be greasy, the haddock mushy, but it still looked better than anything I'd eaten in weeks. I was tempted to go inside but feared Brynn would recognize me.

I heard a car door slam but didn't jump until I heard a voice say, with obvious surprise, "Kathy? What are you doing out here?"

Dean Archer stood a foot away, nervously smoothing his strawberry blond hair. His smile didn't reach to his eyes, which darted between me and the front door.

"Me?" I stammered. "Oh, I, uh—"

"I'm meeting a colleague here," Dean Archer announced. "Fellow from the history department." He glanced at his watch. "He's late. Maybe I'll just wait in my car." He headed back to the parking lot.

"Nice to see you," I said, trailing him to the lot and stopping dead when I saw him climbing into his car. This time I got the make. A Camry. And it was gold, not tan.

twenty-six

The ladies were engrossed in a discussion about epidurals when I arrived at Marcy's shower. "I never even got mine!" one exclaimed. "I wanted it so much, too! I said to the nurse, 'Okay! Now!' and she said it was too late—it was time to push! Next time I'm getting an epidural the minute the stick turns blue!"

"My epidural didn't take!" countered another. Her listeners clucked in sympathy "So I'm lying there with this needle in my spine and an I.V. in my arm, and I'm still in excruciating pain!"

Marcy wasn't there yet since the shower was a surprise (she knew about it, of course, but now she supposedly believed it was scheduled for next weekend). I spotted Marcy's friend Meredith, who I knew reasonably well, and headed across the rose carpet because chatting with her would be slightly less excruciating than standing all alone and looking like a loser.

"Hi, Meredith." She was standing next to the food table: a bonus. I popped a mini quiche in my mouth and spread some artichoke dip on a slice of Italian bread. I smiled (mouth closed) and tried to look genuinely pleased to see Meredith, even as I waited for her to ask if I was seeing anyone.

She surprised me by saying instead, "Here's some free advice, Kathy. If you ever find yourself in the position of giving birth, insist on—I mean, demand!—an epidural."

"Thanks, Meredith." I tried to look amused. "I'll try to remember that." I stuck the bread in my mouth and savored the taste of the artichoke dip, which was made with cheese—Gouda?—and a touch of sherry. It was so much better than that slimy cafeteria food. The dining hall would probably be closed by the time I got back to Mercer, anyway; after the shower, I planned to drop some work off at Jennifer's apartment. It was only three o'clock in the afternoon, but if I ate enough of these things over the next couple of hours, I could call it dinner.

Meredith took a big gulp of her wine. "So, are you seeing anyone?"

"No one special," I said, implying that I was at least keeping myself busy with a smattering of Mr. Wrongs. "Nice house," I said insincerely. It was a few streets away from Marcy's and similarly tasteful from the outside. However, the owners, lacking the benefit of my guidance, displayed an excessive fondness for mix-and-match florals. "Whose is it again?"

"Alex's mother."

"Oh, right." I spotted her across the room. She was

blond and plump and wearing—what else?—a flowered dress. "And what's her name?"

Meredith shrugged. "I've always just referred to her as Alex's mother."

"Hi, Kathy." I turned. It was Marcy's sister-in-law, Pamela. She bared her teeth at Meredith in an approximation of a grin. "Meredith."

Meredith turned red. "How are you, Pamela?" Then, without waiting for an answer, she mumbled something about seeing if Alex's mother needed any help and scurried away. Meredith played a key role in the animosity between Marcy and Pamela. Marcy had never liked her brother's flashy, humorless wife, whom she'd nicknamed "The Professional Shopper." Still, relations remained cordial until Jacob's bris, when Meredith, being both kind-hearted and chatty, tried to make conversation with Pamela, who was sitting alone. Perhaps it was Meredith's basic decency that kept her from recognizing Marcy's sarcasm in the nickname. Then again, maybe she's just dim. At any rate, she shined her big smile at Pamela and chirped, "So Marcy tells me you're a personal shopper."

Pamela, looking confused and suspicious, answered with a careful, "Nooo."

Meredith barreled forward with, "Oh! But I asked Marcy if you worked, and she said you're a professional shopper. I figured she meant a personal shopper. Hey! What a great job! To get paid to shop for other people!"

Of course, Pamela rarely shopped for anyone but herself (and when she did she opted for items such as marked-down mugs). Later, Marcy tried to undo the damage—"All I meant is that you've got really good taste"—but their relationship had been strained ever since. Surprisingly, Pamela always latched onto me at these baby things, presumably because we were generally the only two women whose lives didn't revolve around children. The only difference between us was that I was childless, while she actually had a daughter, a well-dressed, sallow-faced four-year-old with an army of baby-sitters and a habit of hiding under tables at family events.

"I like your shoes," I told Pamela. I did, actually.

"These?" She kicked up her foot and twisted around to see what she was wearing. "I got them on sale on Lord & Taylor. I've got another pair almost exactly the same, but I couldn't resist."

"Well, when you find something that works," I said.

"Did you do something to your hair?" she asked me.

I wrinkled my nose. "I've just been ignoring it, so it's a bit longer than usual. I think I need a new look."

"I don't know," she said, squinting. "The length is nice on you. Makes you look—younger." I stifled a giggle. She touched my bangs. "Some highlights might be nice. Auburn, maybe." And so we were off on a conversation with so much more depth than the parallel one about epidurals.

Marcy looked so shocked when she walked into the living room that I thought she'd been honestly fooled. Later, she admitted that Dan had been coaching her all morning until she achieved a believable progression from confusion to recognition to appreciation. A few days earlier, Alex's mother, the one hosting the party, had let it slip about the date change, but she swore Marcy to secrecy lest the other Alex's mother, the one who'd spilled the beans about the shower in the first place, find out. The two had made up, but Alex's mother—the hostess—liked having something to hold over Alex's mother. The other Alex's mother.

I am not against showers. If I ever get married, I sincerely hope that someone will throw me one. When Marcy got engaged, I threw a tasteful affair in her mother's living room (at the time, I was still living in the Charlestown dump with Tim), where Marcy opened pastel packages containing platters and nighties and an acrylic bagel cutter (that one came from Pamela). When she got pregnant with Jacob a year later, I commandeered her mother's living room again, and the gifts were even better than last time: mobiles and blankies and box after box of teeny-tiny clothes. So I figure she owes me. Of course, at the rate I'm going, my bridal shower gifts are more likely to run along the lines of large-print books and Depends pads.

When Marcy was pregnant with Joshua, one of her new mommy friends threw her a second baby shower. Now that she's about to pop out kid number three, here are some of the things Marcy already owns: one bassinet, two cribs, two changing tables, a front baby carrier, a baby backpack, a bouncy seat, an ExerSaucer, two single strollers, one double stroller, one jogging stroller, a swing, a Johnny jumper, a narrow-mouth Diaper Genie, a wide-mouth Diaper Genie, three diaper bags, seven infant towels, nine baby blankets, fourteen receiving blankets, and a wipes warmer. The first time Jacob's sensitive butt encountered a cold wipe, in the ladies room at the Chestnut Hill Mall, he screamed so loud he made Marcy cry.

"I know how worn out the baby towels get," Meredith said as Marcy opened her fluffy package. Alex's mother (I forget which one) said the same thing about receiving blankets. By the end of the shower, Marcy's household inventory now included ten infant towels and nineteen receiving blankets. Add to that a ducky frame, an unusually ugly Noah's Ark wall hanging, a couple of Toys "R" Us gift certificates and four mint green outfits (Marcy and Dan had chosen not to find out the sex of their baby), and I wondered if Marcy and Dan would have to build an addition on their house just to contain all their crap.

I gave Marcy a gift certificate for a facial because she always looks so happy when she is away from her kids. She thanked me profusely, but the rest of the mommies glared, as if to say, "What else would you expect from a career gal?"

"Great gift," Pamela said, sincerely. "I wish someone had thought of that for me when I was pregnant with Sophia." I suddenly, passionately, wished I had bought some booties and a bib.

twenty-seven

I had never been to Jennifer's apartment, but I had a hunch she owned a lava lamp. She lived near Boston University, her alma mater, and I checked the little piece of paper on which I'd written her address before heading from Newton into the city. It wasn't hard to find her building, a bland white brick structure half a block off noisy Commonwealth Avenue. I spent fifteen minutes circling in search of a large parking space (I've never mastered parallel parking) before I finally pulled into a parking garage that was much farther away from the apartment than I'd realized.

When I finally made it back to the building, a guy in painter's overalls (just a hunch, but I don't think he was actually a painter) held the front door open for me. In principle, I objected to his trusting nature (I could have been a thief), but I was relieved that I'd be able to slip the envelope under Jennifer's door in case she wasn't home. Still, I was hoping she was in. I really did want to see if my hunch about the lava lamp was correct.

Her roommate answered the door. She was a tall, gangly girl with pale skin and short black hair. I'd met her before but couldn't remember her name, just that it was something weird. "I'm Kathy," I said. "I'm Jennifer's—I work with Jennifer. I've got comments for her on some articles she wrote." I said this casually, but, in truth, I was feeling slightly buoyant. Jennifer's articles, while cleanly written, were almost as dull as mine had been.

"Oh, right," she said, airily. "Come on in." I walked into the living room and was hugely disappointed. It was so uninspired: worn rust-colored wall-to-wall carpeting, grayish white walls, mismatched Salvation Army furniture. A small television set sat atop a plastic milk crate. There was not a lava lamp in sight. Also, the place was dirty: unopened mail and crumb-covered plates covered the scratched coffee table, while newspapers, shoes and vast amounts of lint littered the carpeting. I glanced at one of the envelopes on the coffee table. Oh, right, I remembered—the roommate's name was Chrisanna.

"They're in her bedroom," Chrisanna said, tilting her head toward a closed door.

Was I supposed to barge in on Jennifer in her bedroom? College coed or not, I still had my inhibitions. "Can you tell her I'm here?"

"Oh! Okay!" Chrisanna looked honestly surprised, like, "Right! Manners!" She rapped on the closed door and said, "You got company."

Jennifer pulled the door open. She was barefoot but

wearing full makeup, black satin hip huggers and a pink tube top. She had outdone herself. She looked like a hooker on the verge of catching pneumonia.

She looked horrified to see me. I attempted a smile. "Sorry to drop by unannounced." Did she really dislike me that much? I'd always thought she merely disdained me. "But I've got a bunch of handwritten comments on the articles you sent me, and I don't have access to a fax machine."

"Okay. Thanks." Her voice was tight. She took the envelope from me and reached back for her doorknob. That's when I snuck a peek in her room and saw the boy sitting propped up on her bed. Not a boy, though, but a man. He was wearing blue jeans and holding a paperback. I was about to be amused when I took a look at his face.

"What are you doing here?" I asked, honestly confused. And then, even more stupidly, "Why didn't you guys just meet in the office? Richard would have let you in."

Tim stared at me for a minute, then looked away. He rubbed his forehead with the heel of his hand. "Shit."

I felt my lungs contract. "Oh, my God." I said. "Oh, my God!" I looked at Jennifer. Her arms were crossed across her chest. She squinted down at the floor and ground her purple-painted big toe into the carpet.

This is the point where I should have started shouting, "How could you!" It was the time when I should have hefted the closest thrift store lamp above my shoulder and chucked it across the room. Next time I assume a new identity, I'm going to be a violent schizophrenic.

Instead, I turned and ran out of the apartment, down the stairs and out the door. I paused a moment on the

cracked concrete sidewalk, partly because my tears were
making it hard to see and partly because I expected Tim to
appear at any time, at which point I was now fully prepared to scream, "I hate you!"

I started down the street because I didn't want him to
think I was waiting for him. I walked slowly so he'd be able
to see me from a distance, call out for me, catch up to me.

I made it to the parking garage without being pursued.
The attendant took my ten dollars with only a quick
glance at my tear-streaked face. I drove back down Commonwealth Avenue, just to see if Tim had come after me
yet. But he never did.

Marcy knew something was wrong the instant she
opened her door. "What happened?" she asked without
saying hello.

"It's Tim." As soon as I said his name, I began to sob.
She threw her arms around me and held me against her
massive belly.

"The bastard," she said with venom. Then, just to make
sure she hadn't misunderstood my hysteria, she gasped,
"He's not dead, is he?" I shook my head against her shoulder. "Total bastard," she hissed.

I sobbed some more and finally pulled away because we
were still in her open doorway, and I didn't want the neighbors to see. Also, my nose was starting to run, and it would
have been rude to get snot on her dress even though, given
her extensive experience as a mother, she probably wouldn't
have minded all that much.

She led me into her living room and settled me on a
velvety moss green couch, then spread a blanket over my

lap even though it wasn't cold. She darted off to the bathroom and returned with a box of tissues (the kind with lotion), which she set on her cherry coffee table. "Comfortable?" she asked. I nodded, still unable to talk. She headed for the kitchen with a promise to return with a cup of tea.

Marcy came back with a huge glass of wine. "I thought you could use something stronger than tea." She handed me the glass. "I turned on a video for the boys and gave them a plate of cookies. With any luck, that'll keep them happy until bedtime." She sat next to me on the couch and waited for me to speak. When I didn't, she quietly asked, "Is he getting married?"

"No," I said. "I don't know if it's even serious." I took a mouthful of wine and swallowed. "He's sleeping with Jennifer."

Marcy shook her head in confusion. "Jennifer who?"

"Jennifer from work."

Marcy squinted at me, still confused. "Not your secretary? The tacky one?"

"She doesn't like it when you call her a secretary. But, yeah—that's her."

Marcy snared the wineglass from my hand and took a swig, murmuring something about how the fetus was fully formed and in Europe women drank all through their pregnancies. Clearly, she was trying to remember if I'd ever mentioned they knew each other. She was stumped. "But how did Tim ever meet her?"

I was all set to be vague, cover my tracks, keep my promise to Tim not to divulge our big secret. And then I thought: why? I was nervous, though. "Where's Dan?" I asked.

"It's Saturday night," she said. "Where do you think he is?"

"At the office?"

She nodded. "To make up for staying at home with the boys while I was at the shower. Don't ever marry a lawyer. You'll spend all your nights and weekends alone."

"I'll try to keep that in mind."

She stared at me, waiting. I looked at the deep yellow of my wine and ran a finger along the rim, making a little squeaking noise.

"I don't mean to be insensitive," Marcy said. "But we've got maybe twenty minutes before the boys come tearing in here. And that's if we're lucky."

"Okay," I said, finally. "Tim called me a couple of months ago and asked me to work on a story with him. I'll get into the details later. Basically, I've spent the last month undercover, living as a freshman at Mercer College."

For once, Marcy was speechless. Finally, she managed a *"What?"* and I launched into my tale. When I got to the part about pretending to be Jewish, Jacob came in and said, "Josh is stinky."

Marcy blinked at him. "It's probably just gas."

He held his nose. "Uh-uh. He's poopy. Joshy's a pooper."

"Okay, okay," Marcy said hurriedly. "I'll come get him in a minute. Just go back in the playroom and let Kathy and me talk."

He shook his head. "No! I don't want to sit next to him! He's stinky! P.U.! P.U.!"

Marcy sat up straight and spoke slowly. "Jacob. If you'll go back in the playroom now, you can have another cookie."

"I don't want a cookie. I don't like that kind."

"Okay," she said, her voice rising. "You can have one of

the chocolates in the pantry." He stood very still for a moment, and then scurried off to the kitchen.

"So she actually believed you were Jewish? Who would believe you were Jewish?"

"I told her I was half Jewish, half Irish."

"Oh, yeah," Marcy laughed. "That was a popular match in our parents' day."

"Does your mother still refer to me as your shiksa roommate?"

"It was once she said that. Once! I never should have told you." When we were in college, Marcy's older brother, Larry, came down for a weekend. Tim and I were temporarily on the outs—every year or two, we split up for about a week—and Marcy's brother expressed an interest in filling the vacuum. I didn't find him the least bit attractive (I never actually told Marcy that), but when Marcy's mother heard he'd started calling me, she got in a tizzy envisioning little Catholic grandchildren and all the attendant baptisms and First Communions. I truly hated her for her bigotry—moot though it was. In time, however, she acquired Pamela as a daughter-in-law instead, so I guess she's been punished enough: Pamela is not just a bitch; she is a Methodist bitch.

Over the years, I've occasionally wondered if I was too quick to write Larry off. I mean, he was a nice man who later showed himself to be a good husband and father. Also, having hit it big in the Internet boom, he owned not only a mansion in Brookline, but a waterfront house on the Cape.

"It gets worse," I said, continuing my Mercer saga. "Next I was supposed to be a lesbian."

Marcy was leaning toward me, utterly absorbed, when Jacob reappeared in the doorway. "The chocolates are all gone."

"They were there yesterday," Marcy said desperately.

"Daddy ate them."

"When? He's never home."

"Today, when you were at your party."

Marcy lowered her voice. "Please, Jacob. Please. Go. Back. To. The. Playroom."

"It's *stinky*," he wailed.

There was a heavy moment of silence. She looked at me beseechingly. It had been a long time since Marcy had found me this fascinating. She looked back at Jacob and took a big breath for strength. "If you'll go back to the playroom, tomorrow I will take you to Chuck E. Cheese."

Jacob's eyes lit up. He jumped in the air. He ran out of the living room, and we heard him say, "Joshy! We're going to Chuck E. Cheese!"

"You have no idea how much I just gave away," she said to me.

"I think I do," I said. Jacob's third birthday party had been held at Chuck E. Cheese.

"So now you're a lesbian," she said, returning to my story.

"I'm not anymore," I said. "And, really, I never was. It was just this rumor. And there's this guy, Jeremy, who's just so amazing but way too young."

Jacob appeared once again in the doorway. "This better be good," Marcy said.

"Josh stuck a cookie in the VCR," he said.

"There's a video in the VCR."

"Not anymore."

"Okay. I'll get it later."

Jacob turned and began to walk out. "Oh, yeah. And Joshy took off his diaper."

twenty-eight

It was almost midnight by the time I got back to the dorm. It was Saturday night, though, so for many, the party was just getting started. The hallways echoed weirdly from the noises behind closed doors: loud, bass-heavy music, drunken male laughter, girlish shrieks. Walking down the hallway, a door swung open and the noise jumped out. Jake—of Mike-n-Jake—called, "Hello," his face flushed from alcohol. Inside, Katherine, in her usual uniform of jeans and a baby doll shirt, sat on Mike's bed, leaning against his bent knees.

"Mike likes my belly button ring!" she called out.

He reached forward to touch her exposed midriff, but she swatted his hand away playfully. "Careful! It still hurts!"

"Want a brewski?" Jake asked me, holding up a bottle. "Keith's at his parents for the weekend." Keith was Mike's studious roommate.

"Thanks, but I'm beat," I said. In truth, I was wide awake but in no mood to complete a foursome chez Mike.

Turning the key in my door, I checked our erasable memo board. Now that I had a laptop, I mostly received e-mails, but I still got the occasional note on my door. I liked the memo board because it showed all the world that I was loved. From Katherine: "Party in Mike's room! Come with?" From Vanessa: "Hiya! Don't you ever check your e-mail? Thought you might be up for an ice cream. Call me on my cell." There were no phone messages from Tiffany. Apparently, my Uncle Tim had not called. Then again, maybe he had called, and she just wasn't in. I said a silent prayer that she'd gone out with Ethan. I wanted nothing more than to crawl into bed and fall into a blissful coma.

The room was dark, which I took to be a good sign. I turned on the light. Then I saw the lump under the covers. I turned the light off quickly, but not before I caught a glimpse of Ethan's pasty, guilty face.

"I was just leaving," he said, moving in the dark.

"No!" Tiffany yelped.

"It's okay," I said. "Just dropping off my backpack. I'm headed over to Mike's room." I shoved my key in my pocket and tossed the backpack in the direction of my bed. It hit the side and fell to the floor. Leaving, I closed the door as quietly and as quickly as I could.

I leaned against the cold cinder block wall, willing myself not to cry. Mike's party—such as it was—was a possibility, I told myself. At least I could get drunk. But I'd risk designating myself as Jake's woman for the night, a chance I was unwilling to take. Besides, I didn't want to get drunk. I was tired of the fuzzy feeling and the excruciating mornings-after. Alternatively, I could simply go back to my car and drive home. I'd be in my apartment before two. Of course, there was the problem of my car keys; they were in my backpack. I couldn't bear to open that door again. Also, I had a singing rehearsal the next morning.

I was about to lose my battle against the tears when I heard the orange fire door at the end of the hall swing open. It was Jeremy. I was unreasonably glad to see him. "Hello!" I said brightly, scurrying toward him.

He beamed. "You locked out?"

"I should be so lucky." I leaned toward him and lowered my voice. "Tiffany and Ethan are doing it."

He gawked. "No way!"

"Make room in hell," I murmured.

"So what are you going to do?" he asked carefully.

I shrugged. "Keith's away, so Mike's having a party. If you can call three people a party." I looked down the hall, then back at Jeremy. "I'll go if you will."

He thought for a moment. "Or we could go to my room, where we won't have to drink cheap beer and listen to bad music."

"The beer's imported," I said. "I saw the bottles."

Jeremy shook his head. "Mike saves the bottles, then refills them with the cheap stuff. He thinks no one notices."

"Doesn't that make the beer flat?"

"Extremely."

We looked into each other's eyes, and then I looked away. "I don't want to keep you up," I said, forgetting for a moment that twenty-one-year-olds don't actually need sleep.

"I'm not tired," he said. "Come on." He loped down the hall. I followed.

He flipped on his overhead light and hit a switch on his CD player. A familiar song filled the room. "Have you ever heard the Beatles?" he asked.

Surely he was kidding. "You mean that hot new group out of Wisconsin?"

"Sorry." He grinned. "But when Katherine heard this the other day, she asked if it was early Justin Timberlake."

He pulled two beers (imported) from his minifridge, twisted off the tops and handed one to me. "To the first boy band."

Okay! Okay! I should have known better. But what was I supposed to do? Tiptoe into my bed, pull the covers over my ears and try to block out the sounds of Tiffany copulating? I couldn't face the party in Mike's room. I couldn't go home. I really had no choice.

Okay. I wanted it to happen, too. I wanted him to fluff the pillows on his bed so I could be comfortable leaning against the wall. I wanted him to ask me who my favorite Beatle was (John) and to hear that his, against all odds, was George. I wanted him to play the White Album. I wanted him to turn the lights down low, but as the fluorescent lacked a dimmer, I wanted him to turn them off completely. I wanted him to kiss me on the eyelids and cheeks and ears and lips, while running his hands up and down my back. And then I wanted us to lie down together and fall quietly asleep in each other's arms.

It was all going so well until we got to the sleep bit.

His breathing grew ragged. He continued to caress my back, but under my shirt this time, working his way up to my bra. That slowed him down a bit, as it took a few moments for him to realize the bra possessed a front closure. He made up for lost time quickly, however, undoing the clasp with one hand. One hand!

A little voice inside my head told me, "Now! You should stop now!" My loose, flopping bra felt ridiculous inside my shirt. But a second, more forceful, voice snarled, "Oh, the hell with it. Have a little fun." I tried to clear my mind, become one with the moment. After all, if a person is going to do something completely immoral—and this was, wasn't it?—she should at least have a good time. But I kept getting these pictures in my head: Tiffany with Ethan, Jennifer with Tim. I don't know which yucked me out more, but the thought of Tim and Jennifer together egged me on. Tim wasn't the only one who could land a young hottie.

Jeremy drew away slightly and pulled off his rugby shirt. Oh, my! The vision, dim as it was, temporarily cleared my mind. The only chests I'd ever seen like this were on billboards. It was almost worth turning the fluorescents back on. I plunged back to his lips with renewed vigor and ran my fingers through his tousled curls. He pulled my shirt over my head, and I let him, yelping only briefly when it caught on an earring. The bra slid easily off my back. Now I was glad the lights were off. It's not that I have an especially bad body image (which is to say that I dislike my body about as much as most women I know); I just hated the thought of having to see myself half-naked with a twenty-one-year-old. My God! This was wrong! It was!

"I like you," he murmured into my neck. "I really do."

"I like you, too," I said, seeing a glimmer of hellfire in my mind. I tried to concentrate on his astonishing chest but couldn't. I had to get out of this. Suddenly, inspiration hit. This was the age of safe sex! Birth control pills weren't good enough. Diaphragms were out. Foam wouldn't do. We needed a barrier, or the deal was off. "I don't have any protection," I said, feigning disappointment and reaching for my shirt.

"That's okay. I do," he murmured. In two steps, he was at his desk. He opened the drawer, rummaged quickly and easily. Two more steps, and he was back with a foil packet. Pretty impressive for a guy in a dark room.

He pulled back the covers of his bed, pausing when he reached me. I stood up obligingly, and then sat down on the sheet. I tried to think of a nice way to say, "I didn't mean to lead you on," but then he had me flat on my back and was nibbling at my neck, and the words didn't come.

So it happened. The clothes came off, the caressing and stroking and rubbing intensified. Bodily fluids were— well, you get the picture. I waited for some swelling emotion to transport me to ecstasy. It didn't. As aroused as I was, I still felt extremely self-conscious and extraordinarily guilty.

And then it was over. He gave me one final kiss on the mouth, nuzzled his head into my neck and went to sleep. I panicked, knew I'd never sleep, wondered how I was going to get out of there. And then I fell asleep anyway.

I awoke to pins and needles in my right calf. Jeremy's legs were slung over mine (his bed was a single, after all). It was as dark as it had been when we'd fallen asleep. Green lights from the CD player, now quiet, cast an eerie

glow. I checked the digital clock next to his bed: 3:30 A.M.
I carefully slid my legs out from under his. He sighed and
shifted and did not wake up.

I fished around the dark floor until I found my underpants. I pulled them on, and they immediately filled with
a warm wetness. I felt myself blushing in the dark. I
yanked on the rest of the clothes and took a last look at Jeremy before leaving. A faint glow from the streetlights filtered through the Venetian blinds and illuminated his
face. He really was beautiful, like some perfect boy in a
movie. Sleep softened the curves of his face, making him
look even younger than he was. My throat constricted as I
imagined how he would feel when he learned the truth
about me.

If Ethan hadn't left my room, I'd retrieve my car keys
from my backpack, drive back to my apartment and sleep
all day. I'd call Vanessa and say I was sick. Perhaps I'd stay
sick, or perhaps I'd just disappear. Maybe I'd tell Tim that
I didn't want to work with him anymore. I'd tell Richard
that I was chasing a non-story. On Monday, I'd file for unemployment.

I pulled Jeremy's door softly behind me. Then I turned
and gasped. Across the hall, Mike's door was just opening.
If it was Katherine, I was cooked. There was no time for
me to run away.

But it wasn't Katherine. It was Jake. He was wearing
jeans, the top button undone. Tropical print boxers showed
above his waistband. He froze in the doorway. I expected
him to laugh at me, to say, "You tramp!" I assumed he'd
passed out earlier and wondered why he didn't just sleep
off his hangover in Mike's room. But then I noticed his expression: caught. He shot a quick look back into the room,

where Mike lay sleeping under a white sheet, one naked leg spilling off the side of the bed.

Jake and I stared at each other. Finally, I said, "I won't tell if you won't."

"Wow," he whispered. "If I'd bagged Jeremy, I'd want everyone to know."

twenty-nine

There was only one lump under Tiffany's pink bed-spread when I peeked in the door, so I abandoned my plans of deserting my career. Instead, I crawled, fully clothed, under the covers and somehow managed to sleep.

Tiffany was gone when I woke up in the morning, which was just as well since she doesn't approve of swearing, and I uttered some choice words when I realized I was late to my singing rehearsal. As I was already dressed, it didn't take long to get out the door (just a quick brush of the teeth and a rearrangement of the scrunchy), but the girls were singing when I entered the lounge, and Penny gave me a dirty look.

I murmured my apologies and took my place in the half-circle. My stomach rumbled. I longed for a cup of coffee, a granola bar—anything. My harmony was off. I tried to sing softly.

After rehearsal, I caught up to Vanessa and Penny. "I really am sorry," I said. "I overslept. It won't happen again."

Vanessa crossed her arms over her bony chest. "Out partying?"

I blinked guiltily, thinking of Jeremy, then remembered Vanessa's note on my message board. I'd never called her back. "I wish! I had to go into the city for this stupid baby shower. My, um, cousin's pregnant." I rolled my eyes. "It was totally lame."

"I know what you mean," Vanessa said, suddenly softening and rolling her eyes in response. "Last year I went to my cousin's wedding shower. Totally bogus."

"I would have much rather have had ice cream with you guys," I said. "Was it fun?"

Vanessa shrugged. "It was ice cream."

"It was fun," Penny corrected.

"You guys want to get lattés?" I asked.

They traded glances, and then assented at the same moment. Vanessa and Penny seemed to read each other's thoughts, which would have been cute if it weren't so creepy. For a brief moment, I wondered if maybe they were lesbian lovers.

"How well do you know Jeremy?" Penny asked the instant we left the lounge.

"Are you, like, dating him?" Vanessa prodded.

Okay. They were straight.

"I wish!" I said. Something told me they would not buy the he's-not-my-type line. "I think he's still hung up on his ex-girlfriend."

"Ugh," Vanessa said.

"Is she as trampy as she looks?" I asked. Actually, Brynn didn't look any trampier than most of the other girls at

Mercer; she was simply prettier. I wasn't trying to be mean. Okay, I was being mean, but I was doing it for a purpose. I had to prove myself to Tim for one last time. I was almost out of time, and the idea of failure was unbearable.

"Total slut," Penny said.

"Major tart," Vanessa concurred.

Maybe they were just investigating, too.

We strode along the concrete sidewalk in silence for a few moments. Just before we got to our destination, I asked, in a hushed tone, "How many guys do you think Brynn's done it with?"

Loud, tuneless alternative music hit us as we opened the door to the coffee shop, which was called Jitters. Jitters coffee wasn't nearly as good as Starbucks, but its music was much louder and more offensive. As a result, it was always packed. We got in line behind two other jeans-clad, long-haired, slouching girls and squinted at the menu posted behind the counter. "Thirty," Vanessa said, about a minute after I'd concluded that they were both ignoring my question.

"No way," Penny said. "At least fifty."

"Don't forget she was going out with Jeremy for, like, three years," Vanessa said.

"And you think he's the only guy she was sleeping with?" Penny asked.

"Yeah, okay," Vanessa said. "There was that whole rumor about how she was doing Troy while she was going out with Jeremy." They both shuddered. I suddenly remembered the now-old saying: you never just sleep with one person. You sleep with everyone that person has slept with, and everyone that person has slept with, and so on and so forth. I pictured Troy and felt nauseated.

"Ever since they broke up, though, she's going through, like, every guy on campus," Penny said. "She's a total skank."

We ordered our coffees: nonfat latté for me, plain coffee for Vanessa, and for Penny, a banana coconut latté—whatever the hell that was—and an enormous slice of chocolate cake.

After coffee, I headed farther off campus. I'd been longing to return Evelyn Archer's dog book for as long as I'd had it, and now seemed like a reasonable time. Any sooner, and she'd suspect I hadn't read it. I hadn't, of course, except to check a quick description of a golden retriever. That way, if Evelyn asked what dog I'd be getting when I finally came to my senses and realized I needed one to complete my life, I'd have my answer ready. After all, if you had to get a dog, who wouldn't want a golden retriever? I couldn't think of a nicer animal to piss on my carpet and chew my shoes. Besides, they don't live very long.

I could hear the dogs barking before I got to my house. Yeah, that's what I needed in my life. The other people in my apartment building would love it, too. I was hoping no one would be home so I could just leave the book on the front stoop, but when I was a house away, Dr. Archer's Camry pulled into the driveway. I slowed momentarily. Had he seen me? I hadn't run into him since our encounter at the Gray Gull; I'd hoped to avoid him entirely.

He turned off the car and got out. The dogs' barking grew even louder. Evelyn had told me that she put the two nicer dogs in the garage when she went out. She worried about being "a bad dog mommy," but they had a habit of chewing furniture when left alone, and if she put the dogs in the backyard, Altoid might, well, eat them.

I ducked behind the neighbor's bush. The dean hadn't seen me, I was quite sure. As soon as he went inside, I would stick the book by the door and scurry back to my dorm.

To my surprise, a girl emerged from around the side of the house. I recognized her shiny, dark hair. Dean Archer hurried over to the garage, and they disappeared through the side door. The dogs' barking grew wild for a moment, and then it was quiet.

thirty

Richard sent me an e-mail: "Tim's in town. Let's meet Monday." As if I didn't know Tim was in town. At least it meant I could avoid Jeremy, I told myself. And Tiffany, too. She was sitting at her desk when I got back from the Archers' house. She didn't turn around when I walked in, even though I said, "Hi," very casually, as if I didn't know she was a sinner. Tiffany's side of the room was looking barren these days. Ethan said he didn't like Clay Aiken "looking at them." The posters came down immediately. Oddly, I missed Clay's airbrushed face. It was always nice to have someone else in the room whenever Tiffany got into one of her snits.

"Maybe we should redecorate the room," I suggested to Tiffany's pink back (she hadn't changed her wardrobe to reflect her new sexual sophistication; this particular shirt sported a kitten on the front). "We could do something wild—paint it bright blue, maybe. Even a mural could be fun. Have you seen Katherine and Amelia's room? It's really cool."

Tiffany tapped at her keyboard. I dropped my backpack on my bed and turned on my computer (this is when I saw Richard's e-mail; truly, he could have been more discreet). There was an e-mail from Jeremy, too: "Missed you this morning. J." Ugh. I thanked God for technology; at least he hadn't left the message on my memo board.

I sent a message back to Richard, saying I'd be in the office at 9 A.M. Jeremy's message I ignored.

"I have to go to Boston tonight," I said to the dead air. "I'll be back tomorrow afternoon." A month earlier, I would have worried that Tiffany would try to pry my secret out of me. Now I doubted she cared—although I thought I should give her a heads-up in case she wanted to plan a sleepover with Ethan.

"We didn't have sex," she said.

"What?" I asked. Really, I wasn't trying to draw out this conversation; I just wasn't sure she'd said what I thought she'd said.

"We didn't do it. We didn't have sex." Her voice was flat.

"Oh," I said. "Okay." Silence. "It's not really any of my business," I added, hoping to end the conversation.

"He wanted to," she said.

"Oh," I said.

"He said he needs it. That if he doesn't get it he gets all . . . backed up. And if I won't do it, then he'll have to find . . . I don't know. So we did something different. I kissed him. You know, down there."

She removed her hands from the keyboard and placed them quietly in her lap. "So I'm still a virgin." She turned halfway around in her chair. Her dull hair hung in her incredibly sad face. She looked up at me slowly. "Aren't I?"

"I guess so," I said carefully. "But you know, you don't have to do anything you don't want to."

She rubbed her chair with her index finger. "He really likes it," she mumbled. "He says it makes us closer."

"Because he's getting what he wants," I hissed. "Tiffany, don't let him use you."

Her head snapped up. Her small eyes were hard in her puffy face. "He's not using me. He loves me. I shouldn't have told you. You don't understand." She spun back to face her computer and sat perfectly still, seething.

"I'm not saying Ethan doesn't love you," I said carefully, although I didn't for an instant think he did. "I just don't think you should do anything that makes you uncomfortable. Anything that you're not ready for."

She turned back to me and looked me full in the face. "You don't know anything about me," she hissed. "You've always been cute and popular. You don't know *anything*."

I didn't know what to say, so I kept quiet—although a twisted part of me wanted to say, "If you think I'm cute now, you should have seen me when I was eighteen." Instead, I shut off my computer and pulled a pair of jeans and a T-shirt from my drawers and stuffed them into my backpack. I almost threw in a couple of textbooks—I had two papers due this week—but then reminded myself that I wasn't really a college student, after all. The essays were the least of my problems.

"I'll see you tomorrow," I said, holding my voice steady but shutting the door just a bit more firmly than was necessary.

thirty-one

For once, Jennifer was sitting at her desk rather than mine. Tim arrived a few minutes later. Very discreet— as if this were the first time they'd seen each other all morning. They both avoided my eyes. Then again, I avoided theirs, too, so it was hard to say whose effort at floor-gazing was more sincere. My throat hurt from withholding a sob. I'd promised myself I wouldn't cry. Tim mumbled something about caffeine and went in search of the coffeepot. Had he worked at *Salad*, he would have known better. Richard supplied only the cheapest grounds available, resulting in a watery brew that somehow managed to be both harsh and flavorless.

Even beyond the love triangle, it felt weird to be at the office—like going back to elementary school after summer vacation, when you wonder if your friends will still like you and whether your teacher will give you too much homework.

I wore jeans and platform sneakers that I'd picked up at a TJ Maxx on the way home the night before. Assorted sparkly clips held my hair off my face. I wasn't trying to make some kind of a statement; I'd just become so accustomed to teeny-bopper wear that it was easier than putting together something more sophisticated. Okay, maybe I was trying to throw my new persona in Tim's face: You want young? I can do young! But, surely, I wasn't that pathetic. Besides, this way I wouldn't have to stop off at home to change clothes before heading back to campus.

Sheila, carrying two cardboard cups of designer coffee, gave me one of her big, bleached, ultra-fake smiles as she hurried past my cubicle on her way to Richard's office. "*Kathy*! I hardly recognized you! You look *darling*! And so *thin*!"

Five minutes into the meeting, and it was clear: my friends no longer liked me, and my teacher thought I was not working up to potential. Or, even worse, that I *was* working up to potential, and this was as good as it got.

Tim announced that his boss was willing to extend the project as needed. "Clearly, I need to be more involved," he said without looking at me. "I'm going to start hanging out at the bars in Mercer, pretending to be a lonely guy looking for some company." The Snake Pit was the only bar in town, as Tim knew perfectly well. And Gerry had proved useless so far. "I'll base myself in Boston," he continued. "The drive's pretty manageable." The shit! Jennifer maintained a blank expression. Did Chrisanna know she was getting a new roommate?

"One week," Richard snapped. "If I don't have a final story on my desk by then, I'm pulling the plug. You can do whatever the hell you want after that, but Kathy's out of it." Sheila clasped her coffee cup between two hands and gazed at the sloshing liquid inside, while Tim pretended to take notes and Jennifer chomped on her hair.

"I know it seems slow," I whimpered, "but I've been making contacts, building credibility—"

"I cannot believe," Richard boomed, "the money that has gone into this! The clothes, the bedding, the, the"—he grabbed my expense report—"the *alternative music!*"

"It's not like I could bring along my Air Supply CD's!" I squeaked.

"And then there's the issue of your salary," Richard said crisply.

Jennifer stopped chewing on her hair and wrinkled her nose. "You have Air Supply CD's?"

"A month and a half's salary—for what? We're paying you to go to keggers and sing with a bunch of little girls!"

"First of all," I said, trying to sound calm even though my voice was shaking. "I'll have three lifestyle articles for Sheila by Friday."

She perked up. "Terrific!" she beamed, before checking Richard's still-cranky face and setting her attention back to the coffee.

"Second," I continued. "I have not been going to keggers. I mean, hardly at all. And the singing group is part of my research. It's not like I'm doing it for fun." It was quiet for a moment. Richard's nostrils twitched. I turned my head partway toward Jennifer. "The Air Supply CD's were a gift." I shot Tim a poisonous look. "I never listen to them."

Richard concluded the matter by announcing that *Salad* was done covering my college expenses and that he'd continue my salary only on the condition that I coughed up the three articles I'd just (impulsively) promised to deliver by the end of the week. "Our advertisers are coming disproportionately from the lifestyle sector—furniture stores, flooring companies and the like. We need more editorial content to help support the ads." Then he praised Jennifer on her "marvelous" articles (Richard never called anything marvelous unless it came from Sheila) and hinted that we might "expand her role" in the future.

I was in big trouble.

I had planned to accomplish many important tasks during my day in the office, all of which I immediately forgot upon being humiliated in the meeting. Instead, I gave in to my impulse to run and hide.

"We've got to talk," Tim mumbled as I shoved my papers into my bag. "About the investigation, I mean," he added hurriedly.

"The investigation?" I spat. "Isn't there something else we need to talk about?"

"No," he said evenly. "There's nothing left to say."

"How about, I'm sorry for misleading you? I'm sorry for making you look like a fool?"

He closed his eyes for a moment, then opened them slowly. "Let's try to be professional. To just focus on the investigation. We need to sit down and review the facts. We need to see if we missed any angle, any lead."

"It'll have to wait," I snapped. "I've got a full day of interviews scheduled."

"Don't back out now, Kathy," he said. "This isn't about you and me."

"You've made that perfectly clear." Backing out seemed like a wonderful idea.

"I talked to Gerry," Tim said.

"Who's Gerry?"

"The bartender, you know, at that pub."

"The Snake Pit."

"Right. Anyway, he said there's this kid. Troy. He didn't know his last name. But he said to watch him."

"I already have been."

He took a deep breath as if to gather strength and spoke again. "I'll finish this story without you if I have to, but I'd rather have you on my side."

"I've got the inside track," I said as if I believed it. "You couldn't possibly do it without me."

"Just see what you can find out," he said.

My "full day of interviews" was utter crap, of course, but it sounded feasible—especially since I'd promised Sheila three nonexistent articles by Friday.

I fled to my apartment. It looked unusually large and luxurious. Framed pictures! Built-in bookshelves! Curtains! On the coffee table there was a plate of fossilized toast crusts and a rotting apple core, which kind of took away from the overall effect and made the room smell a bit. The carpet was littered with lint and crumbs. Once I moved back home, I vowed, I would keep fresh flowers on my coffee table. I would vacuum more often and stop eating my frozen dinners on the couch.

I carried my plate to the kitchen sink and dropped the apple core into the trash. So it wasn't just the apple that smelled: I'd take the trash out later. Then I went into my bedroom (Look at the size of the bed! And the bedding: no synthetic fibers!) to fetch the vacuum, which wasn't in my closet. I lay down on my bed to try to remember where I'd stashed it and promptly fell asleep.

I awoke disoriented. The shadows in my room told me that it was almost evening. So much for getting anything done. It all came back to me in a rush: Tim and Jennifer, my precarious job situation, the need for three quick articles. I only knew one person who could throw that many topics my way. I checked the glowing numbers on my digital clock: 5:20 P.M. With any luck, he'd still be in the office.

"Kathy!" He sounded far too pleased to hear from me. "I've called your office a couple of times, but they keep saying you're out on assignment."

I cringed. Not that I really wanted to know that Dennis had been calling me—but it would be nice if Jennifer would pass on my messages every now and again.

I asked him if he was free for a "professional dinner," which sounded entirely dopey, as if we would be paid to eat, but which I figured would at least let him know that I wasn't asking him out. We agreed to meet at seven-thirty at a trendy place in the South End.

Next, on impulse, I called Marcy and asked if she could join us. I needed to tell her about my night with Jeremy, needed her assurances that I wasn't a bad person. I didn't want to go into details over the phone, but maybe we could catch some time alone before or after dinner.

"I'm having dinner with Dennis, and I'd rather make it a group thing," I told her. "Besides, I need to talk to you about Jeremy." I'd told Marcy about Dennis, whom she'd just missed meeting that long-ago day in Filene's Basement, but I wasn't sure if she remembered much. She called Dan, and he, miraculously, said he'd shoot to be home at six-thirty. "So he's working shorter hours?" I ventured.

"No. But the bigger I get, the more frightened of me he becomes."

* * *

Dennis and Marcy were engrossed in conversation when I arrived at the restaurant. "You found each other," I said.

They beamed up like old friends—of each other, not me. "Marcy said you were rescuing her from another night of chicken nuggets and Nickelodeon."

"Dennis likes *SpongeBob,*" Marcy announced, rolling her eyes dramatically.

Dennis squeezed her arm. "She's a snob, this one," he laughed. He turned to Marcy. "Give it one more chance."

Marcy shook her head. "That's just asking too much."

When Dennis went outside to use his cell phone, Marcy, without even looking up from her menu, remarked, "When you told me we were meeting Dennis, I thought you meant the Dennis who had a thing for you."

I squinted, trying to get her drift. Her stomach was so enormous, she could hardly pull up her chair. Yes, Dennis was being awfully nice to her, but did she really think he was hitting on her? What I really wanted to talk to her about was Jeremy, and she didn't even care enough to ask.

I was trying to come up with a suitable response to Marcy's inquiry when Dennis reappeared. He looked nice tonight, I had to admit, in a white tab-collar shirt, black jeans and black oxford shoes. He smelled good, too, like a freshly sliced pear.

"What do you think of this place?" he asked, pulling back his chair and smiling at me. I glanced at Marcy to see if she'd noticed the shift in his attention. Didn't she see he was just being polite to her, that he was hoping to win me over by sucking up to my friends?

I looked around lazily. "The whole exposed-pipe thing has been overdone," I proclaimed. "Although I like that they've painted the pipes different colors. Makes me think of the, you know, that museum in Paris."

"The Pompidou," Marcy offered.

I ignored her. "But the black walls . . ." I wrinkled my nose and shook my head.

"What would you do?" Dennis asked. "Royal blue? Red?"

I considered. "Parchment. With colorful prints on the walls. That way, the ceiling would be the focus."

"But I thought you didn't like the ceiling," Marcy said. She wasn't being especially contrary; she was always like this. Tonight, though, I just wasn't in the mood.

"If you're going to have exposed pipes, it's striking to paint them different colors," I reiterated carefully. "Hey! There's an article idea—exposed pipes and vents and stuff as art! Taking the industrial look a step further . . ." I pulled my notebook out of my bag and wrote it down. Dennis gave me the name and number of a designer who specialized in industrial chic. "Any other ideas?" I asked Dennis.

"Black walls?"

"Yes . . . yes! Black: bold or bleak?" And we were off.

After dinner, Dennis, who lived around the block, asked us back to his place for coffee, and I finally felt grateful for Marcy's presence (she still hadn't asked about Jeremy, even in a whisper). Dennis seemed almost appealing tonight, I had to admit, but I still wasn't ready for any kind of physical contact. But who knew? Maybe Marcy had allowed me to see him with new eyes. Really, he was just the kind of sensitive, artistic guy I should be hooking up with.

Dennis lived on the second floor of a lovely brownstone. The South End was still dangerous in places, but over the past twenty-five years or so, it had been reclaimed and restored to much of its original glory. The apartment itself was anything but traditional: plum, mustard and ochre walls, leather arm chairs, blond wood intermingled with cherry. Black and white photographs mounted on broad white mats lined the walls. The overall look was part contemporary, part retro: striking and stylish, certainly, but not quite original. I'd seen the look before, I was certain. I just couldn't put my finger on it.

"Cappuccino? Latté?" Dennis asked, heading for a massive espresso maker that took up most of a black granite countertop. Then it hit me: Dennis's apartment looked just like a Starbucks.

"Latté," I said. "Decaf if you have it." It was really, really hard not to add, "venti, nonfat, with a shot of vanilla syrup."

Marcy asked for a glass of milk as she gazed around in wonder. "Snazzy place, Dennis. You really have a knack for decorating."

He shrugged. "Not me—my ex."

Marcy made sympathetic noises, while I peered at Dennis anew. He had been loved and desired. Maybe I had missed something. Maybe I should open my mind and my eyes.

"At least he had nice taste," Marcy said. "Your ex, I mean." I spun around, tried not to gasp. She often spoke without thinking, but with this, she'd hit a new low. Why would she assume Dennis was gay, just because he had style? The evening had been going so well. Dennis was a sensitive sort. His self-esteem might never recover.

I smiled at Dennis, tried to find words to make the whole thing into a joke. He looked remarkably unperturbed. He pushed a button on the espresso machine, which made a loud whooshing noise. When it was quiet again, he sighed. "I don't know. The place is a little too in-your-face for me. I was pushing for a tweedy, masculine look, but he had to have his way. As always."

thirty-two

So you can't really blame me for going to bed with Jeremy again.

It's not like I went to his room intending to rip his clothes off. I just tapped on his open-just-a-crack door, smiled shyly and sat down on his unmade bed. Sloppy though I am in my own home, I felt a whiff of superiority. It's one thing to be slovenly behind the locked doors of an apartment no one ever visits, quite another to leave your bed unmade with your door open. The beige sheets looked familiar. Surely he had washed them since our romp. Right? Anyway, the bed was really the only place to sit; it was that or the floor. Jeremy was at his desk, his bendy aluminum desk lamp illuminating an over-highlighted textbook. The thing is, though, he got up and closed his door and came back to sit next to me on the bed. He cupped my face in his hands and gazed at me with those green-gold eyes with such pure heterosexual lust that I thought, "This may be the last straight man on the planet—and he likes me!"

That's another thing. After we left Dennis's place, Marcy gushed about what a nice guy he was. She illuminated this niceness by saying, "Dennis told me how you said all your old friends had gotten married or moved away. So he thought you needed a shoulder to lean on." There you have it, from the mouth of Marcy: Dennis had been calling me nonstop because he felt sorry for me. I had reached the very lowest rung on the Ladder of Loserdom. I was so mad, I never told her about Jeremy, even when we were finally alone, and she never bothered to ask.

Still, I contained myself and forged ahead on my quest to set things right with Jeremy. "About the other night—" I looked down at my lap. I fiddled with the braided silver ring on my right hand. After Tim moved out, I'd bought it to replace the turquoise non-engagement ring he had given me for our five-year anniversary. "It wasn't supposed to happen. It just wasn't . . . right."

"I know," Jeremy said softly. I looked up in surprise. Was he about to express his undying apathy? I wasn't sure I could take it. He dropped his hands from my face and stroked my fingers. "When you told me about that music teacher in high school, I just assumed . . ." He looked up at me and smiled gently.

"What?" I asked, honestly perplexed.

"Well, that it was more than, you know, emotional."

Oh, God. Not another retread of my romantic past. I didn't mind the sobbing and lying, really; I just wasn't sure I could remember all the details. "What do you mean?" I asked carefully.

"I thought, you know." I looked at him expectantly. "That you had slept with him."

Okay, now I was truly confused. "What does it matter whether or not I did?" I asked, hedging my bets and sounding a bit defensive.

"It's okay," he said, squeezing my hand. "I just wish I had known. I would have made it more, I don't know, special or something. But I'm really honored to be your first."

So there you have it: *I was so bad in bed that Jeremy thought I was a virgin.* What choice did I have, really?

Afterwards, I crept out of the bed and tried not to feel smug. (In the heat of passion, Jeremy had murmured that I was "a quick study." Ha!)

The hall was mercifully empty. As I turned the key in my door, I said a silent prayer that Ethan wouldn't be there. And he wasn't. Some pimply kid with greasy black hair was there instead. "Huh?" he grunted, the hall light waking him as it hit his face. His exposed shoulders were white and bony and sprinkled with yet more acne. He lifted his head slightly and then let it fall back onto Tiffany's pillow. She never woke up. More likely, she was faking sleep. She usually snored when she was really out.

I closed the door more loudly than was necessary. Slipping back into bed with Jeremy was more appealing than I liked to admit, but sneaking out unseen in the morning would be impossible. Besides, the door had locked behind me as I left, and I wasn't about to wake him up.

At the end of the hall, the orange fire door swung open: Amber. Maybe I could sleep on her floor. But she breezed right by, yapping into her omnipresent cell phone.

I had no choice: I had to go home. Fortunately, I had my backpack with me, car keys inside. So I'd miss another day of classes and another day of investigating. Maybe more. I'd poked around all I could and found nothing, unless you counted Dean Archer's sleazy behavior, but I'd come to the conclusion that the girls weren't hookers, after all. I'd kept a close eye on Brynn and never saw her with anyone else. Besides, if Archer was paying her for her sexual services, wouldn't he take her to a hotel rather than a restaurant? And the other girl; I spent a bunch of nights hanging around her dorm and never saw her again. If she were a hooker, she'd be in and out a lot more. It was time to give up, I suddenly realized. The articles for Sheila were more important than this hopeless investigation, and I'd never get them written from my dorm room.

I heaved a sigh of relief as my Civic pulled out of the dorm parking lot. As unpleasant as my adult life was right now, I was tired of playing make-believe. I'd shared some sweet moments with Jeremy, but my gut ached when I imagined his face the moment he learned my true identity.

My gas tank was approaching empty, so I pulled into a convenience store parking lot. The store was closed—it was almost three A.M.—but the pumps were still open, thanks to the miracle of credit cards and auto-pay. Just a mile from the college, this spot lacked even a whiff of quaintness. Next door was a tire superstore, one of those chains you see everywhere. Across the street was a stark brown apartment building fortified by a cinder block fence. Lights twinkled in two windows several apartments apart, and I wondered if the insomniacs inside knew there were others awake at this lonely hour.

As the gas whooshed into my tank, I leaned against the

side of my car and stared up at the sky. It was inky black tonight, without a single star peeking through. The pump shut off, startling me with its loudness.

A light blinked off in the apartment building across the street. I started my car and was about to pull out of the parking lot when I remembered my apartment keys. Sometimes I shoved them to the back of my desk drawer. There was no point heading back to the city unless I had them, and I hadn't been doing so well on details lately. I pulled into a parking space on the edge of the lot, and killed the engine. Afraid of running down my battery, I shut off the lights. I rummaged through my backpack. The keys weren't in the outside pocket where they belonged. I took a deep breath and stared out at the empty parking lot. Now what was I supposed to do? I opened the backpack's main compartment and came up empty again. Desperate, I dumped the pack's entire contents onto the passenger seat: disintegrating tissues, granola bar wrappers, a syllabus, a dull pencil, a pink gel pen. No keys. I was coming to terms with the idea of sleeping on one of the vinyl couches in the dorm lounge when he walked into the parking lot, head down, hands in the pockets of his oversized pants.

I froze. Had he seen me? I had every right to be here, of course, just as he did. But Troy gave me the creeps. I'd been keeping my eyes open for him, walking by his house at every opportunity, but I wasn't prepared to face him on my own, especially in a dark and deserted parking lot.

He shuffled over to the side of the building, where a sporty silver BMW sat parked under a burned out streetlight. As he pulled out of the lot, I sat paralyzed for one more moment before turning the key in my own ignition and slipping behind him on the deserted streets. At first

I kept my lights off, but then I flicked them on. Hot shot investigative reporter or not, I respect the rules of the road. Besides, it was really dark, and I couldn't see.

He drove a few blocks, then, surprisingly, pulled into a residential area. He wound through a few streets, very, very slowly, almost as if he were lost. The houses here were solidly middle class, wandering neither into the lower or upper ranges of the socioeconomic scale: ranches and raised ranches overlooked tidy hedges and lawns that were turning brown for the season. Little Tikes cars sat neatly parked beside closed garages. There were no street lamps back here, but a porch light was left on every now and again, rescuing the neighborhood from total darkness.

Finally, I had to turn onto a different street; we were the only cars out at that hour, and I didn't want to arouse suspicion. I pulled over and turned off my lights, wondering what was going on, wondering what to do. I went back to where I'd last seen Troy's car, assuming he wouldn't recognize my Civic as the one that had been tailing him earlier.

I would have passed him if I hadn't paused too long at a stop sign, contemplating my next move. I glanced in my rearview mirror and saw the hatchback parked on a side street, lights off, and two still, dark figures in the front seat. They were still there the next time I rounded the block. And then they were gone.

As I pulled into Marcy's driveway, I glanced at the clock: 4:59 A.M. I groaned. Another time of the year, the sky would be glowing with the first hint of morning, but today it was as black as midnight. After I let myself in (Marcy hides a spare key under the mat because burglars would never look there), I crept as quietly as I could toward the television room. When a tall figure loomed in the darkness, I yelped, less from fear of death than from the terror of not being able to sleep for two hours before Marcy got up with the kids.

"What are you doing here?" I gasped at Dan when he turned on the hall light, clad in a flannel bathrobe and holding a mug of aromatic coffee.

"I live here," he said with as little sarcasm as he could muster.

"Well, yeah. I mean, I've heard the rumors. But what are you doing up?"

"Six-thirty meeting." He sipped his coffee, and then used the belt from his flannel bathrobe to rub the steam from his glasses. "Coffee?"

I rubbed my eyes with my fists and shook my head. "I haven't even gone to bed yet." Then I thought of Jeremy and said, "Well, actually, I did go to bed, but I didn't sleep much. Oh, never mind. I hope I didn't scare you."

He shook his head. "I heard your car pull up and looked out the window. I was just coming to unlock the door."

"I was hoping to crash on your couch for a couple of hours."

He nodded toward the stairs. "Jacob's bed's empty. He had a nightmare and ended up with us last night. I'll leave a note for Marcy."

So, rather than waking up in either of my beds or even in Jeremy's, I greeted the morning—which was almost afternoon—from under a Star Wars comforter. As with the television room, Marcy had decorated Jacob's room without any input from me. On the ceiling directly over the bed was a poster of Yoda wielding a sword or saber or whatever you call those laser things. No wonder the kid was having nightmares.

I shuffled downstairs to an empty, tidy kitchen. A note on the counter read,

K.,
I've waddled off to the grocery store.
Help yourself to breakfast. (Lunch?)
M.

P.S. I expect a full report.

On the counter she'd left assorted whole grain cereals and fresh fruit. I ignored them and dove instead for the walk-in pantry.

She caught me. "Cocoa Puffs?" With some effort, she hoisted a brown paper bag onto the granite countertop. Her car keys followed with a clang. The door to the attached garage was open, her white minivan parked inside.

"I can't believe you feed this crap to your kids," I said between spoonfuls. The chocolate had leached into the milk, turning it almost as brown and sweet as the cereal.

"It's the organic kind," she said mildly, presenting me with a towering cardboard cup of hot, expensive coffee.

"You do love me," I said.

"Someone's got to." She meant to be funny, but it stung. Stupidly, my eyes filled with tears. "Honey!" she said, coming over and giving me a squeeze. "Lots of people love you! Everybody loves you!" She then proceeded to list all the people who loved me. It was a pretty good list, even if most of the people on it were blood relatives and therefore obligated to feel some affection.

"Dennis likes you better than me," I whimpered.

"Gay Dennis?" She looked astonished. I wondered why she felt the need to tack his sexual orientation onto his name until I remembered that there was supposedly a Straight Dennis who couldn't wait to get into my pants.

I nodded.

"Are you insane?" she said. "I am a fat, suburban housewife—"

"You're not fat; you're pregnant," I obediently interjected. "You're a grown-up with a grown-up life, and my life is going nowhere. I slept with Jeremy." Her eyes popped wide. "Twice." Her mouth dropped open, and she started to smile. I shook my head. "He's twenty-one years old, and he thinks I'm eighteen. It's not enough for me to mess up my own life, I've got to mess up someone else's as well." I gazed at her cherry cabinets, her granite countertops, her stainless steel refrigerator plastered with Jacob's artwork. "You are so lucky," I sighed.

She stared at me for a moment, and then shook her head wildly. "You've got it all wrong! You are this cool, funky, creative type who's doing this undercover story and sleeping with young studs, and, and, and *living* instead of just cleaning up a big goddamn house day after goddamn day! All I do is give baths and wipe butts and make peanut butter and jelly sandwiches that always end up pulled apart and facedown on the rug. I get up to pee five times a night, and if I actually manage to fall back to sleep, it never lasts long before one kid or another screams that he's wet his bed or pooped in his pants, and my husband's never goddamn home because he's too busy trying to make partner so maybe I can have an even bigger house to clean!"

Now she was the one crying. I was so shocked that my

tears had stopped, and I hugged her tight and rocked her as she sobbed. When she finally quieted down, I asked where the boys were. Jacob had gone to a friend's house after preschool; Joshua was asleep in the minivan.

"Why don't you go lie down?" I suggested, stroking her frizzy hair. "I'll listen for Joshua."

She shook her head. "I can't," she said miserably, smearing tears down her cheeks with her palms. "My cleaning woman will be here any minute."

thirty-three

I spent the rest of the week holed up in my apartment (the superintendent had a key), conducting phone interviews with a bunch of interior designers who I could count on to give a good quote. Normally, I'd work out of the office and interview in person, but this was quicker. Also, it meant I could remain in my bathrobe all day and break into tears without warning. There were two phone messages from Tim ("Where the hell are you?"), both of which I ignored. I had admitted defeat to myself, but I was not yet ready to admit it to Tim. Staying in Boston meant missing precious final days of the investigation, but my job was on the line. Besides, I'd come up empty during the previous six weeks; what made me think this week would be any different?

I sent Jeremy an e-mail: "Out of town for the week. I'll explain later." I hadn't yet decided whether I would tell him the truth or concoct another set of lies upon my return. Maybe I could just sneak my stuff out of the dorm without seeing him. I sent Tiffany the same message, omitting the promise of a later explanation.

By Friday morning I'd sent the articles to Sheila and was back on the Mass Pike. I spent the drive back to Mercer thanking God I was nobody's wife, but just my own person, free to do as I like, responsible only for myself. I almost had myself convinced when I arrived at my dorm and almost gasped aloud when I saw him, there on the bench: the man God intended for me. Why else would he have made me wait so damn long, if not for the chance to begin each day looking at this flawless specimen? Judging from his salt-and-pepper curls, he was forty-something, though his golden skin was smooth, save for crinkles around his brilliant blue eyes. He was conservatively dressed, in a striped Oxford shirt, windbreaker and khakis, but perhaps his tennis shoes hinted at the soul of a free spirit. Or something. I'd never seen him before, yet I felt this immediate connection, this oddly exciting familiarity.

He smiled at me, and my throat constricted so I could hardly speak, and I half expected him to come out with some Harlequin-inspired line like, "I was wondering when you'd turn up in my life."

Instead, he asked if I lived in the dorm, and I thought desperately of a way to tell him that I wasn't really a college freshman, that I was a suitable woman in my early thirties, a touch young for him perhaps, but I could work on discovering my inner trophy wife. But when I said that I did, indeed, live there, he smiled even more warmly, and I panicked, wondering what kind of a pervert goes trawling for teenagers.

But it was even worse than that. "Then maybe you know my son?" he asked, standing up. "Jeremy?"

I gawked in horror before finally squeaking, "I do," as far as I'd get to saying those words in his presence. Next thing you know, I was leading Jeremy's father up the stairs to his room.

Jeremy practically ran over when he saw me. "I missed you," he said under his breath. I pretended not to hear him.

His mother was already there. Apparently, they had had an hour to kill until Jeremy got out of classes. So his father ("Call me Mr. Dunbar") had eaten lunch alone while his mother (who, as far as I could tell, preferred that I not call her anything) browsed in the "quaint shops" on Main Street (which, unless she had discovered some other Main Street that had heretofore eluded me, meant a hardware store, a discount tire center, a liquor store, and the college bookstore). Then again, the situation still seemed weird; couldn't they spend an hour together?

Jeremy's mother was not what I expected. Or, rather, she was not what I would have expected had I ever expected to meet her at all. By Jeremy's account, she was well groomed and brittle, a WASP wannabe. I'd have expected pearls and silk, manicured nails, sleek hair. But while she'd mastered the icy, brittle routine, Mrs. Dunbar's hair was too blond and too big—in fact, all of her was a little too big. Her navy blue dress was conservative but cheaply cut. She'd worked hard on her diction, though, resulting in an accent that landed halfway between Audrey Hepburn and the Kennedys. Apparently, no one had ever told her that the Kennedys weren't Protestant.

"Well, boys," she said, pointedly looking at just the

"boys." She tightened her mouth into something that re-sembled a smile. "Ready for lunch?"

"I thought Dad already had lunch," Jeremy mumbled, scuffing his sneaker on the carpet. He looked about twelve, which would be cute if I didn't already have enough reser-vations about our, er, thing.

"Yes, but I haven't eaten a thing since breakfast," she said, tilting both of her chins up. "Just because your father couldn't suppress his appetite doesn't mean the rest of us should suffer."

Mr. Dunbar crossed his arms and gazed at Jeremy calmly. "Your mother wants lunch. So we'll have lunch."

"But you ate already," Jeremy said, with a hint of a whine.

"I can have a beer," Mr. Dunbar said gamely.

"At one o'clock in the afternoon?" his wife asked.

"A nonalcoholic beer," he said evenly. Then, to his son, "With a shot of whiskey in it." They both guffawed.

I started for the door. "It was really nice meeting you all." I held my hand up in the perkiest good-bye wave I could manage.

"Aren't you coming to lunch with us?" Mr. Dunbar said, sounding truly baffled.

"Oh, I don't want to get in the way of your, you know, family thing."

"But Jeremy has been talking about you for weeks," Mr. Dunbar said. "We've been looking forward to getting to know you."

I looked desperately at his mother, hoping, I guess, for some confusion on her face, some indication that he'd been exaggerating, that Jeremy had not, in fact, mentioned me before today. The look I met was filled with such hatred, though, that I knew Mr. Dunbar spoke the truth.

"Surely Katie's own parents are coming," Mrs. Dunbar said, dismissively. "It is Parents Weekend, after all."

Oh, crap: it was, wasn't it? I'd completely forgotten. I blurted out something about how my parents were in Europe to celebrate their anniversary. Jeremy gawked at me. Shit. "I mean, my dad and my stepmom. And there was no way she was going to miss out on a trip to Europe." I rolled my eyes. "My mom lives in Santa Fe, but she's in Romania. She's on a, like, spiritual journey." I shrugged as if to say, *Just another dysfunctional family*.

Because there weren't a lot of options, we went to The Snake Pit. Except it wasn't The Snake Pit, technically, because the restaurant half was called The Spit. I think that was supposed to refer to a cooking technique, but it never failed to make me look twice at my water glass.

Gerry left his perch behind the bar to take our order. When he saw me, he raised his eyebrows and smirked. He squatted next to the table in that overfamiliar way some waiters adopt so they can be at eye level with you, as if you're some three-year-old they are trying to befriend. But the glint in Gerry's eye was anything but friendly. "Glass of white wine?" he purred. "A nice chardonnay, perhaps?"

I stared at him. His shiny skin gave off the yeasty smell of beer. "Diet Coke," I said.

Still smirking, he wrote down my order and continued through the table. He didn't suggest wine to anyone else.

"They'll sell booze to anyone around this place," Mrs. Dunbar huffed when Gerry had left. "You aren't even twenty-one, are you?" she asked without looking at me.

"No," I answered truthfully. "I'm not twenty-one."

* * *

I called Marcy as soon as I got back to my room. "How are you doing?"

"I'm fine," she assured me. "I'm hormonal. And I think I'm starting my midlife crisis a little early."

"You always were an overachiever." I sighed. "It's Parents Weekend, and everyone else has someone coming."

"Where are your parents?"

"On a barge on the Rhine."

"Not your *real* parents."

"Oh, right." I screwed up my face, trying to remember what I'd told Jeremy's parents. "Mom's in Romania, consulting with a shaman."

There was a moment of silence. "I don't think they have shamans in Romania," Marcy finally said.

I sighed. I hardly even cared whether I got caught anymore. Sunday I'd be packing up. Monday I'd be back in the office, admitting defeat. "Dad and his second wife have left their horse farm in Virginia for a trip to Europe. I keep getting the feeling that it's a last hurrah, and that the stepmonster is pregnant. Horrible to think I could have a sister who's almost thirty years younger than me."

"Twenty years."

I paused. "Oh, shit." I didn't think I could make it through the weekend.

Tiffany's parents were due to arrive at six o'clock. They showed up at five-thirty. Mrs. Weaver, who was all edges and angles, skipped right over hello and moved on to, "You should really wear makeup, sweetheart."

"I *do*," Tiffany shot back. "I just got out of the *shower*. I haven't had *time* yet. You said you'd be here at *six*."

"Six-*ish*," her mother replied evenly, smirking at me and rolling her eyes.

Mr. Weaver, a short heavyset guy, kissed Tiffany on her cheek and then just stood there with his hands shoved firmly in his pockets, while her younger sister, Brittany, walked around the room examining our crates, posters, bedspreads and—I couldn't even believe it—closets. "Brittany!" Tiffany snarled. "*Privacy?*"

Brittany rolled her eyes. "What. Ever." She was thirteen, but she looked more like sixteen. She wasn't pretty—heavy makeup covered an obvious acne problem—but she was tall and had inherited her mother's metabolism. She was all breast and no butt. I had always wondered who size 0 jeans were meant for. Now I knew.

"Stand up and let me look at you," Mrs. Weaver commanded her oldest daughter. Tiffany did so, reluctantly. She wore a fuzzy long-sleeved powder blue sweater and a peasant skirt. Her feet were bare, her toenails unpolished and overgrown. Mrs. Weaver forced a smile. "When you complained about the cafeteria food, I guess I thought—" She shook her head dramatically. "Never mind."

Mr. Weaver rolled his eyes. There was a lot of eye rolling in this family.

"What?" Tiffany asked.

Mrs. Weaver flicked her hand. "Nothing."

"*What?*"

Mrs. Weaver tilted her head to one side. "I just thought you might have. You know. Taken off some of your baby fat."

"I've lost ten pounds," Tiffany muttered.

"Are you sure?" her mother asked, squinting.

Brittany poked though the plastic mesh carryall that held Tiffany's toiletries. "Can I try some of your scented lotion?" she asked, unscrewing the cap before Tiffany had a chance to answer.

"It was nice to meet you all!" I chirped, backing toward the door. "I've really got to get to the, um, library."

"Won't your parents be here for dinner?" Mrs. Weaver asked, suddenly full of warmth.

"They couldn't make it." I shrugged. "They're divorced." I figured that would be enough to convince the self-satisfied and still-married Mrs. Weaver that my parents were too busy with their own lives to think about me rather than make her wonder why I wasn't missing just one but two sets of parents.

"I understand," Mrs. Weaver said with equal amounts of sympathy and smugness. "Then you must have dinner with us."

I stared at her, truly caught unprepared.

"I only made the reservation for four," Tiffany hissed. Wow—she really disliked me.

Mrs. Weaver and Tiffany argued over whether or not I'd be welcome at dinner. "I'm not hungry, really!" I insisted. "I had a late lunch."

Tiffany and I had just about lost out to Mrs. Weaver, who kept saying, "I insist you join us! I insist!" when Marcy poked her head through the door. "I couldn't leave my little sister all by herself on Parents Weekend!" she squealed before I had a chance to say anything. She swept into the room and gave me a suffocating hug. Someone crept in behind her.

"Dennis!" I gasped, stopping short of "What the hell are you doing here?" He turned red.

"Don't sound so surprised," Marcy chirped. "You wouldn't expect me to leave my *husband* at home, would you?"

thirty-four

In honor of Parents Weekend, a gourmet buffet was being served in the dining hall. But it was basically the same swill as always along with some really tough roast beef accompanied by horseradish sauce and "o juice."

Marcy explained herself while Dennis searched for some rolls that hadn't been fossilized from too much time spent under heating lamps. "The twelve-year-old from next door came over to watch the kids until Dan gets home. Eight bucks an hour! Is that obscene, or what? I told Dennis you were doing an undercover story about dorm decorating," she said, slurping mashed potatoes covered in sludgy gravy.

"And he believed it?"

She shrugged. "People generally assume you're telling the truth if you don't give them reason to think otherwise."

I smiled. She was right. "You know, my gig here is almost up, anyway. It really would have been okay if you had told Dennis the truth."

She blinked twice and then laughed with relief. "Oh, thank God. I did tell him the truth. I just didn't want you freaking out on me." She leaned back in her chair and rubbed her oversized belly.

Dennis returned with breadsticks. "At least these are supposed to be crunchy." He took a noisy bite. "I can see why you've lost so much weight. The food here is really revolting."

"Did you think I was fat before?" I asked, narrowing my eyes.

"Of course not," he said soothingly. "You've always looked great. You're just skinnier now, that's all." He settled into a plastic chair. "So tell me about your story, Kath. I love the idea, by the way. Cheap chic, posters beyond the Saint Pauli girl and all that." I remained silent and let him dig further in. From the corner of my eye, I could see Tiffany eating with her family. What was it she had said about reservations? True, there had been a presale for the buffet, but it was covered under the meal plan. She really wanted to avoid me. I should have felt relieved, but I felt oddly slighted, as if the geekiest boy in school had refused to dance with me. I slunk lower in my chair, lest her mother command the family to haul their trays over to us.

"I really admire the way you used a bedsheet to make a curtain," Dennis continued. "It's a very loose look, very contemporary. I'm really looking forward to your article."

Marcy was squirming. I sighed. "She told me, Dennis."

"What?" he asked disingenuously.

"This has nothing to do about decorating," I said under

my breath. "As you know. We'll talk about it later." I took a bite of the roast beef and chewed for a really, really long time until it was soft enough to swallow. "Uck," I said. "Dennis, where did you come up with those breadsticks?"

At the salad bar, I snagged a few packets of breadsticks and crackers. On my way back to our table, I stopped short. Troy sat at a table with an older, yellow-haired woman and a bald, gray-haired man in a blue blazer. Troy had parents? I guess I'd always assumed he had just hatched or something. As I stood there, they threw napkins on their chunky plates and pushed back their chairs. Troy's mother hauled on a long, red wool coat. They left their trays on the table in a most horrendous breach of cafeteria etiquette. If ever I'd doubted that evil lurked in Troy's heart, this sealed it. Maybe he was the key to this thing, after all. There was only one way to find out.

I scurried back to Dennis and Marcy. "Let's move!" I commanded.

"What?" Marcy asked, looking generally perturbed about leaving her food.

"I'll tell you in the car. *Bus your trays!*"

I don't know that a white minivan is the most innocuous of vehicles, especially in a college town where every other kid drives a spiffy little Volkswagen or mini SUV, but I worried that Troy had seen my car before (which also stood out, in that it was far crappier than the roadsters preferred by most Mercer students), so I suggested we take Marcy's instead. Besides, with all the parents in town, there were more minivans around than usual. Marcy, winded from walking across the dining hall, waited on the steps of the dining hall while Dennis and I scurried down the street, keys in hand. When we arrived at the vehicle, we both made our way to the passenger door. We blinked at each other. "I'm used to driving a Civic," I said, cowering in the van's massive shadow.

"I haven't driven since the nineties," Dennis countered.

If I'd driven any more slowly, I would have been going backwards, but I made it to the dining hall without incident. "You didn't scratch it, did you?" Marcy asked. She'd driven with me before.

I glared at her. "Don't start. I'm still mad at you for blabbing, you know."

Once we were safely buckled into our seats, Marcy asked, "Where to?"

I looked at her blankly. "I hadn't thought that far ahead."

Dennis looked crestfallen. "My first car chase, and we've already lost the guy. Who is he, anyway?"

"His name is Troy," I explained. "Tim thinks he's the head pimp."

We cruised the streets. After about ten minutes, I suggested driving by Troy's house.

Marcy swung around. "If you know where he lives, why didn't you say something in the first place?" I fixed her with my best I-still-hate-you stare. She cleared her throat. "What I meant to say was, lead the way."

The house was really crappy looking, in a way that most college kids find cool, with peeling paint and an oversized sagging porch crowded with bug-infested couches. In an effort to curb underage drinking, Mercer had done away with fraternities a few years back. Now groups of pack-minded youths rented crappy houses en masse. Weekends, they hosted notorious parties. Weekdays, they made do with blaring bass-heavy music in the middle of the afternoon.

There he was, on the porch with his parents. "Bingo!" I yelled. There were a few other parents in attendance, but none of them dared to sit on that skanky furniture.

Marcy parked the car. I ducked down. "Don't stop!" I hissed. "We don't want him to see us, remember?"

"I'm sorry if I'm not well-versed in stakeouts," Marcy said. "I'm sorry if I'm just a boring housewife and all I know is how to change diapers and make macaroni and cheese." Her voice was starting to get that quiver.

"Okay! Okay! Just drive around the block. We'll figure something out."

We wound up parking half a block away. Since Jacob was sensitive to heat, the van's windows were all tinted, making us hard to see from behind. We watched in the rearview mirror as Troy's parents climbed into an old sedan and drove away. Troy disappeared into the house.

"Now what?" Dennis asked.

"We wait," I said. I hadn't seen all those detective shows for nothing. Of course, in detective shows, they'd always thought to bring along hot coffee and binoculars. All we had were some fuzz-covered gummy bears stuck to the rubber floor mat and a few Dr. Seuss books. The van was equipped with a VCR, but it only worked when the engine was going.

Finally, Troy emerged from the house. "He's entered our field of vision," Dennis said, very low. Apparently, I wasn't the only one who'd been watching detective shows.

Troy's BMW was parked in front of the house. He started the motor and zoomed away from the curb and past Marcy's van. She turned the key, put on her blinker and slid smoothly behind him. He zipped through a stop sign. She paused briefly and continued, although not so closely as to arouse suspicion. When he reached the main street, he caught the tail end of a yellow light and sped ahead. Marcy glided to a halt at the now-red light. I looked left. I looked right. "Go," I said.

Marcy stared at me. "It's red."

"There's no one coming."

"That's not the point. It's red. It's illegal to proceed until the traffic light turns green, even if there are no cars coming. And look." She gestured out the windshield. "There's one coming now."

A car passed us in the intersection, then traffic was clear again. "Okay, it's clear." The car remained still. "We're losing him!" I wailed.

Marcy turned to face me. "I am eight months pregnant. I have two children at home who depend on me. I'm sorry if I'm a failure as a sleuth, but I am not about to break the law!"

"Um, Marcy?" Dennis piped up from behind.

"Yes?"

"It's green now."

We lost him, of course. We circled around and came up empty.

We retreated to Jitters for some coffee. Dennis did his best to be chipper. Marcy turned stony. I just kept muttering about how this was my last chance.

And then he walked in. Just like that! It seemed improbable, impossible, really, but it wasn't all that surprising when you considered just how few places there were to go in this town.

"It's him!" I hissed. Dennis was so surprised, he splashed some mocha latté out of his oversized mug. Marcy looked shocked, too. In the interest of speed she shoved the rest of her brownie into her mouth. Once she gave birth, she'd probably be on Weight Watchers for the rest of her life. Until then, she wasn't going to miss out on a single pastry.

He walked to the counter. Bypassing the counter girl, he spoke to the short, muscular guy manning the espresso machine. They had their heads bent together for maybe thirty seconds before he left.

"He didn't get any coffee," Dennis said in wonderment.

"This is big," Marcy whispered.

Things went downhill from there. We followed Troy to his decrepit house and sat there for a whole twenty minutes before Marcy had to pee. Dennis waited in the bushes while we drove to the convenience store. Then we returned and waited some more. Finally, we made Marcy turn on the van so we could watch *Toy Story* on the VCR. After that, we watched something that featured a talking mouse. Marcy made two more trips to the convenience store and one to Taco Bell. After downing burritos and super-sized colas, we took turns visiting the convenience store bathroom. "You'll need these," Marcy said, shoving a box of travel tissues at me before I made my pilgrimage. "I finished off the T.P."

Troy's light was on, so we knew he was there. But he was going nowhere fast. At midnight, Marcy said, "How about we take turns watching? I'll do the first lookout. You can catch some sleep."

I sighed. "You should get home. I'll come back later in my car."

Marcy was silent. Dennis was silent, too, but that was because he was sprawled out in the last row of seats, fast asleep.

"Dan and I had a fight," Marcy finally said. "I called him from the Quick Mart and told him I might be out all night on a stakeout. He said I was acting like an adolescent in the midst of a midlife crisis."

"That's an oxymoron," I said.

"I pointed that out. I also said he pulls all-nighters all the time. And that tomorrow's Saturday and maybe it wouldn't kill him to spend a little time with his sons. He said that he was thinking about going into the office tomorrow, and since I'm the primary caretaker, it is up to me to be home whatever day of the week it is."

We were quiet. Dennis started to snore. I took Marcy's hands. "You pretty much have to stay."

"I think I do."

We got lucky. Troy turned out his light at one-thirty. I was all set to give up when I grabbed Marcy's hand. "Wait!" In the dim light, we saw him walk a half a block past his Beemer and unlock a beat-up blue van. "The chase is on," I murmured, sounding far less cool than I'd intended.

We didn't have to drive far. Mercifully, we hit only green lights. Troy turned onto a quiet street not far from Dean Archer's house and pulled into the driveway of a raised ranch with a few lights burning inside. It didn't exactly fit the stereotype of a whorehouse, but I suppose any house could work as long as it had enough bedrooms.

I wondered why he didn't simply go to the front door instead of slipping around to the back. We pulled around the corner and slid to a quiet stop. We checked Dennis and then left him in the car like a sleeping baby we were reasonably sure wouldn't wake up.

The street was a little short on bushes to hide behind, but the house next door to the raised ranch (which was merely a ranch and, in this light, appeared to be some unnatural shade of green) boasted a Little Tikes log cabin in the backyard. We squeezed inside (Marcy just made it) and peered out the window.

"Now what?" Marcy asked.

"Now we wait until we see a john or a prostitute show up."

"And then what?"

I chewed my lip. "I haven't gotten that far. I'm not even sure this is the whorehouse. It could just be a meeting spot."

"I've never liked the word *whore*," she said. "Prostitute sounds less seedy. More like a job description and less a statement of character." She ran her finger along the log cabin's textured siding. "Maybe I should get one of these little cabins for the kids."

I stared at her. "It's *plastic!*"

"You're such a snob."

"You're the one who lives in Newton. I don't think they even allow these things in Newton."

She grabbed my arm. "Look!"

Next door, a short, solid guy with his head down, hands in pockets, slipped through the back door of the lit house.

"The coffee guy?" Marcy asked. I nodded. "Now what?" she whispered.

"I wish you'd stop asking me that."

"Maybe we should wait until a girl comes out. And then we tail her."

"We're good at that," I said.

We feared our stakeout in the plastic log cabin, which lacked so much as a plastic chair, would stretch until morning, but only a few minutes passed before Troy came scurrying out the back door.

"No girl," Marcy said.

"No, but he's got . . . a TV!"

The short guy appeared a few minutes later, carting some rectangular electronic contraptions. "VCR," I guessed. "And maybe a DVD."

"We have one of those," Marcy whispered. "But I've never figured out how to use it. Besides, most of the kids' movies are on video, and I don't want to march out and buy a whole new set on DVD."

"Do you think they're shooting porn in there?" I ventured. "And Troy's going back to his place to check out the movies?"

Marcy squinted at me. "Porn movies? Would you get your mind out of the gutter? They are not making porn movies. *Duh*! They're *robbing* the place."

I stared at her. The *duh* was unnecessary, I thought, but she was right. We'd just uncovered the culprits behind the recent spate of burglaries.

When the thieves slipped into the house again, we scurried out of the cabin and back onto the street. Well, I scurried; Marcy lumbered. She really was huge. I was half expecting a movie moment where she clutched her belly and moaned, "The baby is coming!" But she just farted a couple of times and murmured something like, "Wait till I tell Dan about this!"

Dennis was a little hurt that we didn't include him in the chase (that's what we called it, although I suppose it was more of a stalk), but he found some consolation in being able to accompany us to the police station. "I know it's a total cliché, but I just love a man in uniform," he confided.

We'd called the police from Marcy's cell phone and then, on their instructions, drove to the Mercer Police Station. "We don't get to see the takedown?" Marcy asked.

"Do you really want these guys to know who turned them in?" I asked her. "They might even take down your license plate." Her eyes grew big. The police station would be just fine.

We filed a witness report, although it was merely a formality. Responding to our tip, the police were able to catch Troy and his partner with their hands in the cookie jar. I mean that literally: that's where the homeowners, who were out of town, kept their spare cash.

Burglary wasn't Troy's only vice. In the van's glove compartment, the cops found enough cocaine "to light up a herd of elephants." Apparently, Troy had used his pawn-shop profits to invest in drugs, which he sold on campus for an enormous profit.

I tried to be vague about my reasons for staking out Troy in the first place, but I finally came clean: I was an undercover reporter, following an unrelated story at Mercer College. I tried to leave it at that, but then I noticed that they weren't smiling at me as much anymore or thanking me for finding the elusive burglars. I finally freed myself by dropping Dean Archer's name and recommending they call him in the morning.

As we left the station, I was flooded with elation. I had my crime story, and it wasn't tawdry or dirty. I had helped the police and the community. I could pretend that I had come to Mercer to report on the lives of college students and had merely stumbled upon a bigger story.

I was free.

thirty-five

When I crept into our darkened room, I was afraid I would interrupt Tiffany with yet another anonymous man, but she was sprawled out on top of her pink bedspread, alone and fully clothed. Had she added binge drinking to her list of newfound vices? At least it wouldn't give her any diseases, I reasoned—in the short term, anyway.

I retrieved my laptop from my desk and unhooked the modem. The cord fell with a crash against my metal wastebasket. I swore softly and checked Tiffany. To my relief, she didn't stir.

The library was empty. For Parents Weekend, the students were all tucked into bed early, their bellies full of chicken cordon bleu or salmon if they were lucky enough to have parents who took them to a real restaurant, or with chewy roast beef if they were like the rest of us.

I found a carrel and plugged in my computer. I was

physically exhausted but mentally buzzing. I braced myself for the usual panic that hits whenever I start something new, but it didn't come. I'd been preparing myself for this moment for months now and couldn't wait to get to the end.

> Mercer, Massachusetts is the quintessential college town: small and picturesque, with white clapboard houses and centuries-old trees. The college that bears its name does the town aesthetic justice. With a central green flanked by looming brick and marble buildings, it has the feel of a miniature Harvard and the aspirations of becoming another Williams or Amherst. Appearances can be deceiving, however.

I went on to make less-than-flattering remarks about the student body, which I described as being "generally white and affluent, frequently spoiled." I referenced the flashy autos, the gold cards, the flat-screen computers.

> But for some students, the goodies are never enough. Perhaps they look with envy at students even wealthier than themselves. Or maybe they are so bored with privilege that they find themselves irresistibly drawn to society's underbelly.

The story of Troy's accomplice was especially tantalizing—and frightening:

> As for Robert Sanchez, he turned his job of reliable coffee maker into village spy. He knew his regulars: who they were, what they drank, where they lived. When

faithful customers failed to show up for a daily cappuccino, he would stake out their houses to see if they were merely sick or, as he'd hoped, out of town.

From there, I described the spate of household robberies plaguing Mercer and ended with my own heroic role in ousting the culprit—who just happened to be Mercer's premier drug dealer. I left out the Little Tikes log cabin.

As I finished proofreading the article for the second time, the sky outside the library turned a murky gray, signaling the approach of a nasty New England autumn morning. I typed a quick message to Tim, attached the file, and sent my story out over the Internet.

Trudging back to the dorm, I realized just how exhausted I was. Perhaps now I could finally collapse.

Tiffany looked just as she had when I'd left her: fully clothed and sprawled out on top of her pink bedspread. There was just enough gray light leaking through the warped metal Venetian blinds to allow me to grope my way around the room. I should have been tired, but I'd passed the exhaustion mark long ago and continued to feed off my adrenaline buzz. I looked at my hard little bed. I hated it. Never, ever did I want to sleep there again. My first impulse was to simply run for it: pack up my computer and a few other essentials and hit the road. In two hours, I could crawl between my cold Egyptian cotton sheets, stroke the dense, natural weave of my comforter, and fall into a long, deep sleep, uninterrupted by shouts, music or carnal encounters. Later I could sneak back for the rest of my things, perhaps when Tiffany was out (for all her unseemly behavior of late, she never missed a class).

My laptop and I got halfway down the hall before I

recognized the stupidity of this plan: better to sleep now, pack later and make a clean, final break. Later, I would wonder what would have happened if I had followed my impulse to flee.

I took my plastic bucket down to the bathroom, where I scrubbed my teeth and washed my face. Free of makeup, my face looked suddenly older, and I wondered if any of my dorm-mates had ever noticed the fine lines around my eyes. They were tiny but hardly invisible and fully inexplicable on the face of an eighteen-year-old.

Back in the room, I shrugged into my barely-there nightgown, the only thing I could stand to wear in this chronically overheated building. Suddenly the exhaustion that had been crouching in the corners of my body leapt out. My eyes and limbs ached with fatigue. I wondered how long I'd have before Tiffany, an incorrigible morning person, popped out of bed and opened every drawer and door until she was sure she had awakened me. It was with that black thought that I took one last look at her before slumping onto my bed. I wanted to see if her sleep was showing any signs of lightening, how long I had until she'd wake up.

The room was brighter now, the light for once more yellow than gray. I'd sometimes thought that Tiffany was prettier asleep than awake, her complexion all pink and white and smooth, her rosebud mouth free of tension, her too-small eyes peacefully closed. But something was wrong. I should have noticed it earlier. Tiffany was not the sort to pass out on her bed. Tiffany was the sort to arrange her pillows just so, to place a glass of cold, clear water on the bookshelf behind her bed, to smooth her sheets around her until there was barely a wrinkle. The light was no longer gray, but her face still was.

I crept over to her bed. Hardly breathing myself, I bent my ear next to her mouth. I thought I heard something, but I couldn't be sure.

"Tiffany?" I whispered. Louder now: "Tiffany?" Nothing.

I grasped her arm, gently at first, then harder. "Tiffany? Wake up!" I was shaking her now, squeezing her arms and rocking her from side to side. She was warm, I noticed in some corner of my brain. Still warm.

Hours later, at the small local hospital where Tiffany had her stomach pumped, they let me see her. She was still sleeping but noticeably pinker. On my way out, I recognized a guy from the emergency crew who had come to our room with a stretcher. I asked him what I'd said when I'd called. I honestly couldn't remember. "You said your roommate had killed herself," he told me.

"I thought she had."

There should be a lot more to say: about the outpouring of sympathy, about Tiffany's recovery, about my acceptance of responsibility or at least of deeper empathy. I should be able to tell you about a later encounter, a nice lunch, perhaps, when a more-mature Tiffany made her peace with a more-mature me. Maybe I should tell you how we became friends, with me acting as the big sister I never was and that Tiffany never had. But the truth is, I never saw her again. And though I was almost giddily relieved that there still was a Tiffany not to see, once I'd sent a short, sympathetic note to her parents' house in Buffalo, where Tiffany was sent for "psychological healing," I felt downright euphoric at the idea of a Tiffany-free future.

Still, it is hard to put her out of my mind. There are times when I am driving, or grocery shopping, or trying to fall asleep, and the what-ifs shoot uncontrolled through my brain. What if she'd taken prescription sleeping pills instead of the over-the-counter kind. What if she'd used a razor blade. A noose. A gun. What if I'd driven away, or fallen asleep. What if I had simply been her friend.

Statistics tell us that, while four times as many women as men attempt suicide, four times as many men actually succeed. I tell myself that Tiffany didn't really want to die, that her act was a cry for help. The alternative scenario is just too cruel: that the botched attempt was simply one more of Tiffany's failures.

Most of the hall slept through the whole thing. It was Saturday morning, after all. When the emergency medical technicians had left, I considered crawling into bed. But if I'd hated that room before, now it was unbearable. I left behind my posters, the bedspread and some of the duller textbooks. The rest of my things I stuffed into my wooden crates, and, when those were full, into plastic trash bags. I hauled the lot out to my tiny car and sped away through the chilly morning.

I got back to Boston in just under two hours, a new—and final—record. I found a parking spot quickly; Saturday mornings, the streets are emptier than usual. I hauled my stuff up the stairs in three trips. Once I'd locked the apartment door behind me, I made a final call to the local hospital to make sure that Tiffany was going to be okay. They told me that she was awake and that the college had called her parents.

It was ten o'clock in the morning. Jeremy would be waking up just about now. He was the last thing I thought of before I fell into a dull, heavy sleep.

thirty-six

"I hate it," Richard said. "I HATE IT."

I stared at him and took a few deep breaths to keep from crying. "It has everything," I said, my sweaty hands gripping the sides of the molded plastic chair. "Youth, crime, drugs. Class warfare. A chase scene. Even a surprise ending." My voice quivered like a little girl's. "It has *everything*."

He stood up and leaned over his pretentious desk. His cologne assaulted my nose. His nostrils were so close, I could see the curly gray hairs that needed trimming. "It. Has. No. SEX."

I took another deep breath. And another. When that didn't work, I chose a focal point: a lighthouse on one of the magazine covers that hung behind his desk. At least I'd taken something from all those childbirth discussions Marcy's friends were always having. "Perhaps you underestimate the American public. Perhaps they want more than sex."

He collapsed in his chair and laughed meanly. He rubbed his hand over his face, then shook his head and stared at the ceiling in haughty bafflement. "No one ever lost money from underestimating the American public." He leveled his gaze. "And you can quote me on that."

He pushed his speakerphone button, and the dial tone blared. He rifled through his Rolodex, hit the buttons, producing a series of high-pitched beeps. The phone rang once before being answered by a crisp, "Tim McAllister."

"Tim. Richard here."

There was a long, pained sigh on the other end, followed by a resigned, "Yeah."

"You got Kathy's story," Richard said, more a statement than a question, though I hadn't actually told Richard that I'd e-mailed the piece in the early hours of Sunday morning.

"Got it."

Richard narrowed his eyes at me. "And?"

For a moment I held out hope. What did Richard know? The man only held a position of power because of smarter ancestors. Tim would come through, if not personally, at least professionally. Finally he spoke. "I don't know what she was thinking. We never talked about any burglary story."

Richard leaned toward me and tried to hold my gaze. I picked a new focal point, this time a black scuff mark on the wood floor. Richard's shoes were always too shiny. "And now that you've had a chance to read the final version, what do you think? Was it worth all that time and expense?"

Tim's laugh lacked mirth. "Maybe we can sell it to the *Mercer Weekly Gazette* for twenty bucks. If there is a *Mercer Weekly Gazette*. Seriously, Richard, I don't know what to say. I thought Kathy could pull this off. Obviously, I made a mistake."

They said their good-byes, and Richard hung up. My breathing was completely out of control. I was hyperventilating. "I'm sorry that the crime I uncovered wasn't tawdry enough for you," I said, finally.

"You were sent on an assignment, and you blew it." For once, he spoke softly. It was far less wonderful than I'd always imagined. "Seven weeks, and you uncovered nothing." He shook his head. "I don't think you even tried."

"I tried." My voice trembled, but not too badly. "I asked questions. I tailed people. I looked around dark corners. And I *did* uncover things. Dean Archer is banging half the girls in the senior class." There. That got his attention. "His wife doesn't have a clue. The administration doesn't have a clue, or if they do, they're pretending not to notice. Don't you get it? *There is no prostitution ring*. There never was. That girl in Tim's office was making it up." I sat up as straight as I could manage and forced myself to look at Richard's face. "The burglary was all I had to go with. I didn't write about a sex scandal because there *was* no sex scandal."

He stared at me. I really, really wanted him to yell. Finally he hit that goddamn speakerphone button again. The blaring tone made me jump. He pushed another button, and eleven tones raced past each other: redial.

"Tim McAllister."

"I've got Kathy here," Richard said.

"Kathy," Tim said evenly.

"I was here before. When Richard called you." My voice did that preadolescent squeak thing again.

He was silent, undoubtedly trying to recall the exact words he'd said. "Ah," he said, finally.

"Remember Dean Archer?" Richard asked.

"Sure," Tim said, slowly, watching his words. "I had to convince him to let Kathy in."

"What did you think of him?"

"Where are you going with this?"

"Just play along." Richard's essential smarminess was returning.

"He was, you know, normal. Boring but nice."

"According to Kathy, he's fucking half the senior class."

Tim was quiet for a moment, and then he laughed. It was not a pretty sound.

"I exaggerated," I said. "I only saw him with two girls. And one may not have been a senior."

"Even better," Richard said. "Two girls in, what? Seven weeks? Impressive."

"If such things impress you," I murmured.

"Tell Tim how you got your information," Richard instructed.

I should have just walked away. My career at *Salad* was over, that much was clear. But I still felt the need to save face, to show I'd done my job and dug my dirt. I still felt the need to prove myself to Tim, even if he was turning out to be a bigger shit than I ever imagined. "Once I was walking around the campus in the middle of the night— you know, to see if anything seemed out of place." This was the time I was skittering home from the library, terrified of my own shadow and wishing I'd packed a rape whistle. "I heard some rustling in the bushes, so I hid in the shadows until I could see who it was."

"And it was Dean Archer?" Richard asked.

"Yes."

"You're sure?"

"Pretty sure. It looked like him. It looked like his car. He was with this dark-haired girl. He kissed her good night."

"And the other time?"

"There were two other times, but once was with the same girl. At least I think it was the same. I didn't really get a good look at her the first time. I went to his house to drop off a book, you know, just to stick it in the mail slot when I thought everyone was out. As I got near the house, he drove up. I was about to say something, when I saw her come from the side of the house and scurry into the garage with him. She must have been waiting. The dogs barked like mad."

"They did it with dogs?" Richard asked, sounding positively gleeful. Honestly, the man is both a moron and a pervert.

"The garage has a door that leads into the house," I said. "It's less obvious than the front door. And the dogs they keep in the garage are less psychotic than the dog they keep in the backyard."

"Did you look in the windows?" Tim asked.

"No!"

"Do you know who the girl was?"

"No. But I saw her going into an upper-class dorm, so she must be a junior or senior."

"And the other time?" Richard asked steadily.

"Brynn," I said, my voice gaining strength. I could make it appear that I'd learned everything I had about

Brynn through my unquenchable journalistic curiosity and not because she used to be hot and heavy with my boyfriend. My ex-boyfriend. That young guy who I'd gotten naked with against my better judgment.

"Does Brynn have a last name?" Richard asked.

"Spalding," I said. "She's from Pennsylvania. I thought she might be involved in the prostitution ring—before I discovered that there was no prostitution ring. So I tailed her until I found her waiting for Dean Archer."

"In his house?" Richard asked hopefully.

"A restaurant, two towns away."

"Maybe he was just talking to her about her classes."

"Maybe."

"Where'd they go next?"

"How should I know? I left after that."

Richard exhaled, clearly fighting the impulse to scold me for not being more of a voyeur. "Anything else?"

"That's already more than I ever wanted to see."

"How do you know the girls aren't prostitutes?" Tim asked.

"I don't," I admitted. "That was the first thing I thought of, but—I don't think so. I saw nothing to indicate this was anything more than an affair. Well, two affairs."

"What about Archer's wife?" Tim asked, his voice flat.

"I don't think she knows." I'd always assumed Tim had been faithful during our time together; suddenly, I wasn't so sure.

"But what's her story? She wife number one?"

"Two at least. Possibly three. Younger than he is but a lot older than these girls. He's got kids from previous marriages. She's got dogs. The dogs get more attention than the kids from what I've seen. I have a feeling he left his last wife for her, but I don't know that for a fact." I finally recognized the gnawing feeling in my stomach. I'd been mistaking it for humiliation, but at some point it had morphed into fear. "Why are you so interested in Dean Archer?" I asked slowly.

Richard shrugged. "Always enjoy a good bit of gossip."

thirty-seven

Despite their original agreement to give *New Nation* the edge, Tim and Richard released the story on the same day, three weeks after I had cleaned out my desk and said goodbye to my co-workers. In lieu of the usual catboat or sand dune, *Salad*'s cover pictured university gates (not Mercer's, I noted), along with the heading, "Sex on Campus: The Story of a Dean, Two Students, and an Undercover Reporter."

I called Tim the minute I got back from the newsstand, hating the fact that I still knew his number by heart.

"You used me," I said.

"If you had done your job in the first place, I wouldn't have had to."

"How could you stoop so low?" I asked, my voice cracking. "Do you know what this is going to do to his wife? To those girls?" In an afternoon on campus, Tim had discovered the second girl's name: Missy. He had even gotten her to talk to him about the affair after telling her that she wasn't Dean Archer's only "little friend."

"The guy's a slime," Tim said. "He deserves to be exposed."

"Oh, *he's* a slime? What about you? What the hell were you doing kissing me when you were going out with Jennifer?"

"I wasn't going out with her yet. And besides, I was drunk."

"That's the best you can do? *Because I was drunk?*"

"That's the best I can do," he said quietly.

Finally, I took a deep breath and said what I should have said years ago. "Fuck you!" I yelled and slammed down the phone.

Dennis and I were three and a half hours into a Home and Garden Television Network marathon when the doorbell rang. For the first time in two years, my gut didn't cry out, "Tim!" I no longer dreamed that he would show up unannounced some night, begging for forgiveness. He was not the type to beg, I now realized. And I'd gone past the point of forgiveness.

Had I been alone, I wouldn't have answered the door. It was pushing eleven o'clock at night: too late for kids selling candy or missionaries selling God—not that I'd be inclined to let them in, either. But with Dennis, I felt safe. In the four weeks since I'd rejoined the adult world, we had spent a lot of time together. We talked about everything: men, upholstery, careers, shoes. He was recovering from an unrequited crush on his boss, John, while I, of course, was trying to repair my broken heart, though who had broken it was up for debate. Dennis was like a woman, only better because he could double as a bodyguard or wedding date. Also, he'd helped me redo my living room. Now the walls were taupe, the armoire and coffee table a flat, distressed black. We'd stuck some black and white postcards in oversized white mats and hung them in a straight line, gallery style. Dennis had even brought over his sewing machine—despite all my years of doling out decorating advice, I never did learn to sew—which he used to make denim slipcovers for my couch and chair and sumptuous throw pillows in red Southwestern prints.

I was making the most of my unemployment.

"You want me to get it?" Dennis asked. I looked at the door and almost said no, but curiosity got the better of me.

"Do you mind?"

"Of course not, honey." I love this man. I really do.

It was Jeremy. I stared at him from my perch on the denim couch. He stared back. Then he looked at Dennis, who gaped at him with naked lust.

"Dennis, this is Jeremy," I finally squeaked.

Dennis turned his head to look at me, blinked twice and regained his composure. We had already reached an agreement about men. He got all the gays, and I got all the straights. The bisexuals, neither of us wanted to touch.

"I was just leaving," Dennis said breathlessly.

"I'll tape the end," I said. We were nearing "the reveal" on our favorite design show, and while I appreciated his quick exit, I didn't want to push the limits of our friendship.

"Don't worry about it," he said solemnly.

I nodded, speechless. Dennis was a true friend.

After he had gone, Jeremy continued to stand by the

door, looking around the apartment but not at me. I stood up but stayed near the sofa. In a larger apartment, we would have been really far apart. As it was, only a few feet separated us, but it felt like miles.

"Nice apartment," he said, finally.

"Dennis is just a friend," I said.

Jeremy shrugged. "Well, yeah. It was pretty obvious that he was gay."

"Right," I said. Clearly, mine was the weakest gaydar on earth.

Jeremy's hair had grown a bit in the past month, making it even curlier and more unruly. He wore a plain navy sweatshirt over frayed jeans and high-tops. At the college, he'd looked comparatively mature. Here in my apartment, he looked soft with youth. I wasn't sure if my urge to take him in my arms was carnal or maternal. The confusion was unsettling.

"Do you want to sit down?" I asked.

He shook his head and looked at the floor.

"Can I get you anything to drink?"

He shook his head again.

"Food?"

"No."

I sank into my couch. He stayed rooted to his spot by the door. "I'm sorry I lied to you," I said.

He looked up. "I don't take it personally." He held my eyes. "You lied to everyone."

I willed myself not to cry. "I was doing my job," I said without conviction. "Chasing a story that never came to anything. All that stuff about the dean—I didn't write it, and I never meant for it to be printed."

He snorted. "Right. So you were just hanging with us

for—what was it? A slice of life? To see if times had changed?"

I shook my head. "That was the official story. Truth is, I was chasing a rumor. Turned out to be false. This girl who'd gone to Mercer said there was a prostitution ring on campus. I got this stupid idea that Brynn and those other girls might be involved. So I followed her." I picked up one of my lovely red-patterned pillows and clutched it to my belly like a shield against guilt. "I never meant for anyone to get hurt."

"She's dropped out of school," Jeremy said. "Brynn."

"I'm sorry," I whispered. "Maybe she'll finish up somewhere else. No one outside of Mercer will even remember the story."

"It made it into the Boston *Herald*."

"Page twelve. Below the fold. Nobody read it, trust me. And if they did, they've already forgotten." Richard might never get over the fact that the wires hadn't picked up the story about Dean Archer's liaisons. Last I'd heard, he and Tim were still fighting over who was responsible for my expenses. Tim said Richard had agreed to share them from the beginning; Richard said that Tim had assured him there was a story worth investigating.

"Brynn's parents divorced the year before she left for college," Jeremy said. "She's a nice girl but—how do I say this? Emotionally unsteady. And a little too fond of sticking stuff up her nose. All those girls she hung out with were. She was trying to get clean, but now . . . I don't know."

"Are you still in love with her?" I squeaked stupidly.

He laughed, but not in a nice way. "Is that why you did this to her? Because you were jealous?"

"No!" I said. I wasn't, was I? "I never even wanted to go

undercover. And I'm sorry I did. I'm sorry I hurt Brynn.
I'm sorry I hurt you."

"I'm fine," he said evenly.

We were quiet for a while. My heart was thudding. My
armpits were damp. "Why did you come here?" I asked
softly.

He shrugged. "It all seemed so unreal. Like, I'd just
imagined you and you'd never really existed."

"I was real."

He shook his head slowly. "I don't think you were." He
turned and reached for the doorway, pulled the door open
and stopped. He turned back halfway. "The hookers are run
out of The Snake Pit," he said to the door. "Guy named
Gerry is the pimp. Brynn was never involved." He turned
his head slowly, bore into me with his green-gold eyes.
"You could have just asked me. I would have told you."

And then he was gone.

A few days later, the Boston *Herald* proclaimed,
"Dog Mauls Mercer College Dean." Below, in smaller but
still-bold type, it read, "Dog Trainer Wife May Have
Planned Attack Following Public Revelations of Adul-
tery." Not only was the story on the front page, it was
above the fold. Actually, it was below the fold, too. It was
the whole page. The *Globe* ran the story, too, though less
conspicuously. It had some useless old stories about global
warming and Middle Eastern bombings on page one.

I called a couple of my friends at *Salad*, but all they
could tell me was that Richard had been behind closed
doors all day. I called Sheila.

"I've been meaning to call you," she squeaked as soon as she heard my voice.

"It's okay," I said.

"No, it's not," she said. "You're my friend. I know you and Richard have had your differences, but that doesn't change anything between you and me."

"Thanks," I said, not knowing what else to say.

"I keep hoping you'll show up at the gym," she said.

"I go during the day now. It's less crowded. And someone less annoying than Stacey teaches the aerobics class."

"Right," she said, her voice trailing off. Then, "So . . . no job yet?"

"No," I said. "But I've got some good leads." Also known as the help wanted section.

"If you ever need a recommendation . . ."

"Right." The silence grew uncomfortable, and I was about to hang up when I remembered why I'd called in the first place. "Did Richard see the paper this morning?"

"Oh, yeah. He can't decide whether it's good news or bad news."

"How could it possibly be good?" Leave it to Richard to find a silver lining in a broken marriage, a ruined career, a humiliated, possibly felonious wife, and a disfigured man on life support.

"Well, he's happy to get *Salad*'s name out there. But he's not so happy with the way it was described."

" 'A regional, lightweight, ad-heavy magazine with national pretensions?' " I quoted.

"Something like that." One of the papers described *New Nation* as "a redundant Internet 'zine' with little funding and less attention."

"Richard's been on the phone all morning," Sheila continued. "Trying to sell the rights to the story."

"What story? *My* story?"

"Of *course* not," she gushed. "Just the information he picked up on his own. Not many people know this, but Richard is a gifted journalist."

thirty-eight

Sometimes things have to get worse before they get better. I thought I'd reached bottom, but I was wrong. While I sat home, eating microwave brownies and drinking wine (I seemed to like it sweet these days), the local papers and television stations followed the Archer's story. Then, because it was a slow news week, the story finally hit the national media with a new twist. "How far will the media go to uncover a scandal?" asked one major newspaper. Another proclaimed that "*Salad* magazine, a heretofore unknown regional monthly, sent a reporter out to search for scandal—any scandal—at a quiet college campus. Not surprisingly, she found it."

Among all the reports, the gist was the same: I had gone undercover for no good reason. I had uncovered marital infidelity ("Hardly a newsworthy item in this day of disposable marriages" commented one editorial, ignoring the dean/student issue). My publisher and *New Nation*, "*Salad*'s Internet arm" (Tim would hate that, I noted with a rare smile), had tried to make a splash with the story and failed. "No one paid any attention—except the university trustees, who are in the process of terminating Archer, and, of course, his wife, who is being held in a local jail under charges of aggravated assault."

As much as the media condemned our muckraking, they positively delighted in the whole dog-mauling angle. They talked about previous dog-mauling incidents and their legal ramifications. They described Dean Archer's injuries in repulsive detail. They quoted dog psychologists. I'd never even known there were dog psychologists. Or, rather, I'd heard of them but always assumed they were an urban myth. There was a lot of speculation as to whether Mrs. Archer had truly sicced the dog on the dean or whether she had simply failed to call him off. All surmised, however, that the question would have been moot had *Salad* magazine never come digging at her doorstep. "Could a lawsuit be imminent?" One asked. I made a frantic call to Dan, who assured me that, while Richard's ass could be on the line, mine was free and clear. Another rare moment of joy.

A couple of reporters waited outside my building. "No comment," I yelped, fleeing back inside. I only vaguely noticed a camera flash. It wasn't long before my "adult" picture was being broadcast alongside my Mercer "pig book" picture. My Mercer picture actually looked slightly more mature; I vowed to get a decent haircut once I got another paycheck. (Richard had given me two weeks' severance, which he had the nerve to call generous.)

On their request, I drove out to Mercer one last time to

make a statement to the police. I reiterated the facts that had come out in the original news story, while making it clear that I had not written the article myself, nor had I agreed to being tape recorded or quoted. In fact, I said, I had initially written a story about the burglaries and about the Mercer Police department's valiant efforts to fight big city crime in a small community. (Okay, perhaps I'd retained a touch of bullshitting ability.) The cops still held me in their good graces for ending the burglary headache. One even suggested I consider an in-depth feature on the department. I said I would sketch out some ideas and call them if I could find an especially punchy angle. I was telling the truth, believe it or not; unless I landed a salaried position, I would have to scrape by as a freelancer.

The police station was less than a mile from campus. I drove the mile with my brain turned off. I found a spot outside the dorm and turned off the car. But I didn't get out. I told myself I just wanted to see it one last time, for closure. But I've never been good at deceiving myself. I was staking out the dormitory in hopes of seeing Jeremy.

After fifteen minutes, Katherine strode by with some guy I didn't recognize. They walked with their hips bumping, their hands in each other's back jeans pocket. I slumped in my seat, and she didn't see me. Five minutes later, Amelia passed with a guy from our dorm. Tanner? Trevor? Something like that. He was small and fair and bookish. He and Amelia wore identical navy blue backpacks that seemed too heavy for their small frames. He looked at Amelia intently and briefly stroked her hair, which was growing out and not nearly as spiky as before. Then they, too, disappeared into the dorm. All I had to do was open my car door and run up behind them—"Hold the door!" (I'd left my key on my dorm room desk)—and I'd be back in my old world, Katie again, wise beyond my years. Except I couldn't, of course. If Jeremy were any indication, I was hardly a hero in these parts.

I tried to imagine Jeremy, what he would be wearing, who he would be with. That's what got me. What if he showed up with Brynn? But no: he'd told me she'd dropped out. Still, there were plenty of other pretty, age-appropriate girls vying to walk along with their hand in Jeremy's back pocket.

I turned my key in the ignition and headed away from the campus. On impulse, I pulled into Chantal/Cheryl's parking lot and walked up to her gloomy front door before I lost my nerve.

I was about to leave when the door swung open. She was wearing her flannel bathrobe, her tangled blond hair wet from the shower. "Hey, Woodward—where's Bernstein?" She was the first person in a long time to look pleased to see me.

"Bernstein and I are no longer on speaking terms," I said.

"The nerds are always the biggest assholes. Didn't I warn you?"

She poured me a glass of chilled pinot gris—in a Reidel glass, no less. One of her clients, an unreformed wine snob, had bought her two Reidel glasses for every varietal imaginable. "Aren't you impressed that I know who Woodward and Bernstein are?" she asked.

"Not really. You always struck me as being smart," I said, surprising myself with the truth of my statement.

"Yeah, whatever." She took a sip from her own over-sized glass (perfect for her pinot noir). "One of my regulars, he teaches this class, Ethics in Journalism? He likes to stand up and lecture to me while I sit on a chair and pretend to be one of his students. And, like, listening to him talk about Joe Klein or something gets me so hot that I start taking off my shirt, then my bra. And I rub my nipples and start to moan like this: *Ooohh . . . Mmmmnnn*." She smirked. "Then he tells me to pay attention or he's gonna fail me. And so I say, 'I'm so sorry, Professor, it won't happen again.' But he says it's too late, he has to punish me. So he drops his pants and I blow him."

She shrugged, took a healthy gulp of her wine, and flicked some lint off her bathrobe.

I gawked at her. "Ethics in Journalism? I took that class."

"How was it?"

I thought for a moment. "You know, now that I think about it, the instructor did always seem kind of distracted."

I took another gulp of my wine and put the mostly full glass on her coffee table. I stood up to leave. "I don't think I'll be coming back to Mercer, but I was just wondering, and this is nothing I'm going to write about, but was there ever any hooking going on at the college?"

She hesitated. "A couple more trips to Denny's and I probably would have told you."

"Gerry?" I asked. "The Snake Pit?"

She smiled. "You found out anyway. Figured you would—hotshot reporter and all. I saw your picture in the paper." She sounded genuinely impressed, which made me feel even more ashamed.

I felt like I should press a wad of money in her hand, offer her some kind of ticket out of her life of desperation. But the truth was, she probably had more money than I did. And she didn't look so desperate.

"Take care," I said lamely.

She tucked a damp lock of hair behind her ear. "I'll be okay. You take care."

I had only one more thing to do before heading back to the city, and I half expected myself to chicken out. If I'd seen anyone I'd recognized, I would have fled, no question, but when I walked into The Human Canvas, the place was empty except for the legendary Thor. True to reputation, a tattooed snake slithered over the bridge of his nose. His right bicep read, MOTHER. Sweet, except when he turned, I read the left bicep: FUCKER.

"You do belly buttons?" I asked.

thirty-nine

"How could I have missed it?" Dennis and I were eating salads at an old, crowded McDonald's. I couldn't believe I had fallen this far. "I mean, I met Gerry," I said, spearing a cucumber. "I thought he was a sleaze. And yet it never even crossed my mind that he might be involved."

"Tim didn't exactly help," Dennis said. Dennis had never met Tim, but he hated him nonetheless. "He told Gerry you were reporters. You never really had a chance. How's your salad?"

"Crappy. Yours?"

"Crappy. We should have gotten french fries."

"Tim's not entirely to blame," I said, stirring the excessive ice in my oversized Diet Coke. "I got so fixated on Troy and Brynn and the Red Hots. Something could have been going on right under my nose and I wouldn't have noticed."

"What could have been going on? What could you have possibly seen?"

"I don't know," I said. "Something out of the ordinary. Girls coming and going at odd hours."

"In college, everyone comes and goes at odd hours," Dennis said. "Next time, will you please let me take you out to lunch?"

"You took me out once this week already."

"If you won't do it for yourself, do it for me." He reached over with his plastic fork and took a bite of my California Cobb salad. "I think yours is better."

"You can have it," I said, shoving the plastic container over. "I'm too depressed to eat."

"Oh, shit," Dennis said, pulling out his silver cell phone. "There's this potential client John told me to suck up to, and I totally forgot to call him this morning. Do you mind?"

"Of course not," I said, as he punched in the numbers.

"I swear," he mumbled, "sometimes it feels like John is my pimp."

I started to smile and suddenly froze. "Oh my God," I gasped. Dennis looked quizzically at me as he asked for the client, who was, not surprisingly, out to lunch.

"What?" He asked as he closed his phone.

"It was right in front of me the whole time."

Dennis swore it was the most exciting opportunity of his lifetime. I was afraid of pushing him into something he didn't want to do. I knew how that felt.

"I want to do it," he said. "I swear. Can I wear a wire?"

"I'm not the FBI, Dennis. I don't have a wire." I did have

the mini tape recorder I used for interviews, though.

I picked Dennis up after work, and we battled our way through Boston traffic. Mercer seemed even farther away than usual.

Main Street was dark and quiet. I dropped Dennis off in front of The Snake Pit. I didn't dare go inside; Gerry had a good memory for faces.

I spent the next hour and a half at the Denny's by the highway, where I wolfed down a BLT and nursed a sweet cup of lukewarm tea. I looked around for Cheryl or her friend the hostess. They weren't there. I opened a novel and tried to concentrate but couldn't. Outside, vehicle lights shone red, white and yellow as they whizzed along the highway.

Finally, my cell phone rang. Dennis was at the gas station.

I pulled into a parking space and turned off the car. "You were right!" he said as soon as he'd closed the door.

I took a deep breath. "I was hoping I was wrong. Did you see her?"

He shuddered. "More than I really wanted to, if you know what I mean."

Here's what happened: when Dennis entered The Snake Pit, he sat at the bar, just as Tim and I had done last summer. He ordered a beer from Gerry ("I really wanted a Lemon Drop martini, but I thought that might seem too gay"), who asked, "You new around here?"

"Just passing through." Dennis glanced from side to side as if he were afraid of being overheard. "I'm kind of lonely right now," he stage-whispered.

After a bit of back and forth, Gerry finally cracked. "There's a college here in town, and some of the girls, they're pretty friendly. I can make an introduction if you want."

"What kind of girls?" Dennis asked, with a look he described as "B movie heterosexual lust."

"Pretty ones. Clean ones. Tall, short—whatever you want."

Dennis pretended to consider. "Any thin ones? I don't like fat girls. The skinnier, the better."

Gerry's face lit up, and he disappeared to make a call. When he returned, he handed Dennis a slip of paper. "Monique will be waiting for you at this address. Apartment's across from the gas station."

("Monique!" I broke in at this point in the narration. "Couldn't they come up with something a little more original?" Really: you've got to wonder what they call the whores in Paris. Debbie and LeeAnn?)

At any rate, Dennis walked to the apartment. "I almost called you, but I thought that might ruin my cover. Anyway, it wasn't too far. A mile, maybe. It was freezing, though."

When he rang the doorbell to the second-floor apartment, a high nervous voice called out, "Who is it?"

"A friend," Dennis answered. Then, remembering the name he'd given Gerry, he said, "John." ("Fitting," I said.) He pushed the record button on the tape recorder in his overcoat pocket.

She opened the door wearing a short black negligee. "She looked so cold," Dennis said. "No clothes, no fat—" He shuddered. Her pale blond hair hung limply along her heavily made-up face. Her upturned nostrils flared with fear.

"I've been waiting for you," she said, moving aside to let Dennis in. She closed the door behind her.

Dennis took a few steps into the room and smiled shyly, unsure of what to do or say.

"Did Gerry tell you about the scholarship fund?" she squeaked.

"The—what? Oh, right. But I didn't get the, um, the prices."

"They aren't prices," Amber said, digging her painted toes into the brown carpet. "They're donations."

"Right," Dennis said. "And what are the, um, donor levels, exactly?"

"Okay." She cleared her throat. "Fifty dollars makes you a friend. For that, I will be friendly to you."

"How friendly?"

"Quite friendly."

"And would I be, uh, friendly to you?"

"No," she said. "It would be a one-way friendship."

Dennis stuck his hand in his pocket and inched the tape recorder up. "Just so we're clear," he enunciated. "Fifty bucks for a blow job?"

Amber was silent for a moment. Then she continued in a shaky voice, "A hundred dollars would make you an entry-level donor."

There was a pause, then Dennis giggled nervously. "That's actually kind of funny."

Amber was silent. It was not funny to her. "Which do you want?" she asked.

"Is that front-entry or rear-entry?"

"Front only. A hundred dollars."

"Is that . . . all?" Dennis asked. "Are there any other options?"

"From other girls, yes. Not from me. I'm still too . . . new."

"What are the other options?" Dennis asked.

"Look," she said. "If you want someone else, I'll call Gerry. There are girls who will do—they'll do anything. Anything. I'll call Gerry."

"No!" Dennis said. "I just want you. Look." He opened his wallet and pulled out five twenties. "This is for you."

She took the money and nodded. "You want to take off your coat?"

"No, thanks," he said. She looked puzzled. "I mean, not yet."

She nodded. "I'll be right back. Make yourself at home. I mean, comfortable." She disappeared into the bathroom. When she returned, she was naked, her collarbone and ribs jutting out like a starved child's. Which is what she was, really. She began to walk toward Dennis.

"No!" he gasped, retreating. "Please! Put something back on—your nightgown or maybe a robe."

She collapsed on the bed and buried her head in her hands. "It's because I'm too fat, isn't it?"

"No! It's nothing like that," Dennis said, pulling down the bedspread and wrapping it around her bony shoulders. "You're beautiful—really, you are."

She looked up at him, her splotchy face soaked with tears. Snot dripped from her upturned nostrils. Her red lipstick smeared from the left side of her mouth down to her chin. "Do you really think so?"

Dennis crouched down next to her and gazed into her face. "I have a confession to make. I didn't really come here for sex."

Her eyes grew wide. "Oh my God. Are you a cop? Because my parents would kill me if they ever found out."

"No," Dennis assured her, shaking his head. "I'm a writer. I'm, I'm writing this screenplay. About a hook— about a prostitute. Young, beautiful, really a good person."

"Sort of like *Pretty Woman*," Amber whispered.

"Exactly!" Dennis said. "Only a little more introspective. Kind of like *Pretty Woman* meets *My Dinner with Andre*."

"I didn't see that one," Amber said.

"It doesn't matter," Dennis said. "All that matters is that you seem like my heroine. Crystal. You're vulnerable like her. And maybe a little lost."

She looked up with wide eyes and nodded.

"I was thinking," Dennis said. "Maybe I could pay you for your time. Kind of a consulting fee."

She agreed.

Dennis asked if she minded being taped; she said no. (As it turned out, she hadn't been taped without permission, anyway; Dennis's overcoat pocket was too thick to let any sound through.)

"How long have you been doing this?"

"Since October. It hasn't been too many times, though. Gerry says I have to work on, like, getting regulars."

"How many times have you done it?"

"This would have been the sixteenth."

"How much money does Gerry get?"

"Half."

"Half! Doesn't that seem unreasonable?"

"I kind of think so. But the other girls think it's okay. And I'm new, so I don't want to make trouble. It's just till the end of the year, till I graduate. Then I'll move away and it'll be like it never happened, you know?"

"How many girls are there?"

"About a dozen, I think. Gerry doesn't tell us much about each other, but a few of us know each other, and we talk."

"Why do you do it?"

"Because I need the money, mostly. Most of the kids here, they have these awesome cars and they take these awesome vacations and they can buy anything they want. Anything! CDs, shoes, really cool jeans . . . and I'm, like, the poor kid who's going to be paying off my loans till I'm totally ancient, like in my thirties or something. Besides, I thought it would be exciting. And not so hard. I mean, it's not like I'm a virgin. Whenever I've had sex with guys at school, it was always like I was floating over my body, just looking down, you know? Like they say what it feels like when you die. So I thought it would be like that."

"And is it?"

"Sometimes. Except sometimes I feel something."

"What?"

"Like I can't breathe. Like I'm being smothered."

"Have any of the men hurt you?"

"Not where anyone could see it."

When he finally turned off the tape I was crying silently, like I do during sad movies.

"Police station?" Dennis asked.

I nodded and turned my key in the ignition.

forty

Marcy had her baby induced on a Sunday, the only day she could guarantee that Dan could get away from work. It was another boy, Thaddeus. "Have you heard of any other kids named Thaddeus?" Marcy asked. I hadn't, and I complimented her on her originality. In truth, I was just so relieved that she hadn't given Jacob and Joshua a brother named Jonah or Justin or Jared.

"The name better not catch on," she said, nuzzling his velvety head. "If it catches on, just remember I was first."

Dennis came with me to the hospital, but he got antsy. He associated hospitals with death. Also, while he was awed, he said, by the prospect of new life, he had a little trouble getting beyond the blood and the breast-feeding. When Marcy opened her cornflower blue hospital gown midsentence (the sentence being, "The episiotomy was only a half an inch long this time, but I'm still going to need a week of sitz baths"), he turned white, then red, then blurted out something about needing a Diet Pepsi and fled from the room.

Marcy moved Thaddeus's open mouth to her breast. He rooted briefly before latching on. When Jacob was a newborn, Tim used to rant about Marcy's insistence on breast-feeding in public. "Can't she go into a bathroom to do it? Do we really have to watch?"

"The baby is *eating*, Tim," I shot back. "When the baby poops, she'll go into the bathroom to change him, but there's no reason he can't eat in the living room."

"She doesn't always go into the bathroom when he poops," he grumbled. And yes, in the midst of an intimate dinner party (I'd served chicken parmesan with a smooth chianti classico), Jacob, aged two months or so, emitted a shockingly loud intestinal grumble, after which his mother placed him on the kitchen counter, a few feet from the table, and exposed his seedy mustard poop for all to see. When she was finished, she tossed the diaper into the kitchen trash. She never repeated the performance, however, so I suspect Dan had a word with her.

Something sparkled on Marcy's wrist. I touched the bracelet. "Sapphires?"

"Not bad, huh?" She held out her arm, and the dark blue stones glowed in their platinum setting. When Jacob was born, Dan had given her a strand of pearls. For Joshua she received diamond earrings. This baby thing was good business.

"It's gorgeous," I said, fingering the stones.

"You can borrow it when you get married," she said. "You know, something borrowed, something blue. It's a twofer."

"Sounds like a plan," I said. "Now all I need is a guy who looks good in a tux."

"Details." She took her arm back and switched the baby to her other breast. "I wish my milk would come in. This kid's hungry."

"I got some new jewelry, too," I said, pulling up my shirt to expose my midriff.

"Oh. My. God." Marcy gawked at my gold navel ring. "You really are eighteen."

I let my shirt drop back down and shrugged. "Youth fades. Immaturity lasts forever. You hate it?"

She thought for a moment, then shook her head. "It's kind of cool. Plus, I admire your daring. Let me see it again." I pulled my shirt back up. The ring was a small gold hoop: entirely tasteful except for the fact that it was stuck in my navel.

"Didn't it hurt?" she asked.

"Yes," I said. "But probably not as much as childbirth."

"Probably not." She detached Thaddeus and rearranged her gown. "Just promise me you won't pierce your tongue. If you pierce your tongue, I won't be able to eat with you anymore."

"It's a deal."

I held out my arms for Thaddeus. I'd spent enough time with Marcy's babies to be a master burper. I buried my nose in the baby's velvet head and breathed deeply. I nudged my shoulder into his belly and began the gentle patting of his back.

"The troops are here!" Dan announced, barging into the ridiculously small room with Jacob and Joshua. Joshua wore a sweatshirt that read, I'M THE BIG BROTHER!—a hand-me-down from Jacob. He clung to Dan's neck.

Jacob pranced over to my side and peered up. "That him?"

"That's him," I said, squatting down to give him a better look. The receiving blanket fell open, revealing Thaddeus's white plastic navel clamp. I felt an instant bond.

"He looks like Yoda," Jacob said.

"No, he doesn't!" I insisted. (I thought he looked more like Larry King.) "He looks like a baby. A beautiful baby."

"I like Yoda better than babies," Jacob said.

"Ah. Then Yoda it is. And he's a boy. Your mom gets to be the only girl in the family."

"Nu-uh," Jacob said, shaking his head. "You're part of the family, and you're a girl, too."

That's when I fled for my diet soda because, honest to God, I started to cry.

forty-one

I never had to crawl to Sheila for a recommendation.

As things turned out, my fifteen minutes of fame weren't all bad. Mitch Lambert, the owner of Mission Accomplished, saw my picture in the paper and got my number from Dennis. "You ready for a career change?" he asked with little preamble. I was.

Before I went in to talk to Mitch, I fantasized about a future in furniture design and glamorous research trips to Paris and Milan. I thought Greece had lots of potential, too: all that bright white and vibrant blue. Instead, Mitch offered me the job of Communications Director. That meant writing press releases and ad copy (no advertorials yet, but I'm waiting), creating brochures and placing ads, which I finally convinced a skeptical Mitch were the key to achieving greater editorial space. When he asked me whether or not it was worthwhile to buy a full page in *Salad*, which in the midst of financial hardship was offering bargain basement rates, I didn't hesitate. "Nobody reads *Salad*. Trust me."

I also write the company newsletter, which always includes a feature that begins, "We're all proud of our employee of the month!" It took just three short months for me to get my own employee of the month award—surprising, since management is usually passed over in favor of store clerks and warehouse guys. I made fun of it to my friends, but secretly I was proud. I hung my plaque on the side of my tan cubicle, which was bought just for me and smelled like a new car.

For the first month, my line to everyone outside of the company was that my job was just a stopgap measure designed to get me through tough times until I could resume my writing career. But then a funny thing happened. I woke up one Monday morning and realized I couldn't wait to get into the office, which was located in Boston's tony Back Bay, above Mission Accomplished's flagship store. I'd just learned a new graphics program, for use in laying out a brochure about sectional couches. Over the weekend, I'd thought about the layout, the copy, the paper stock. The project demanded neither the art of literature nor the craft of reporting, but it was something I never imagined work could be. It was fun. Besides, if truth be told, more people would probably read my couch brochure than had ever read one of my *Salad* articles.

So, after all those years of calling myself a writer, I changed my tune. "I work in PR and marketing for Mission Accomplished—you know, that furniture store." And, surprisingly, no one's eyes glazed over. I was still an

Interesting Person. That's the thing about jobs for "creative types." You can't afford a house or a decent car, but lawyers and accountants will always buy you drinks because they assume you are somehow smarter or nobler than they are—even if you've spent your day writing about coil springs.

My job certainly impressed Max. He was a junior associate at Dan's firm, short and fit with close-cut brown hair and crinkly blue eyes. His five o'clock shadow revealed flecks of red. He had a tendency to rock back and forth on his feet when he had to stand too long, like he was filled to the brim with sparkling energy that might burst out at any moment. "He might be a little young for you," Dan warned with utter sincerity. Marcy guffawed.

They invited him to Thaddeus's bris so he could meet me. "I thought it was a weird thing for him to invite me to," he later confided. "But he's my boss, so I couldn't say no." The thought of Dan being anyone's boss jarred me. It was just so, well, grown-up.

Max and I fell into an every-Saturday-night thing, then we added Tuesdays and occasional Thursdays. I had long since stopped believing in love at first sight. Now I tried to convince myself that "growing into love" was not only possible but positive: mature, logical and long-lasting.

Max taught me to play tennis (at least passably), and we shared a passion for ethnic cuisine. At twenty-seven, he seemed like AARP material after the college life. He preferred television to books but was considerate enough to wear earphones if I was trying to concentrate on something else. Off the tennis court, he didn't make my pulse quicken, but maybe that was a good thing.

*   *   *

Shortly after I started my job, Tim showed up at my door. It was a Friday night, and I was expecting Dennis, so I answered without even peering through the peephole. I blinked and realized with bitter satisfaction that I didn't want him there.

"Can I come in?" He asked after a moment of silence. I nodded and moved out of his way. He strode over to the couch and sat down. He looked up, waiting for me to sit. I didn't. He stood up, not wanting to feel himself at a disadvantage from being lower than me. Dogs are like that, too.

"I just came from the hospital," he said.

Stupidly—this was Tim, and Tim made me stupid—I thought of his parents. "Is someone ill? Your mother's okay, isn't she?" I asked, genuinely concerned. I'd get over Tim, but I'd never get over losing his parents from my life.

"I went to see the dean. He's out of intensive care now."

"Oh. Right. How is he?"

"They wouldn't let me see him. But the nurse said he'll be okay, though he's going to need some plastic surgery. Dog took off most of his ear."

I winced. "Did you really think he'd want to see you?"

He shrugged. "It wasn't a social visit. I'm after a story."

"What story? His pain and suffering? Or his wife's? There wouldn't even be a story if we hadn't gotten involved. Doesn't that bother you?" At her husband's urging, the police had never filed charges against Mrs. Archer. They didn't have any proof that she'd instigated the attack, although they insisted she have the dog destroyed. Knowing how she felt about her dogs, she probably considered Altoid's execution a worse punishment than her own incarceration.

Tim ran a hand through his hair. "Of course it bothers me. But I started this thing; now I've got to see it through. I'm just doing my job." Where had I heard that before? "*New Nation*'s reputation has really suffered. Advertisers don't want to touch us. I've got to salvage what I can out of this story."

This was my moment. I could tell Tim that I'd cracked the case after all, that Gerry, his big source, had been at the center of everything. I could tell him that I'd put Gerry out of business—without hurting the town or the girls involved. Dennis and I had handed the tape over to the Mercer Police, who said they'd heard rumors about the ring but never believed them. Dennis described the girl he'd seen as "kind of average weight, brownish hair." That was okay: with the tape in hand, the police were able to extract a confession from Gerry. With my encouragement, they decided against pursuing the girls. "You start arresting Mercer students, you're apt to set off another media frenzy," I cautioned. "Besides, Gerry's the real criminal. With him in jail, they'll be too scared to carry on."

But I didn't tell Tim any of this. "Count me out of it," I said.

"I already did," he said softly.

I stared at him. "Then why are you here?"

"I just thought I should try to make peace or something."

"Is that supposed to be an apology?"

He blinked. "Actually, no."

I nodded. "You want something? Coffee? Water?" He

shook his head. I willed him to say something. He didn't. I willed him to leave. He didn't do that, either.

"You should probably get going," I said rudely. "If you've got a flight to catch. Or—" It hit me: of course he didn't come all the way up to Boston just to see me. "Are you staying at Jennifer's?"

"Yeah."

"Oh." The familiar stab: just when I thought it was gone forever. "So you're still together?"

"Yeah."

I tried to think of something nice to say about her. She's nice? No. Funny? No. A good dresser? God, no. "She's a good writer." I gulped. I hated to admit such a thing.

"What?"

"Her writing. It's good, I think."

He shrugged. "I wouldn't know."

"Haven't you read it?"

"Just her fiction. And you know me and fiction—I'm not much of a judge."

"But you can tell if it's good, can't you?"

He shook his head dismissively. "I don't read much fiction except for mysteries. So what do I know?"

"What genre? I mean, I always thought Jennifer wrote literary fiction."

He shook his head. "Science fiction romance."

I paused. "You mean she writes science fiction and she writes romance? Or she writes romantic science fiction?"

"Romantic science fiction."

"I didn't know there was such a thing. What does that mean? Alien dating?"

He started to smile. "I think the term is 'intergalactic mating.' Or sometimes 'cross-species pollination.'"

"Oh my God." I smiled in spite of myself. In spite of everything. "Cyberbabies?"

"No babies," he said. "Fully grown pod people. They emerge from eggs following a twenty-year gestation. Makes life a lot easier for their parents."

"But what a disaster for all those diaper manufacturers and Montessori schools." We laughed, and I remembered how it felt. Once, we'd laughed together often. But that had been a long time ago, maybe years before he left. More soberly, I asked, "If Jennifer's such a lousy writer, why do you stay with her?"

"I didn't say she was lousy," he said. "I said it wasn't my thing. And, anyway, I don't really care what she writes. I just care about who she is. She's so . . . honest. She really doesn't give a damn what anyone thinks. I've never met anyone like that before. She's just so totally her own person. And I think she's good for me. She makes me look at life differently. Makes me think about what matters."

I cut him off before he could start telling me how great she was in bed. "If you don't care about her writing, why was mine such a big deal?"

He stared at me, confounded. "Because I thought it mattered to you. I just wanted something to matter to you. Something other than me."

The doorbell rang. I jumped. I'd completely forgotten about Dennis. I opened the door and Dennis strode in. "There's a faucets and fixtures show in Medford. You want to go?" He stopped dead when he saw Tim. "Hello?"

"Dennis, this is Tim. Tim, Dennis."

"Ah," Dennis said, the light dawning. "Tim." The unspoken end of the sentence—"the unfeeling shit who broke your heart and ruined your career"—hung in the air.

Tim sprang up from the couch. "I'd better get going." I nodded. At the door, he hugged me stiffly but for longer than I would have expected. My gut began to hurt. *Just go. Just go. Just go.*

Tim looked up at Dennis and back at me. "I'm glad you found somebody," he whispered solemnly. I opened my mouth to set him straight, then shut it and nodded. Everybody deserves a little dignity now and then, even me.

When the door shut (softly; far too softly), Dennis took me in his arms before I'd begun to sob. But then I let loose. When I was done soaking his silk shirt, he strode into the bathroom and came back with a box of tissues. I wiped my eyes and blew my nose only to find it hopelessly stuffed. Dennis pushed my hair back from my face. "The guy from the college was *much* hotter."

It was another Friday night, months later, when my phone rang.

"It's Jeremy," he said. My pulse quickened, and I hated myself for it. We exchanged stiff hellos. Then he said, rather flatly, "I got a job in Boston. Starting in July. I just thought you should know. Like, in case we run into each other or something. I just didn't want you to be surprised."

"Well, congratulations," I said. Damn that pulse. "I'm working in the Back Bay now. Will you be anywhere near that?"

"Framingham."

I paused, confused. "That's, um, not really Boston. It's about a half hour, forty minutes away." Surely he knew that already. "The chances of us running into each other are pretty slim."

"Right," he said crisply. "But you never know. And like I said, I just didn't want you to be surprised."

"Thanks for the heads-up." The silence was so painful, I wondered why neither of us made a move to end the conversation. Finally, I spoke. "Are you seeing anyone?" Who said that?

A pause. The quickened pulse had morphed into a pounding thud. "No. You?"

Shit. I could lie, I thought. But no: I'd lied to Jeremy enough for one lifetime. "Yes. But only on Saturdays. And alternate Tuesdays." Max and I had dropped the occasional Thursdays, both claiming to be too busy, but mostly feeling too closed in.

"Oh," he said. And he was disappointed, I could tell—or maybe I just wanted him to be.

"But today's Friday," I said quietly.

I could hear him breathing. Maybe his heart was thudding, too. "And tomorrow?"

"Tomorrow's Friday, too."

Max was relieved to be cut loose. He did his best to act hurt, but then he confessed that he'd been carrying a torch for a secretary in his office ever since he'd joined the firm, but he hadn't asked her out because she was a working-class girl from Revere with a killer accent and no college education. "Besides," he said as kindly as he could, "I've always felt that there was a bit of a, um, generation gap between you and me."

I smiled tightly and sent him on his way, wondering what I'd ever seen in this shallow twerp.

* * *

Jeremy graduated with distinction. I didn't attend the ceremony, as we both agreed it would be too weird. Besides, his parents were having some trouble accepting our relationship. During our one tense dinner, his mother, after a couple of martinis, asked about the health of my ovaries, which I told her were, to the best of my knowledge, in tiptop shape. As much as I disliked his mother on other grounds, I understood her concern. I, too, thought Jeremy deserved better—or at least younger—than me.

"Are you sure you aren't just staying with me to piss off your parents?" I asked, mock jokingly, one night. He was lying on my couch, his head on my lap, while I stroked his curls, which were set to be chopped off in a couple of days in preparation for his new job.

"I've already told them I'm not going to medical school," he said. "That's pissed them off enough already."

Marcy and Dan had us over for dinner. I expected it to be uncomfortable, for my friends to set a place for Jeremy at the children's table or to at least send me knowing smirks. Instead, Dan nodded to me in the kitchen, as I scraped plates into the sink. "You look happy," he said.

"I am."

"That's all that matters."

Jeremy rented an apartment in Framingham with three other guys from Mercer, but he spent most nights at my apartment and did a reverse commute out of the city. Each morning, he put on one of his three suits and a dress shirt he had ironed the night before. He looked handsome, of course, in spite of his cheap suits, but I liked him best when he came home and put on sweats and a T-shirt after neatly hanging his suit and shirt in my closet. He seemed lighter without that suit, more himself. His job was in ad sales for a radio station. "I never knew you were interested in radio," I said when he first described the job to me.

"Neither did I," he laughed.

After a few weeks of rude receptions to his cold calls and a paycheck that seemed so much smaller after the taxes had come out, he asked me if work ever got any better, and I told him sometimes, but not always. It was as honest as I could be. He talked about architecture school for about a week, then he moved on to ideas about social work, real estate or teaching. Dennis, who I still saw as much as possible, although he, too, was seeing someone, suggested that Jeremy find a sales position in the interior design industry. "Between the men and the women— honestly, no one would say no to you." Jeremy laughed (and blushed), but said he secretly coveted a recliner with a drink holder and couldn't really see getting excited about upholstery and "curtainy things." I think he fell a bit in Dennis's estimation after that, although Dennis continued to describe him as a "nice, nice boy."

I tell him he should save his money, buy a backpack and spend a year in Europe. "You'll never regret the things you did," I tell him. "You'll only regret the things you didn't do."

"Would you come with me?" he asks every time.

"No, but I'd wait for you," I say. We leave it at that.

One Sunday, Jeremy looked up from circling every entry-level ad in the help wanted section and sighed. "I really envy those people who grow up knowing exactly what they want out of life," he told me. "Like, they're five years old, and they say they want to be a veterinarian when they grow up, and twenty-five years later, that's exactly what they are."

I put down my coffee and walked over to him. I held him tight and told him that knowing what you want takes the fun out of life, that true joy come from the surprise.